THE CHRONICLES OF NIGHTWOLF

C.R. BEAUMONT

THE CHRONICLES OF NIGHTWOLF

THE FOUR FAMILIES

TATE PUBLISHING
AND ENTERPRISES, LLC

The Chronicles of Nightwolf
Copyright © 2014 by C.R. Beaumont. All rights reserved.

No part of this publication may be reproduced, stored in a retrieval system or transmitted in any way by any means, electronic, mechanical, photocopy, recording or otherwise without the prior permission of the author except as provided by USA copyright law.

This novel is a work of fiction. Names, descriptions, entities, and incidents included in the story are products of the author's imagination. Any resemblance to actual persons, events, and entities is entirely coincidental.

The opinions expressed by the author are not necessarily those of Tate Publishing, LLC.

Published by Tate Publishing & Enterprises, LLC
127 E. Trade Center Terrace | Mustang, Oklahoma 73064 USA
1.888.361.9473 | www.tatepublishing.com

Tate Publishing is committed to excellence in the publishing industry. The company reflects the philosophy established by the founders, based on Psalm 68:11,
"The Lord gave the word and great was the company of those who published it."

Book design copyright © 2014 by Tate Publishing, LLC. All rights reserved.
Cover design by Jim Villaflores
Interior design by Caypeeline Casas

Published in the United States of America

ISBN: 978-1-63185-280-0
1. Fiction / Thrillers / Suspense
2. Fiction / Occult & Supernatural
14.03.28

Contents

Prologue

Salem Town
April, 1692

THE NIGHT WAS calm, a rarity in the time and place where the family of Nightwolf resided. Recent events had led to the persecution of perceived and sometimes real witches, placing several families in danger, and thus steps were now being taken to try and preserve the future. Gentle clouds drifted across the moon which illuminated the old standing grove of Oak which served as their meeting place. If the gods favored them, then they would be successful and find a way to protect the families and ascend more than one from each line into the power which was passed down for centuries from father to son or mother to daughter. Quiet footsteps echoed in the darkness, softly treading the forest floor and taking two toward the oaken grove, a hallowed-out center amongst a circle of trees where the moon might look down and see the work of whoever wished to worship there.

Delicate hands prepared the kindling for a bonfire at the center of the circle, showing cautious practice and skill when placing the sticks and logs in their proper place. Still, the soft echoing of footsteps came, alerting those who stood within the circle of two approaching. The first sound as the two entered came from a young girl, her hair was as red as fire and her eyes glittered like jade in the morning sun, a soft sigh escaped her lips followed by a slight smile.

The two who entered the circle of Oak looked almost identical, save that one was noticeably younger than the other. It was obvious that they were brothers. Long black hair was carefully pulled back by a red ribbon; their eyes seemed to shine like emeralds in the moonlight, resonating the power that they held within.

"All is prepared?" The older of the two asked as they came to stand in front of the girl.

"Yes, Mick, all is ready. The others are all patrolling the forest to ensure that the hunters don't stumble upon us this night." She answered him with quiet tones as her gaze drifted to the younger brother, a soft smile tracing her lips for a moment.

Mick nodded once and began moving to the northern quadrant of the circle of Oak trees where a simple marble altar rested; it was adorned with various items for the upcoming ritual which was to be performed. The young girl watched Mick quietly for a long moment before speaking once again.

"You are certain that this ascension will work without any complications? It is the rule that only one per generation is allowed you know?"

Mick turned, looking back at her with a concerned glance and then nodded, "Yes, I am aware of the tenets, but this is something that must be done to help try and preserve us. There are too many hunters about for us to be so utterly alone now."

She nodded once, her eyes drifting back to the younger brother for a long moment, settling on his with what could only be interpreted as a look of love. He seemed to return her look, his eyes tracing over her for a short moment before turning to focus on his brother, who was now staring at them both.

"Is it time brother?"

Mick nodded silently for a moment before responding, "It is. Are you ready?"

"I am. Let us begin."

The younger brother moved to the eastern section of the circle of Oak and waited patiently, the young girl following him to stand by his side and taking his hand for a moment while whispering softly to him, "You better remember me…"

He smiled briefly for a moment, as Mick began walking around the circle, chanting and casting out salts and water around its edges. The light of the moon shown down brightly, perhaps as a sign of acceptance of their ritual, and the clouds seemed to part as Mick moved to the center of the circle and lit the bonfire. The flames illuminated the scene in an almost eerie light, however, causing shadows to dance along the edges of the trees and between them.

The soft chanting echoed out from Mick, seeming to drift through the air like a warm summer's breeze, dancing among the leaves of the trees around them and then finally settling upon them. His movements took him around the circle once more before stopping in front of the two, his eyes tracing over them for a long moment before he spoke, his tone deep and somber, "Bride, is it true that you come of your own free will and accord?"

"I do."

"Groom, is it true that you come of your own free will and accord?"

"I do."

"Above you are the stars, below you are the stones, as time doth pass, remember… Like a stone should your love be firm; like a star should your love be constant. Let the powers of the mind and of the intellect guide you in your marriage, let the strength of your wills bind you together, let the power of love and desire make you happy, and the strength of your dedication make you inseparable. Be close, but not too close. Possess one another, yet be understanding. Have patience with one another for storms will come, but they will pass quickly. Be free in giving affection and warmth. Have no fear and let not the ways of the unenlightened give you unease for the Gods are with you always. Once you kiss know that you shall always be bound, no matter time or place, no matter life or death, you shall be eternally linked. Do you both understand this?" Mick intoned as he continued the first part of the ritual to marry them, knowing that the second part was the dangerous one.

The two nodded once, intoning together, "We do."

Mick nodded once more to them and laid a delicate green and gold sash across their hands, tying them both together, "You may now kiss and seal the pact."

The two looked at each other a long moment in silence, their breathing echoing in their ears and hearts pounding in their chests the only sounds for that time, and then they softly kissed, sealing the pact to be bound together. They held the moment for a long time, not seeming to want to leave that perfect time, but then the kiss broke and they turned looking at Mick once more.

"Now it is time for you to assume your mantles of power. Are you both ready for the tasks that lie ahead?"

The two nodded once and Mick continued the ritual, "Two who are bound from the four families shall bring salvation to the world, protect it from darkness, and lead people back from damnation. Two, who bear the marks of the families shall join in union as has never done before and usher in a new era for the families and the powers we hold. You two have been chosen and wed. Now, as is written, you shall receive the mantles of power which has been passed down from your forefathers and mothers unto you."

The two embraced each other closely for a moment and then turned toward the altar in the northern section of the circle, calmly walking toward it hand in hand, still bound by the green and gold sash.

Mick continued speaking as he methodically moved to the center of the circle, "As with the passing of time so must pass the power of the ancestors to the children, may they now accept their power and their blood cleanse the future to come!"

The two stopped in front of the altar and stood there in muted silence for a moment, the girl taking up the athame from the stone surface with a graceful gesture and then turned to look at her new husband. Her voice was soft and caring as she spoke to him, "Hold out your hand for me husband, I shall draw your blood to bind us further and bring us into our power."

He nodded quietly as he held out his hand and with one fluid motion, she cut across his palm with the ceremonial knife, a shallow cut, but deep enough to draw out a large amount of blood. She then turned the blade hilt toward him and he took it in his free hand. His voice was just as caring as he spoke, his accent seeming filled with British formality, "Hold out your hand for me Wife, I shall draw your blood to bind us further and bring us into our power."

She smiled faintly and held out her hand to him, his own motion was as graceful as the wind, cutting her palm, and then placing the athame back on the altar. They both looked up to the moon then, joining their bloody hands and held them up, still bound in the green and gold sash, speaking clearly and with purpose, "We now accept our mantle of power and our responsibility to the families, as husband and wife we shall do our sworn duties!"

They paused, almost hesitantly at the end of their words as the sky seemed to cloud, blocking out the moons light from the circle of Oak, darkening the area to nothing but the light of the now dying bonfire and the shadows dancing amongst the trees. The wind hissed vaporously through the leaves, giving warning as howls erupted in the woods and the sounds of a hunting party filled the glade with shouts of anger and puritan prayers to cast out demons. The two watched the edges of the grove fearfully as the night ever more darkened and the wind picked up, brewing a storm, the sounds of witch-hunters drawing ever closer. Mick cursed quietly under his breath and cast a glance back at them, his voice low and stern, "Flee, I shall distract them while you escape… let them not catch you or we shall all be doomed to darkness."

The two nodded and looked back up to the sky, attempting to finish the ritual hurriedly, "Hear us! We call for the power of our ancestors, as is our right on the night of our marriage and ascension! We call for the blessings of the gods and the four corners for which our houses represent! Hear us!"

The sky flashed with lightning striking the altar and illuminating the circle in a horrifying sight. Mick turned, looking back at the two, his eyes widening as he witnessed the surge of electricity around them both, their faces etched with pain and agony, and then all was dark and silent. The sounds of hunting dogs filled the night with the sounds of the storm, and Mick knew that the worst was yet to come…

The altar was gone, as were his brother and his wife; naught but ash and rising smoke remained, barely illuminated in the dying bonfires light. He stared at the spot for a moment longer before drawing a horn from his sash and blowing hard on it to sound the retreat for the families which patrolled the forest, trying to hide the circle of Oak with spells and illusions. Then, Mick fled, turning toward the darkness and ran for his life.

Dreaming of You

A lapse in time, a lapse in rhyme...
A lapse in all believed to make sense...
Pictures of games, pictures with names,
And it all jumbles together to make no sense...
Maybe it's the pressure, maybe it's the pain,
Just take an aspirin, and try to forget it all again...

October 2008
Week 1, Thursday

Steven awoke sweating profusely, soft cursing escaped his lips as he looked around his dark room and came to realize where he was. The dream had come to him once again; it was becoming more of a nightly habit and was seriously aggravating his sleep over the past few weeks. Sighing heavily, he climbed out of bed and ventured to his bath. As he turned on the water so that it would run hot and steam up the room, he undressed and draped his night clothes across a bar in the bathroom. Looking into the now fogging mirror, his mind wondered as to why the dream was becoming more frequent now. Every time he awoke from it, he felt as if he was singed all over, as if burning from the inside after being hit by lightning. Shaking his head, he slipped into the large tub and relaxed back, turning off the water while the steam rose up, partially hiding him from view as he closed his eyes.

"I simply don't get it... usually my dreams mean something... but now... this one is so repetitive and... it doesn't make any sense to me. I would never marry so young... least of all to someone I don't know," he mumbled to himself as the water eased away the tension from his muscles.

He didn't really care to check the time, though he knew that the day brought the first day back to school, his senior year in high school and he wasn't particularly looking forward to it after the previous summer. So much had happened over the last few years that it made his head hurt from thinking of it, not to mention his heart. But then he pushed that deep aching back down, believing that the past was to be left where it was, behind him. Still it did not stop the dreams or the occasional twinges of pain when something reminded him of Ruby, the girl he had fallen in love with the previous year and lost.

He scowled silently to himself as he tried to clear his mind, the dream always made him think of the past for some reason, as if living through it hadn't been enough. Sighing softly, he rose from the bath and let the drain loose before grabbing a towel and dried off. He used the towel to wipe off the mirror once he was done and then leaned on the sink counter staring at himself for a long moment. His own sapphire eyes stared back stoically at him, his long raven black hair hanging loosely around his muscular shoulders making him look like some sort of young barbarian shrouded by the mist still hanging in the air around him. A soft sigh escaped his lips, as he grabbed a black silk cord and tied his hair back after combing it out. The start of the day was still hours away, but he already felt tired just as he always did when having that dream. His eyes drifted about for a moment before he moved over to his closet and mulled over what to wear. He never really dressed to impress anyone, just to feel comfortable, thus his usual selection came to his mind first. His hands moved pulling a set of black dress pants off a hanger along with a green silk shirt. Deliberately, he dressed and then headed downstairs to forage around in the fridge for breakfast.

His typical morning consisted of the same waking, bathing, dressing, and breakfast. Steven wasn't one who enjoyed change and usually kept to his routine every day, at least as much as he could. The fridge yielded orange juice and eggs, which he quickly cooked and scrambled up. His manservant was always irritated when he cooked, probably because Steven rarely cleaned up his own mess, life with money had made him lazy in the department of housekeeping for the most part, and thus he never worried about it. Finishing the eggs, he placed them on a plate and ate quickly, making sure he didn't spill anything on himself. He always hated it when he got clumsy and spilled food on his clothes, but then he realized that sometimes it couldn't be helped. Setting down his glass after he finished his juice and meal, he stood and made his way out of the kitchen and to the front drive of the mansion, which he called home. His car sat parked outside the front door, a shimmering green Porsche convertible coupe, which seemed to echo a restlessness he held from his younger days.

As he approached the car, he spoke quietly just above a whisper, "Boucliers vers le bas."

The surface of the car shimmered evenly with what seemed like a static charge before returning to normal just before Steven opened the driver's side door and climbed in lowering the top down. He loved to feel the wind in his face as he drove, even in the middle of winter, but as for now the summer heat was only just ending and leaving the cool fall seasons breeze to begin. Steven turned the ignition and put the clutch into gear and then sped out of his driveway toward school. He liked speed, but his eyes were always watching everything around him. His driving was something he took entirely too seriously, but it had prevented a great deal of mishaps in his life since he first got behind the wheel. Several minutes later, he was pulling into the school parking lot and rolling into the space he had reserved for the past two years of school. If nothing else, there was something to say about having money, and that was that one could get nearly anything they wanted with the right price.

As the car rolled to a stop in the parking space, he exited the car and grabbed a leather satchel from the passenger's seat and slung it over his shoulder. His fingers flicked the switch to raise the top on the car and he turned, mumbling under his breath back toward his car, "De boucliers."

A slight static shimmer covered his car for a brief moment before leaving a noticeable sparkling shimmer across its surface as Steven began walking toward the entrance of the school. The previous summer had left his mind wandering, still skimming over events in which he counted himself lucky to be alive still. Sighing softly he pulled his class schedule from his back pocket and flipped it open giving it a brief look.

Period:	Time:		Class:
0	7:30-8:30	—	—-
1	8:35-9:35	—	12th lit.
2	9:40-10:40	—	Calculus
3	10:45-11:45	—	Business Concepts
4	11:50-12:50	—	Lunch
5	12:55-13:55	—	Art 102
6	14:00-15:00	—	European History
7	15:05-16:05	—	—-

"Hrm… finally a light schedule," he said to himself as he entered the building and proceeded through the halls.

Steven ignored the soft whispers of the other students as he passed by them and had to restrain himself from smirking on more than one occasion when they gave him frightened and paranoid glances. He was just beginning to realize the value of superstition, especially after the previous year when no one would leave him alone. Now they all backed away from him and got out of his way as he moved through the crowded halls toward his first class. Arriving early in Literature, he took a seat near the front of the room and waited for everyone else to file in. The five desks around him remained empty up until the late bell rang and a girl came speeding in and sat in the desk directly to his right. A slight frown crested his lips in irritation as he glanced over at her ever so slightly before turning his attention to the teacher.

The teacher lectured on about Shakespeare and his plays and jotted notes on the black board for the students to copy down and study. Steven kept his notes in a sectioned tablet, scribbling down everything that the teacher wrote and said in an organized fashion. The girl who now sat to his right leaned over discretely to peek at his notes, causing him to snap the notebook shut quickly and glance at her with a raised brow. She backed away to her own notes quickly and Steven reopened the tablet and resumed taking his notes. Soon the bell rang and everyone shuffled out of the class to move through crowded halls toward their next period. Steven walked easily through the halls, the crowds parting like the red sea as he moved down the center of the hallway. Sarah, the girl who sat to his right during literature, leaned over to one of the other students in the hall after noticing how everyone moved quickly out of his way and lowered her voice to speak, "Who is that guy?"

The freshman looked up at her with a rather shocked expression, his voice low and hissing in slight apprehension, "That? That's trouble, stay away from him or you'll regret it!"

Sarah blinked in surprise at his expression and response as the boy darted off down the hall through the now reforming crowds, though she couldn't help it as her eyes wandered down the hall after Steven, following him with mute curiosity. Sarah wore loose fitting jeans and a white T-shirt which was covered mostly by a jean jacket that matched her pants. Standing at about five feet and seven inches, her mid-back length vibrant, fiery red hair made an amazing contrast with her jade green eyes. Her figure was graceful and slender, moving nimbly as she went to her next class. Looking at her schedule she groaned inwardly noting that it was calculus, she hated math more than anything in the world. Sighing, she entered the room and glanced around for a moment for an open seat and noted with some surprise that the only five available were once more around that strange boy. Taking a slow breath she moved over and sat to his right once again.

Steven's brow knotted in frustration before he forced it to relax as the girl from his literature class once more sat beside him. *Must be some new girl*, he thought to himself in mild frustration as he pulled out his notebook and pen with a graceful move. The bell rang and the teacher entered the class closing the door quietly.

"Morning class, I'm your calculus teacher for the year. Now, I know you're used to all this Mr. this and Mrs. stuff, but you can just refer to me as Coach A, is that clear?" The teacher began with an easygoing smile and a clear voice.

The class voiced their agreement and Coach A began writing formulas on the board while explaining how they worked and were used in the real world. Steven yawned quietly as he took notes and began to think he should have picked a more challenging class when he glanced over and noticed that Sarah had begun dozing off. He leaned over just an inch and smacked her hand with the back of his pencil before moving back to his notes as she nearly jumped with a start. She began looking around wildly for a moment to see who had smacked her, noticing only others students taking notes or dozing off due to the sheer boredom of numbers and equations. Turning in surprise, she looked at Steven as she rubbed her hand some, "Did you see…"

Ring!

Steven simply stood, tossing his notebook in his pack, and walked out of the room leaving Sarah sitting there with her mouth open. She turned, her cheeks noticeably reddened at the rudeness, only to see that some of the other students were watching her with nervous and horrified gaze as they quickly left the room. *What the hell is so bad about this guy to cause everyone to be so damn afraid of him*, she wondered as she gathered up her books and shoved them in her own pack. Soon she was on her way to business concepts, which she dearly hoped would be more interesting than calculus.

Steven sat in the boy's bathroom on the sink counter smoking a cigarette as he lazily tapped the water faucet off and on. The late bell rang and he swore quietly to himself, he hated being late for anything especially class, but he wasn't truly worried about the prospect. Mr. Fergus in business would understand, Steven reasoned to himself as he put out the cigarette on the counter and left the bathroom heading toward class. He entered the room quietly and took his seat, which he discovered was once more beside Sarah's. *The gods must be punishing me for something.* He thought to himself as he pulled out his note pad and pen.

Sarah watched Steven enter the Business class late and take the last open seat, beside hers, but what surprised her most was that the teacher didn't even stop lecturing when he noticed Steven's late arrival. She also noted that Steven frowned briefly when he looked at her upon entering the room and began wondering why he was being so rude to her. She sighed softly and decided that she would break the ice when the teacher was done lecturing and began to wonder as to what she could say.

Mr. Fergus lectured on about the laws and principles of marketing which usually applied to major corporations as Steven yawned and began lounging back in his chair while noting that Sarah was taking notes furiously. *What a nerd*, he thought to himself as his eyes lingered on her for a moment, his face remaining expressionless. The other students scowled when they thought he wasn't looking, everyone who had been in the business classes knew that Steven was the teacher's pet and could get away with anything if he really wanted to with little to no disciplinary action. Rules were for everyone else, they would say, but not him. Mr. Fergus gave out an assignment and went into his adjoining office, half-closing the door and allowing the students to work on their own.

Sarah leaned over toward Steven with a smile, her voice soft in an attempt to be sweet and charming, "Would you like to work together?"

Steven glanced over at her and snapped back sharply, his voice frigid, "No."

Sarah blinked with a blank stare, taken aback in shock by the cutting tone in his voice and then turned toward her own work with an indignant look crossing her face. Steven filled out his worksheet quickly and carefully stuffed it into his sectioned notepad before lounging back once more in his chair yawning ever so slightly. Sarah looked over at him, surprised at how quickly he had finished, and then blurted out at him in a hushed tone, "Hey? You're already done?"

Steven glanced over at her, his brow arching, though the iciness in his tone remained firmly in place, "Yes."

"But you didn't even open the book!" Sarah exclaimed sarcastically trying her best to ignore his tone.

Steven looked at her with a puzzled and nearly amused expression crossing his face, "Look, why are you talking to me? Aren't you scared or something, or are you just ignorant of who I am?"

She turned red for a brief moment as her eyes widened before turning away anger and embarrassment clearly etched across her face. Steven chuckled with mirth as he leaned back a little more in his chair, but his reaction caused her temper to get the better of her and she moved almost reflexively nudging the off balanced legs of his chair with her foot ever so slightly just enough to send him slipping backwards.

Crash!

The quiet whispers of students swapping answers suddenly stopped, filling the room with an almost deathly silence as everyone glanced nervously over in the direction of Steven and Sarah. Steven slowly rose from where he fell on the floor and dusted himself off putting his chair back in place before he resumed sitting in it.

"You'll pay for that," he hissed under his breath just loud enough for her to hear him.

Sarah felt a chill run down her spine, and goose bumps swept across her skin as if touched by an arctic wind when he spoke. Still, she turned, determined to face him with a smile; but, as she met his eyes with her own her face paled and drained of all color whatsoever. She could feel the storm brewing inside him as those icy blue eyes turned a stormy and seemed to reach into the very depths of her soul searching out her most private thoughts and feelings for weakness with a cold and calculating malice. She sat there frozen in fear as the rest of the class seemed to be watching the two holding their breath in anticipation of the worst.

Ring!

All the students immediately leapt up from their seats at the sound of the bell and barreled out of the classroom, dropping their assignments haphazardly in the box on their way out. Steven calmly rose and put his own work sheet in the box as he began to head out the door.

"Hey, Steven! Have you got a minute?" Mr. Fergus yelled from his office causing Steven to stop in mid-stride a moment.

Turning with a charming smile on his face, he nearly ran into Sarah who was leaving right behind him, but his motions seemed akin to floating as he moved back just out of her way and kept them from touching. His voice was calm and relaxed as he spoke then, "Yes, Mr. Fergus? I have time."

Sarah stepped out of the room, but paused just for a moment, upon hearing how rich and deep his normal voice was she stopped just outside the classroom and turned to look back curiously. As she looked into the room, she noticed he was watching her and once their eyes met once more she felt something inside her stomach jump. Those sapphire wells of his eyes seemed to tell her that there was nothing that could be hidden from him, no matter how personal, and the thought frightened her a bit. Shivering she turned quickly and went to lunch, trying not to think about it.

"Steven," Mr. Fergus began with a smile, "Have you considered what you'd like to do for an apprenticeship yet for the class?"

"Hrm… You know what I'd really like to do Mr. Fergus, teach or sub in for a teacher here… if only for a short period of time," Steven answered with a thoughtful look on his face, "That is of course if there is an opening for such."

Mr. Fergus's eyes widened as did his grin, "I'll see what I can do for you Steven, I'm sure that something will open up for you here."

Steven nodded with a smile and turned leaving the room and heading to lunch.

Sarah entered art class and gasped in surprise noticing that Steven was sitting at a table in the back of the room. She moved through the room and sat at the table beside his and took out her pad and pen. Glancing sideways at him, she noticed that he seemed to be working on some type of pen and ink drawing. Another girl entered the class and moved across the room to come and sit beside Sarah at her table, a tall brunette with dark almond colored eyes and a golden tan, "Hi! I'm Angela, the head cheerleader. You're the new girl, right?"

"H-hi, yeah, I'm Sarah. Nice to meet you," Sarah answered, surprised by the girls outgoing nature.

Soon everyone was seated and Mr. Pedgoint, the art teacher, closed the door signaling the start of class. He was a sixty-year-old art teacher who was desperately overweight and wore spectacles so thick that some students joked he could see the surface of mars. Setting a bowl of fruit on a stand in front of the class, he instructed that they draw a still-life portrait of the fruit in the medium that they preferred the most. Sarah watched as Steven put his current drawing face down on his table and then pulled out a fresh sheet and began to quickly sketch the assignment with his pen. She watched in fascination as he seemed to get the proportions just right and flow through the movements of shading like a cool falls breeze through the trees. She sat in awe as he finished his picture and merely stared at him and the drawing with disbelief, *It looks so life like, almost like you could reach out and pluck it from the page.* Had she not just seen him draw the sketch she would not have thought it possible for such a thing to be drawn as opposed to being a photograph.

Angela poked Sarah a bit hard in the side whispering to her in a warning tone, "Hey? What are you doing? Don't stare at him, he's *dangerous*!"

Sarah turned around some looking at her with a raised brow for a moment, "Dangerous? You've got to be joking, right? I mean yeah his eyes are a bit unnerving, but…"

A boy with short red hair and wearing worn holey blue jeans and a white T-shirt covered by an expensive black leather jacket leaned over toward the two girls, his almond brown eyes seeming to shine blissfully with mischief, "Yeah! They say he murdered his whole family and buried their bodies somewhere off in the woods, but the police never found anything…"

"Nah!" Sarah whispered back eyeing Devin in slight curiosity and excitement.

Angela gave the two of them a stern look before looking over at Steven fearfully, her tone growing more hushed, "Yeah, it's true… and they also say he's some type of witch or something."

Sarah turned her head noticeably looking over her shoulder at Steven for a moment, and then turned back quickly toward the other two the instant she realized he was now watching them all very closely, her voice barely audible as she whispered to them, "He's watching us!"

Sarah's still life suddenly floated up off the table and then to the floor as they all gasped in surprise. Angela whispered in a near hiss as fear seemed etched on her face, "I told you he was a witch!"

Devin snickered causing Angela to blush in embarrassment, "The windows open, it's the wind, and don't tell me that you believe in all that fairytale crap?"

Angela's expression changed, turning a deeper shade of red, "It's not a fairytale! I heard that he hexed some poor freshman last year and that the kid died the very next day!"

Devin, unable to contain himself, burst out with laughter loudly enough catching the rest of the class's attention.

"Mr. Lion!" The teacher roared across the room, "Is there something you would like to share with the class that would amuse us all?"

Devin defiantly stood up, a wide grin spreading across his lips, "Well Mr. Pigeon, it would be my guess that with your telescopic vision, which I might add could see Uranus, you would be able to *see* what was so funny. You know, using that latest spy glass technology and all…"

The whole class burst into a fit of uncontrollable laughter, with the exception of Steven, who Sarah noted had returned to working on his original drawing and was paying little attention to the scene at hand.

"W-Well! I-I never! T-to the office M-Mr. Lion!" The teacher roared pointing at the door viciously.

On his way out the door, Devin intentionally turned his head toward Mr. Pedgoint making pigeon noises. The class roared again with laughter as Devin made good his escape leaving the teacher trying to quiet the uprising. Steven stealthily placed a hand over his mouth to conceal a slight snicker as Sarah turned to see his reaction to such a display of immaturity.

Ring!

Steven picked up his stuff and left the art class to go to his last class of the day. Sarah went on a hunch and followed him simply to discover that she was right and they indeed shared the same class once again at the end of the school day. Entering history, Steven picked a desk in the front row, though this time he wasn't surprised to see Sarah trailing in behind him and taking the desk beside him. In fact, he would have been more surprised after the day's events if she hadn't shown up and done so. Stealing a glance at her as she sat down, Steven had to admit she was quite attractive, if not a bit over feisty. He then turned his attention to the slender new teacher just out of college who was to be their history teacher. Her shoulder length brown hair accented with blond highlights seemed to make her light brown eyes shine more so than normal, and adding to her beauty. Steven managed a smile as he noticed that almost every other guy in the class was practically drooling all over themselves at the sight of the new teacher.

He yawned happily as he leaned back in his desk and pulled out his pad and pen. The teacher wrote her name on the board in large letters, "Miss Callum," before she turned facing the class.

"Hello, students, I'm your new history teacher, Miss Callum, and we're going to start off the year with the French revolution. Now if you'll turn in your books to page..."

Steven, in boredom, began to drift-off into oblivious thought already bored with the subject when a loud thud against the classroom window caught his attention. He looked over and saw a chalk board eraser lying on the ground just below the window and its dusty imprint clearly outlined on the glass. Then he noticed that Miss Callum had stopped speaking and was staring at the eraser in disbelief while everyone else in the class was staring at him in fear, save one, Sarah who looked up from her notes and then around the class with a rather confused expression.

"Uh... anyway... Mr. Nightwolf, why is it do you think that Napoleon..." Miss Callum tried starting again.

"Napoleon met defeat in 1814 by a collaboration of major powers. Prussia, Russia, Britain, and Austria. Napoleon was then exiled to the island of Elba and Louis XVIII was made the king of France. In September 1814 the Congress of Vienna met to discuss problems and issues arising from the defeat of France. In February 1815 while the congress was in session Napoleon escaped from Elba and returned to France. Many veterans of his former campaigns flocked to his side to recreate his army, and on March 20, 1815 he again took the throne of France. The Battle of Waterloo was one of the bloodiest in modern history. During the fighting of June 18, French casualties totaled about 40,000, British and Dutch about 15,000, and Prussian about 7000. All in all he suffered defeat due to poor planning, lack of communication, and a problem with dealing with the truth that he could be defeated. His ego was a very big motivation in his achievements," Steven answered interrupting her and causing her to raise a slight brow in surprise.

"Yes, that is correct, Mr. Nightwolf," She replied back regaining some of her composure.

Ring!

Sarah jotted down his name quickly along with the rumors she had heard throughout the day in her notepad. *Steven Nightwolf. What an unusual name*, she thought to herself as she shoved the notebook into her bag. She waited for him to leave the classroom before proceeding to follow him at a distance she believed wouldn't attract his attention. Steven walked along the halls and then exited the school, moving along the outside walls until he reached the front and leaned against one of the pillars which stood as prominent icons of the entrance to the school. He tapped his foot lightly as he folded his arms and relaxed back against the pillar sighing softly. Sarah waited as the last bus pulled away before moving through the shadows along the wall to get closer to where he was in the hopes of seeing why he was still hanging around after school. As she crept closer, she froze in place as she heard his voice knowing by its closeness that he must be just around the corner from her.

"I know you're there, Devin, so you may as well come out now that everyone is gone…" Steven said in a casual dry tone.

Devin emerged from the shadows near the pillars trying to seem as if he walked around the corner. Sarah's eyes widened in curiosity as she peeked around the corner witnessing the scene in astonishment. He wore a cheesy grin as he spoke to Steven in a happy joking tone, "No you don't."

"Oh really?" Steven answered in a sarcastic tone as he canted his head to the side.

Devin leaned against the pillar next to him in a lazy fashion with a raised brow. "You know what? You should come to the club tonight... I've got some new tunes I'd like you to hear."

Steven's brow knotted in concern as his tone turned more serious, "You know I hate crowds of people, Devin."

Sarah sneezed and walked forward around the corner attempting to look as if she was just now rounding the bend and not listening in on their conversation. The movement off to the side caught Steven's eye and he turned his head to see Sarah coming around the corner.

Cursing under his breath quietly he mumbled to Devin, "Gotta go man..."

He abruptly turned and began walking toward the parking lot as if he had just exited the school. As he reached his Porsche, he muttered under his breath and the surface of the car cracked and sparked with electricity for a moment before returning to normal. Sarah gasped in awe as she watched the display in surprise, partly because he was driving a Porsche and partly because she had just witnessed a lightning display ripple across the surface of the car. Glancing back, Devin noticed Sarah with a curious expression on her face as he spoke, "Nice car, huh?"

"Y-yeah... did you see? I mean the car... oh, never mind," Sarah stammered in disbelief as she watched Steven drive off.

"Oh, about that car... You might want to stay away from it and not even get to close to it."

"Huh? Why?" She asked turning toward Devin with a curious expression.

"Well for one, the security system is state of the art, so take my advice and don't even get near it," Devin answered her with a firm look.

"Whatever..." Sarah trailed off looking back in the direction that Steven's car sped off in.

"Hey, don't take it from me then. But, there was this guy who tried to vandalize it once and he got the hell shocked out of him..." Devin continued with a shrug.

"Really? Who might that have been?" Sarah mused as she turned away from him and began to walk away losing interest.

"Oh, just some dumbass freshman," he answered in a flat blunt tone.

Sarah turned looking at him with an inquisitive look for a moment, "So what's around here to do anyway?"

Devin grinned slyly for a moment as he casually walked toward her, "Jamesville? Well there's this really boring museum, the lake, the cinema down town, or there's this club just on the outskirts of the industrial side of the city called The Clubhouse—"

Sarah raised an eyebrow cutting him off, "The Club house? And what's that all about?"

Devin reached into his pocket and pulled out a business card handing it to her with a wink, "Here"

She took the card and flipped it over in her hand looking at the small map on the back, "So what time's it open?"

"Be there tonight around seven," he answered with a smile.

"Alright, I suppose I can ask Angela for a ride..." She mumbled to herself while nodding some.

Devin shuddered in disgust at the name and scowled some, "Sure, if ya like 'em dumb."

"Huh? What, you don't think she's the perfect dream date like every other guy in school?" She teased a little.

Devin's expression grew flat for a moment, his tone matching as he answered, "Let's put it this way, I don't like sluts."

Sarah blinked in shock for a moment before she said anything else, "Guess you two don't get along, huh?"

Devin nodded quietly in response. Sarah gauged his mood carefully a moment before continuing on, "So… is Steven going to be there?"

Devin quirked a brow and gave her a penetrating stare for a long moment as if trying to figure something out, then he relaxed some and answered casually, "No, I don't think so. Why, would you like to see him there?"

Sarah blushed turning away some, "No! I just don't want to go anywhere that he hangs out that's all."

Devin chuckled softly as she turned and began to walk away briskly.

"So you're coming tonight, right?" He called after her, grinning wildly like a Cheshire cat.

Sarah turned calling back over her shoulder as she kept walking, "Maybe."

Shrugging as she walked away, Devin turned his head to the left to feel the gentle caress and whisper of the wind across his face and ears, "Oak…"

He raised an eyebrow in bewilderment as he sighed and put on his mirrored sunglasses, "Yes Kari, it's a tree… What do you want now, wind god?"

The wind only hissed its laughter as he moved through the parking lot to the place where his Harley was parked. Opening the saddle bags, he pulled out a dark red helmet and put it on casually before tossing his pack into the same bag and snapping it shut. Devin then pulled out a pair of black leather gloves and put them on before sliding his leg over the seat and zipping up his leather jacket. Smirking to himself, he kick started the engine causing the bike to begin to hum smoothly. A chill ran down his spine for a moment and he turned his head sharply toward the tree line, his eyes scanned the area and he could have sworn he saw a figure there a just a split second before standing in the woods wearing a green cloak, but as he did a double take, he saw nothing more than the wind dancing among the trees. Sighing softly he chucked it up to his imagination playing with him or the wind playing her usual games.

Revving the engine some he pealed out of the parking lot and onto the main road. As he pulled up to the first red light he flipped down his visor and turned his head taking note of the red corvette convertible beside him on the road. His eyes trailed over the occupants for a moment as he noted Sarah in the passenger seat and Angela in the drivers turning and smiling at him.

"Hey there stud," Angela yelled over at him, "Wanna have a little fun?"

Devin practically gagged until he realized she had no idea it was him on the bike, but then he smirked to himself deciding to play along and nodded without saying a word to her. Angela looked at Sarah and then to the two other cheerleaders in her back seat who had gotten a stupid grin across their faces.

"Well girls, let's make him chase us," She giggles as she revved her engine waiting for the light to change colors.

"Catch us if you can stud!" She yelled over at Devin as she gripped her steering wheel tightly and smirked mischievously.

The light turned green and Angela slammed her foot on the gas blazing a trail of burnt rubber down the road, as Devin revved his bike's engine allowing them a headstart. Sarah's expression turned pale as her hands clenched into a death grip along the dashboard of the car. The corvette flew down Main Street as Devin's dark red Harley sped after it, slowly catching up. Upon reaching downtown, the two red darts zipped past Highlander Mall where a squad car was parked and waiting for people to speed by. The two sergeants in the car yawned in boredom when the alarm went off on their speedometer and the corvette flew by at blinding speeds. The driver of the squad car fumbled in frustration trying to start the engine of the squad car and spilled his coffee in his lap causing a yelp of pain followed by loud cursing. No sooner had the cop started the car and its sirens when Devin sped by like a red lightning bolt no farther away than two feet from the driver's side window causing the driver to cuss once more and knock his partner's coffee over into his partner's lap.

"God Damn it!" The man in the passenger's seat yelled followed by a series of swears as he fanned at his crotch wildly.

The squad car squealed onto the road and after the two speeding red darts in hot pursuit. Devin heard the sirens and checked his mirror to see the police cruiser in heavy pursuit behind them.

"Oops…" He said hitting a blue button on the dash of his handle bars causing one of his saddle bags bottom to open and litter the road way behind him in spiky caltrop nails.

The squad car hit the spiky tacks at full force and the sounds of bang like gunshots echoed from the tires as the vehicle spun off the road and into a ditch. One of the cheerleaders hearing the sirens looked back out the rear of the car to see the cop car spinning out of control.

"Angela!" She yelled as she reached over the seat grabbing her shoulders forcefully and causing Angela to jerk the steering wheel and the car to fishtail out of control.

Devin pulled his bike up to the side of the car quickly as he saw it going out of control and took his chances diving off his bike and into the driver's seat, landing in Angel's lap as she sat there in a frozen panic. Pushing Angela into Sarah's lap, he took the wheel of the car and fought desperately to regain control and slow the vehicle down. Fighting with the wheel for several moments he straightened out the car and eventually brought it to a complete stop before he dived out of the car once more and down the adjacent hill the road was on tumbling out of sight through the dense tree line. Angela erratically pulled herself back into the driver's seat and yanked up her emergency break as she began shaking and crying loudly. Sarah sat motionless, staring into space with little to no color in her face as the other two girls tried to calm Angela back down to a reasonable state.

Devin tumbled down the hill, hitting trees and shrubbery all along the way, loud swearing left his lips with everything he hit. His foot caught a stump and he began to flip faster which only served to dizzy his head and bruise him more. Feeling himself stop rolling over ground and beginning to fall, he closed his eyes tight letting out a panicked scream when he suddenly stopped and felt as if he was floating back up. Hazily opening his eyes, he watched himself float up out of the trees and back out onto the road where he was abruptly dropped on his rump. Looking up and blinking in confusion, Devin's sight met the view of a big rig barreling down the highway about to run him over. He in took a deep breath as he blinked and looked again to see that time seemed to freeze in place. His eyes darted around in confusion and shock as he noted a figure standing on the side of the road wearing all black with a black-cowled cloak staring at him silently. The cowl seemed to move ever so as its shadows hid the face of its owner, as if a soft breeze was still drifting around the man from out of nowhere.

"Now what the hell is going on here?" Devin yelled as he threw his hands in the air in frustration, "First, I see some fool dressed in a green cloak, and now I'm seeing one in black? Am I dead?"

Devin became quiet and solemn as the figure deliberately approached and spoke in a whispering voice that seemed devoid of all emotion and feeling which sent a chill along his spine, "Be more careful, monsieur Noirlion, can't have you risking your life for just anyone, now can we?"

Devin stared speechlessly up at the figure for a long moment before finding his voice once more, "W-what? Who are you? I don't have to worry my watcher is… wait a minute! You're not my watcher… but you saved my life, why?"

The dark figure raised his hands and extended his arms as he spoke, "You must find that which will complete the circle, for you have two of the elements but lack the others…"

Devin blinked as he pondered with a confused expression, then a look of realization crossed his face, "The others? But how do I find them?"

The figure laughed with a hallow gusty sound as he gradually dissolved into mist, leaving haunting words behind in his absence, "It's all right in front of your eyes, you will know when the time is right Devin Noirlion…"

Devin stood and walked to the side of the road staring in awe as the big rig honked its horn and barreled by him. He sighed as he lit up a cigarette and a loud explosion from the other side of the road caught his attention, as he saw parts of his bike flying through the air.

"Damn it!"

Shaking his head, he took another long drag off his cigarette and began walking home through the woods mumbling to himself, "Mom's gonna kill me when I get home and she finds out about my bike…"

GLAMOUR

The wonderment of passion,
It's colors are purple and red...
The glow from thy window, tis a shimmer...
Yea, but a soft glimmer of the warmth you hold...
Like a candle in the wind...
Fighting, struggling, to n'ere allow the cold in...
A golden halo rides upon your fiery hair...
And eyes of jade, with innocence, are also there...
Just one sweet smile upon your lips,
Tis all I need to lift my spirits...

October 2008
Week 1, Friday

STEVEN SAT UP in his bed shaking his head and panting as he wiped sweat from his brow mumbling to himself, "Damn, that was a messed up dream. I hope Devin's alright."

He crawled out of bed and put on his pants as he began to head downstairs to the kitchen, his tone decreasing to a mumble as he walked, "Why wouldn't Devin be okay anyway? I just saw him at school no more than an hour ago, and it was just a crazy dream anyway."

Sighing he shook his head as he entered the kitchen and moved over to the fridge and pulled out a beer. Popping the cap off the bottle he took a sip and decided to call his friend up and lay the nagging feeling he had to rest.

Devin arrived at his home an hour or so after his bike blew into many pieces and tried with all his might to sneak in and past his mother who was vacuuming the living room. He crept in, cautiously turning the knob of the antique wooden door. Mrs. Noirlion had her back turned toward him and in that he sought out his escape up the stairs directly in front of the door. He took one step while thinking to himself, Okay, she can't hear me…

He took another step as her voice reached his ears with an inquiring tone which caused him to halt in place, "So, how was your day son?"

"Er… uhhh… fine, just fine… only one small problem…" He answered in low tones trying to keep a cool composure while standing in the foyer, his face dirty and clothes torn and bloody.

She deliberately turned and gave him a penetrating look over with a brow half-raised, "What… small… problem?"

Devin tried to appear nonchalant and shrugged as he replied, "Oh… I kind of got into a small car accident, but everyone is okay."

She looked at him questioningly for a long moment, "Did you use your powers?"

Devin looked down and shook his head, "No ma'am… but I wanted to. I ended up saving four girl's lives… but when I jumped to their car from my bike—"

Before he could finish she interrupted him with a near growling tone as her face began to turn red, "What happened to your birthday present?"

Devin kept his eyes down shrugging dismissively, "It… ah, well, it blew up."

"*What*?" She screamed at him.

"It's wrecked. There was nothing I could do! I was trying to save the girls and…" he pleaded in earnest while biting his lip nervously.

"And your bike paid the price, didn't it?" she interrupted shaking her head in anger.

"B-but it wasn't my fault..." He began to choke out.

Mrs. Noirlion was about to say something further when the phone rang pulling her focus away from Devin. She hesitantly picked it up still eyeing him with irritation and spoke quietly for a moment before handing the phone to Devin, "Its Steven, don't take too long, I'm not through with you yet, son."

Devin gratefully took the phone and let out a long sigh trying to speak calmly, "Hey, what's up man?"

"Devin? Are you alright? I just had the weirdest dream that your bike blew up and some other weird shit happened to you," Steven's voice crackled over the phone into Devin's ear.

"Well it was no dream for me man, my bike is dust..." Devin answered in exasperation.

"Damn. Well, tell your mom that it wasn't as bad as you thought and that I'm getting it fixed right now. Just be ready to come over and get the new bike before we leave out for tonight," Steven answered back over the phone, though his tone registered signs of slight shock.

"Thanks for letting me know man," Devin played it out with a slight grin, "Mom might not be quite so mad now... yeah... bye."

He hung up the phone and met his mother's gaze with a charming smile.

"Well?" She asked in suspicious tones.

"Steven found my bike and says it wasn't as bad as I thought, he'll have it fixed and ready for me to pick up by six tonight," Devin answered happily.

"You're real lucky to have Nightwolf as a friend you know, if it weren't for him you'd probably be in a world of hurt right now, if not dead..." She leveled her gaze at him once more while speaking before breaking into a smile, "So go get your bike and try not to wreck it tonight, okay?"

Devin grinned wider and nodded as he rushed up stairs to shower and change his clothes.

Steven lounged on the couch in his living room flipping the buttons on the remote so that the channels ran back and forth on the TV when the doorbell rang.

"I've got it master," Alfred the butler intoned as Steven was about to hop up and trot to the door to see who it was.

Instantly, he let himself fall back into the plush cushions of the couch and heard the door open and Devin cheerfully greeting Alfred at the door. Soon Devin popped into the living room with a broad grin spread across his face.

"You really saved my ass, man, how'd you know I was in an accident anyway?"

Steven nimbly sat up for a moment and looked at him curiously, "I told you, I had a dream… I can't explain it, it was weird."

Devin's brows wrinkled curiously for a moment and then he sat down to lounge in the chair beside the couch, "Well it doesn't matter anyway, our powers are totally different so maybe it's something new you're figuring out how to do…"

Steven sighed heavily for a moment, "It's not the only weird dream I've had lately… oh never mind…"

Devin glanced over at him even more curiously and decided to try and cheer him up some, "So, you're coming to the club tonight, right?"

"Huh? What club? Oh… Yeah, go on ahead. I'll be there in an hour or so. Need to take a shower first." Steven answered as he started to rise off the couch.

Devin grinned mischievously as he spoke in a light whiney tone, "Sarah was asking if you'd be there."

Steven shot him a look before breaking into a grin, "Well, we'll just see what we see, now wont we?"

Devin chuckled as he stood and waived bye before heading out and then riding off on his new bike.

Steven drove through the industrial side of town and briefly glanced at the time display on his CD player on the dash, mumbling it to himself, "Seven thirty-five pm already."

"Damn, I'm late," He cursed softly under his breath to himself.

Taking a turn into a dark alleyway he quickly pulled his car to a halt and parked behind the night club known as The Clubhouse. Turning off the Porsche he opened the door and stepped out and whispered into the darkness. The air around the car shimmered and he took a look at himself in his window. He was wearing black slacks and a button up long sleeved shirt of the same color. Waving his hands across his face and hair he mumbled the words to a spell and his appearance began to shift noticeably into someone else. His hair turned a light blond and a goatee grew out of the same color across his chin, his eyes also deepened in color seeming to become a dark forest green. Smiling to himself in satisfaction Steven made his way around the large building to the iron entrance door with a sliding peep hole. He knocked three times on the door causing a hollow sounding boom to echo in the alley way and then the sound of sliding metal followed as the hole slid open.

"Noirlion," Steven said calmly with a perfect French accent.

The hole slid closed and the sound of metal bars moving to unlock the door followed just before it was swung open, a large bouncer greeting Steven's sight.

"Welcome to The Clubhouse, sir, enjoy your time with us," the bouncer stated as he waived Steven in through the door before closing and relocking it with a heavy iron bar.

Steven nodded politely in response as he quickly stepped through the door and proceeded up the entry stairs to the main dance floor of the establishment. He deftly made his way past the bar and across the dance floor around people toward the DJ booth where Devin was putting out the latest and most popular tunes. As he stepped up to the request window Steven looked

Devin straight in the eye before speaking with a slight grin, "So, Devin, what do you think?"

Devin squinted for a moment in the low lighting of the club and then grinned chuckling in surprise, "Steven?"

"Yes, though I believe that it will be Sebastian for tonight my friend," Steven answered with a broadening sly grin.

"I like the glamour, it's an interesting touch to see you with blond hair and a goatee," Devin replied grinning back widely.

Angela and Sarah walked into the club with and easygoing pace and looked around to see if there was anyone they knew around. Sarah was wearing tight blue jeans and a low cut white t with Angel written across the back, while Angela was putting on an appearance in a high-waist black mini skirt and a sheer silk blouse with the top three buttons undone. Seeing Devin at the DJ's booth talking to some guy they'd never seen before caused a spark in the two girls attention and they walked over smiling curiously.

"So, who's your friend, Devin?" Angela asked looking Steven over with a gluttonous look in her eyes.

Steven turned toward them with a charming smile, "Sebastian, and pleasure to meet you…" he trailed off as he gently took Sarah's hand and kissed it in a gentlemanly fashion, which caused her cheeks to blush brightly.

Devin looked up from his tapes and CDs and forced a smile, "Hello… Angela," though his tone barely remained civil.

"Ahem…" Steven coughed, "Mayhap we should have a drink or two, yes lovely ones?"

Devin nodded toward them with a relieved look showing on his face, "Yes, show them a good time, Sebastian."

Steven nodded once and led the two of them to the bar, arm in arm, and ordered some screwdriver cocktails and a Long Island Iced Tea, though as he ordered the iced tea he pointed to Angela and discreetly slipped the bartender a hundred. The man nodded quietly in acknowledgement and turned to make the drinks quickly.

"So, Sebastian…"Angela began batting her eyes seductively, "Has Devin said anything about me?"

Steven turned looking at her with a slight smile and turned his tone to a deeper more seductive one, "I dunno… maybe."

"Anything interesting?" Angela persisted trying her best to match his charming bravado.

"No…" He replied flatly turning back to the bar to check on the status of the drinks.

Angela's expression darkened as she realized she had met more than her match in the game of seduction, but it changed back to charming as soon as he turned around once more.

"Awe, c'mon. You can tell me," she said wrapping an arm around his shoulders and looking into his eyes.

Steven smiled charmingly at her even though her touch really made him want to gag and leaned in whispering softly to her, "Well… I think he might really have the hots for you, but he's just too nervous to say anything."

Angela's eye's brightened. "You really think so?"

Steven turned once more, retrieving the drinks from the bar counter and handed Angela the long island ice tea and Sarah one of the screwdrivers.

"Oh yeah. I'm sure you two would get it… I mean get along great together," he lied smiling to her the whole while, not even hinting that he was doing so.

Sarah nearly sprayed the first sip of her drink all over the bar and Steven patted her back gently as she coughed. Angela took a drink of her ice tea and sat down on a stool before speaking again, "So do you think I should go talk to him or something?"

"Yeah! I think that's a great idea," he answered nudging her in the direction of the DJ's booth gently.

Angela rose and walked over to the booth and smiled up at Devin after taking another sip of her drink. Devin smiled back down at her, chuckling under his breath as he noted the long island ice tea with the pink umbrella in it, mumbling under his breath, "Oh my god, he didn't…"

"Wanna…"—hick—"dance Devin?" Angela asked taking another big gulp of her drink.

Steven chuckled softly to himself as he watched the exchange between Angela and Devin for a moment and then turned his attention to Sarah with a charming smile, "Do you dance beautiful Irish angel?"

Sarah looked at him nervously sipping on her drink, "Um… I don't know how to dance."

"Ahhh… well, 'tis not so hard as it looks," he gestured around to the people already on the floor dancing and grinding away, "Just follow my lead."

He gracefully took her hand gently and led her onto the dance floor with a cat's grace to his movements. Devin still looking at Angela with a sly smile answered her politely, "I would, except that I am DJing right now. Perhaps in a moment, yes."

Angela gave a silly smile as she took another drink and half-stumbled out onto the dance floor. Devin noticed that Steven and Sarah were walking out onto the floor as well and began to change the music up as he spoke into the mic, "Alright you all! We're gonna slow it down a little. Fella's if ya ain't got a girl then find one and win her heart through the song…"

Devin finished changing out the tapes and Boyz II Men began to play over the speakers. Steven led Sarah around the dance floor allowing her to get used to his slow steps and rhythm. Soon she had her arms wrapped around his waist and was keeping perfect pace with him while looking into his eyes and smiling up at him happily. He leaned over and whispered softly into her ear, "See, you dance beautifully little Irish angel…"

Sarah blushed deeply and bit her lip as she continued to looking into his eyes once more. She couldn't help but to feel like there was something familiar about him, but then dismissed the idea as he gently leaned in and kissed her on the cheek and making her mind spin in delight. Angela, trying to dance, staggering into people, made her way to the center of the dance floor where she began to sing slurred words along with the song. Everyone around her began to back away as she stumbled to her knees and abruptly passed out face first into the floor with her butt in the air. Devin, watching the whole scene, was barely able to keep control of his laughter as he thought to himself, *Yeah, that's about right for her*.

Steven stifled a chuckle as he broke away from Sarah and moved over, picking Angela up off the floor and carrying her over to the DJ booth and setting her down on the stairs near it.

"Hey, Devin!" he shouted up above the music of the club.

Devin, still shaking his head and chuckling in mirth looked down at Steven and the unconscious Angela.

"Think you can get her home safely tonight, Devin?" Steven asked with a slight grin.

"Ugh! Why me?" Devin responded with a disgusted look.

"Because fool, you're the only one who won't take advantage of her in this... er... incoherent state," Steven answered as he watched the drool drip down from the side of Angela's mouth onto her blouse.

He lifted one of Angela's hands and let it go allowing it to fall limply to the floor in demonstration. Sarah obliviously walked over and stood beside Steven putting her arms around his waist partly in affection and partly for support. Steven then noticed that she was now on her fourth screwdriver and remembered that he really hadn't even touched his yet. Devin put his left hand to his ear and spoke into a mic attached to his headset. Steven raised an inquiring brow, as Sarah seemed to notice Angela finally.

"What happened to Angela?" She exclaimed in surprise.

"Ah... too much to drink I believe," Steven answered flatly.

Devin removed his head phones as a backup DJ entered the booth from the back and took his place at the turn tables. Sighing and exiting the booth he moved down to where Angela was sitting and knelt down waiving his hand in front of her face irritably, "Ello? Anyone home?"

Steven chuckled unable to contain himself, "Out like a light old friend."

Sarah's face showed both surprise and concern, but the alcohol was already robbing her of her senses. Steven noticed her leaning on him even more, her eyes half-closed and then decided that it was time to take her home. He picked her up in his arms gracefully and began to leave, calling back over his shoulder toward Devin, "I trust that you'll take care of 'little miss show it all', right?"

Devin nodded as he rolled his eyes. "Alright, I'll handle it."

Steven laughed aloud as he went down the stairs carrying Sarah out the door of the club. He left the building and walked around through the alleyways to his car, carrying Sarah the entire way. Pausing as they approached he mumbled and caused the security system to deactivate before he opened the passenger's side door and carefully put Sarah into the car and buckled her in. Sighing softly he closed the door and walked around the vehicle and entered in on the driver's side and started the engine before nudging her.

"Huh?" she said partially asleep and mostly drunk.

"I need your address, angel," he said smiling to her once more.

"1323, Wicca Circle," she mumbled turning in the seat and going back to sleep.

Steven shook his head with a soft laugh as he pulled out of the alleyway and began driving toward her house. Devin groaned irritably as he leaned down and picked up Angela over his shoulder and carried her outside to his bike. Even though he really detested the girl, he knew that Steven was right about making sure that no one took advantage of her. Sighing he set her on the front of the bike and then pulled two helmets out of his saddle bag, placing the spare one on her. Then he swung his leg over and strapped on his own helm before kick starting the bike and pulling out of the alleyway himself. He knew where her house was, about a block from the school, and he knew what it looked like. Speeding away from the club he drove in silence down the dark streets of Jamesville toward her house. Several moments later, he was pulling into her driveway and cut off his engine to coast in so as not to wake her parents. Taking off his helm as he pulled to a stop in front of her porch where he paused noting the white swing they had sat in last year.

Memories came flooding back to him in a torrent and he had to check himself to hold back tears. Just that previous year they had been dating, they sat together in that very swing. Then one day, when they were sitting together another guy pulled into her driveway and said that they had met at a club over the weekend while Devin was working. He gave her and Devin a copy of the pictures which had been taken from that weekend. Angela denied it all, telling and begging Devin, swearing that she had been drugged and didn't remember anything about it. Devin didn't believe her. Their argument lasted for only moments, but in the end he believed that she had been running around him and thus he left. Loving her but hating her at the same time, even now he was torn with emotion. Shaking his head he sighed softly and rose off the bike before lifting her up and carrying her onto the porch and laying her down gently in the swing. Taking his spare helmet off her he paused looking at her face in the moonlight, and for a brief moment he remembered how happy they both once were. Notably taking off his own helmet Devin knelt down and kissed Angela softly causing her to stir some and then jumped off the porch quickly.

He put his helm back on and mounted his bike kicking the engine to life and pulling out of her drive leaving her to wake in a haze to stare after him as he sped away. He sped down the road toward his home, his mind now full of thoughts he no longer wanted and his heart heavy with emotions he wished he didn't feel. He cried as he drove, if only to ease himself from what he felt.

Pulling into the driveway of Sarah's house, Steven turned off the car and opened the doors. He stepped out of the car and moved around to the other side and carefully picked Sarah up in his arms and carried her to the front door of the house where he after a moment's hesitation knocked on the door. Soon he could hear the sounds of footsteps followed by the sound of the dead bolt unlocking before the door opened revealing a woman in a long night robe.

"Mrs. Roanoak?" He inquired politely as he looked her over a moment.

"Yes?" She asked squinting her eyes and searching her robes for her glasses.

"I've brought your daughter home. She fell asleep in the car, so I've carried her up the stairs to make sure she gets to bed safely," Steven answered honestly.

Mrs. Roanoak pulled out her glasses and slipped them on exclaiming in slight surprise, "Sarah? Is she okay? What happened?"

"She's fine, Mrs. Roanoak," Steven reassured her softly, "Her friend Angela brought her to the club, but they both had a little too much to drink. So I thought it safer to bring her home rather than to let either of them drive in their condition."

"Oh, thank you, sir," She said ushering him inside, where he gently laid Sarah on the couch in the living room.

"You have no idea how grateful I am, especially after how her father died."

Steven nodded as he bit back his curiosity before turning to leave, "Just make sure she stays out of trouble, ma'am."

Something in the air caused them both to pause as Steven turned back looking at her, their eyes meeting for a brief moment.

"You're not what you appear to be, are you, old wolf?" She said as they stood there in total fascination of each other for a brief moment.

Steven noticed that his glamour had faded, his hair was black once more and the goatee was no longer on his face. His hands reflexively rubbed his clean-shaven chin for a moment as a sudden note of fear struck in the back of his mind before he forced himself to calmly speak, "Things in life seldom are what they seem to be, milady…"

Mrs. Roanoak nodded, her eyes filled with unknown wisdom and power, "Yes, I know that all too well lad. But still, you should try to win her as yourself first… then maybe the two of you can play with glamour."

Steven examined her curiously for a long moment and then thought quietly before speaking again, "How did you know my family name? And why aren't you afraid of me like everyone else… when you see my unusual abilities?"

She smiled warmly at him a moment, "We are the same but different old wolf, besides I think you'll figure it out soon enough."

Steven nodded politely turning once more, "I would appreciate it if you didn't tell her who I really am, milady, might ruin her reputation at the school. The prospect of the school witch bringing her home and all… besides, I'm not supposed to be a nice guy according to rumor and I do have to keep up appearances…"

She chuckled softly and nodded once to him in understanding, "Rest assured heir wolf that she will only know when the time is right, until then, your secret is safe with me."

Steven smiled as he bid her good night and left the house moving to his car with a soft sigh of relief. He was soon driving home in silence, his mind thinking and wandering about the evenings events and he caught himself smiling every time he thought of Sarah though he wasn't sure why. He pulled down the drive to his mansion and parked near the entry way before turning off the car and exiting to look about briefly. Shaking his head to try and clear it he entered his home and went straight to his room and flopped down onto his bed and he began to drift off to sleep quickly and dream.

Shadows and Solidarity

Far away, far away…
Is the darkness far away?
Dost thou know of what thy speaks,
Or dost death come upon wings your soul to reap?
O' the lost souls of the dead,
Some good, some bad, and some unread…
Yet, it cares not, from me to thy…
While my fallen cousins break bread of rye…
Silent, silent, is their sleep…
Darkness is creeping and the mourners weep…
Tis a veil of blackened mist,
Crawling, crawling, at the ground with an evil hiss…
It lies in wait only for thy…
Smirking…
Knowing…
That ye shall die…
Stalked now, arrogant prey,
Is it you which shall die this day…

Tiara Swordfish, an older woman in her mid-sixties, walked through the dense woods near her home. The thick old trees were like a blanket unto the night, comforting, protecting her against anything that would try to scare or harm her. Her blond hair now turning silver glowed radiantly in the moonlight like star fall as she walked. She wore a deep blue velvet robe, which echoed the voice of the sea that was passed down from generation to generation for as long as she could remember. Her hair was long and cascaded down her back, usually left loose and free, it was now bound back at her neck by a single black silk cord.

Her figure was slender and shapely despite her age and she held herself proudly and confident, no doubt from years of experience.

Tiara knew that something strange and dangerous was coming back into the world, and that was why she once again embraced the old ways as she had in her youth. Though there had been times in the recent past where she had to use her skills, this was by far different. This time she knew that it was no longer her responsibility to act; however, she hoped that perhaps she might glean a vision or two to help ease her mind tonight for her dreams of shadows and destruction troubled her greatly. Visions of flame and death had been filling her mind for several nights now, and she wish to put an end to the charade of mystery. She paused in her motions momentarily, the moonlight reflecting brightly in her dark blue eyes which surged up like the tide before a storm as she surveyed the grove surrounded by a circle of five oak trees, all old and wizened by time. Her mind went back to her youth when she danced on many a night naked around the bonfire offering homage to the gods and conducting rituals in the moon's soft light with others who were as she was. She smiled fondly at the memories, for she had only been a year younger than her granddaughter Valerie when she had gained the mantle of her families power over water and though she had fallen in love with one of the others there who participated with her, it was a forbidden love, and the consequences of such were known to the families after their troubled past.

Then she sighed softly and sadly realizing that her granddaughter Valerie had shown no signs of power or of awakening to the family's heritage whatsoever. Perhaps it was naught to be, but Tiara refused to accept that in any regard. She stepped into the circle of trees and walked to an old altar in the northern section.

"Reveal thy true nature," she said in clear tones.

The surface of the altar shimmered like the surface of a pool sending out a soft blue light as symbols of magic raised up from its surface along with the tools for ritual work. She then went to a wood pile just outside the circle and began collecting up the timbers for the bonfire which would be set for this night. Taking the wood she began stacking it teepee style at the center of the circle in a fire pit made of polished blue marble. Tiara then fitted five bars across the top of the pit, placing them into slots which had been carved into the stone forming a pentagram. Carefully she lit the wood and watched the fire come to life giving of light and heat to the grove against the cool night air. She then returned to the altar and retrieved a small cauldron which she took to the brook that trailed just outside of the grove to the west.

Kneeling down, she filled the cauldron with its crystal clear waters before returning to the comforting warmth of the grove. Once inside the circle her movements were fluid as she stepped toward the center and placed the full cauldron on the star configuration which was suspended over the fire pit, placing it just so that she might look into it when the time was right. Her steps then took her to the northern section of the circle, where she began to speak in a crisp and clear voice, despite her age, "House of Oak, guardians of earth, come watch over my visions. I ask for your protection this eve."

The transparent apparition of an elder from the House of Oak could be seen shimmering into existence to watch over that section of the circle. His outfit seemed to match that of a woodsman of old, and his axe looked deadly and sharp as he took up his vigil. Tiara then turned and stepped to the eastern section of the circle and began to speak once more," House of Wolf, guardians of Air, come watch over my visions. I ask for your protection."

A light mist began to permeate the eastern section of the circle but no apparition appeared. Though surprised, Tiara knew to keep her mind on the task at hand as she turned once more and proceeded to the southern section of the circle. Her voice rung out into the night as she spoke again," House of Lion, guardians of fire, come and watch over my visions. I ask for your protection."

The transparent spirit of an elder from the House of Lion began to flicker into existence as if made of the same flames that it guarded. His attire was that of a knight, and his sword and shield seemed alive with flame as he took up his vigil at the southern section of the circle. Tiara then turned once more and proceeded to the western section of the circle, a smile on her lips as she spoke once more," House of my ancestors, House of Fish, guardians of water, come and watch over my visions. I ask for your protection."

The spirit of Tiara's mother shimmered into existence, a long formal gown was her dress, and she smiled fondly at her daughter before taking up her vigil in the western section of the circle. At that moment the circle of tree's seemed to pulse with energy and a silvery blue line sprung forth around its edges illuminating the area in light and power. Tiara smiled warmly as her steps took her once more to the center of circle and her eyes gazed down into the now bubbling cauldron. She waived her hand in a rhythmic pattern above the waters causing them to spin and churn in a counter clockwise motion, darkness and light rippling across their surface.

"Show me the malefactor of my dreams that I may know his true form," she intoned aloud, her voice firm and commanding.

The water within the cauldron bubbled and hissed as the sky began to cloud over and a breeze bearing the stench of old battle fields wafted through the air. Tiara covered her mouth as if warding something off, stifling a gag at the rotten stench, her eyes searching the waters for their vision as a shadow nefariously emerged across the rippling surface. It was darker than the blackest night and its eyes burned as if a light with molten lakes of lava. There was no good in its visage; it radiated hate and fear... and death. The circle pulsed as the cauldron exploded in an exhale of steam and hissing water, causing Tiara to step back in shock and surprise, but then her eyes darted to the south where the cause of the disruption occurred. There in the air just outside the boundaries of the circle lying in wait the shadow of her vision. Its claws seemed sharp and dripped with the blood of the innocents it had killed in life, for it was not living now. Tiara attempted to calmly regain her bearing, staring at the fiend, stunned, and paralyzed with fear as a deep chill crawled under her skin screaming at her to run, to get away before this creature took her as well in its dark embrace.

The shadowy thing approached the boarder of the circle and the silvery blue light began to flicker and fade away as if snuffed out of existence. Her soul filled with terror as her stomach twisted in disgust and panic. The only sound filling the now quiet night air was the thing's raspy hissing breath, which seemed to echo throughout the darkening grove. She opened her mouth; everything in her very soul wished to scream, yet nothing would come out.

Its talons clicked with a soft echoing sound as they began to reach for her, the blood dripping off of them like some decaying thick red oozing jelly. She wished she could close her eyes, scream, run away, but was frozen tight in terror. Just mere inches from her, its talons recoiled as lighting flashed in the night air and struck it, causing it to cry in pain and terrifying anger. The sound echoed as if a thousand dying babies all called out in misery, and shook Tiara to her very core. Her eyes moved, the fear barely subsiding as she watched another figure emerge, though this one from the mist in the east which still hung on the ground like some condescending tone which refused to submit to the will of something so foul. The figure was a man, cloaked in black and flowing like the wind as he sped across the circle closing the space between himself and the visage of darkness. His hand flickered from under his cloak and a blade appeared, lashing out at the thing as if like the lightning which had previously struck it. Tiara watched the battle, unable to grasp what had just happened; was she not a mere moment from death just a second ago? Who was this man who stood in place of the ancestors of the east?

The two fought blow for blow, light and dark clashing in fireworks of sparks and smoke. Then it was over as the man jabbed expertly and hit home with his blade causing the thing to wail once more and flee into the night's darkness as quickly as it had arrived. The man leaned on the blade, which Tiara could now see was a silver katana, his free hand lightly holding his right side as the clouds almost immediately cleared from the skies and the moon once more illuminated the grove in soft silvery light. As the light shimmered across the blade, Tiara could see symbols ancient and perhaps long forgotten etched along its blade, almost seeming to make the sword glow with a heavenly light.

Clearing her throat, she finally regained her voice and spoke a little shakily, "Are… are you the guardian of air? What… was that thing?"

The man steadily sheathed his blade as he turned still grasping his side, only his stormy grey blue eyes seemed to echo out from the darkness of his hood.

"Demon," his voice hissed like a winter wind, cold and crisp, "And no, I am not the guardian to the house of wind, dear lady, yet, somehow you summoned me here for your protection. Be thankful to the gods this night, for it could have easily been me that was driven away this eve."

The man turned, leaving the now darkening circle when Tiara called after him, "Wait! I can heal you if you are injured…"

The figure paused momentarily in his steps, never turning as he spoke once more, "No, I shall survive, besides you said you were here to see… not get involved."

She stood there staring at the figure, for despite the man's saving her life and appearing from the mist, she couldn't help but to feel that this was not at all so strange as it seemed, he even seemed familiar to her in some way but she couldn't place it. Then she summoned up her voice once more to ask one final question, "But, you are of the House of Wolf, are you not?"

The figure turned passively, his eyes flashing as if lightning themselves for a brief second before he responded to her while turning away, his tone as frigid as a polar wind, "I don't know what you're talking about…"

Tiara stood there in shock for a long moment at the man's answer, for whatever she had expected to hear that certainly wasn't it. The figure began to mist away like a light fog upon the wind in the early morning as she called out once again in curious desperation, "Then who are you?"

The only reply was the wind hissing laughter in her ears as the man completely faded away with the mist. Gradually regaining her composure, she began collecting up her ritual tools and placing them back upon the stone altar, whispering a soft spell to hide them with illusions before returning through the thick woods to her home. Her mind was now reeling with more questions than answers thanks to the eve's events and she had expected to have walked away with the opposite as with many past readings. A soft sigh left her lips as she entered the home and languidly made her way up the stairs of the old Victorian-styled home. Her soft footsteps came to a halt outside her granddaughter's door as she turned the knob and peeked in smiling at the sight of her sleeping peacefully. A long heavy sigh escaped her now and she gave up a silent prayer of thanks to the gods before heading off to bed herself.

October 2008
Week 1, Saturday

Steven awoke at noon rolling over with a groan and instantly grabbed his side nearly screaming in agony. As he haltingly climbed out of bed, he examined the long gash across his side and then the blood soaked sheets and bed spread. His breath hissed out from him as he swore and tested his steps gingerly, "Damn it! These dreams are just getting too real for my liking."

Quickly he grabbed his long silk robe and made his way downstairs to the kitchen where he ran into his butler reading the morning paper.

"Morning, Alfred," he said through a sharp stab of pain as he entered the kitchen and made his way to one of the stools at the center counter.

"Master Steven, late night?" Alfred responded quizzically, his ancient eyebrows somewhat raised in concern.

Standing once more Steven made his way to the fridge and pulled out a bottle of orange juice, which he promptly downed and then set on the island counter before a grin spread across his face and he responded, "Yes, actually… I danced with a very charming young lady last night…"

He took another long drink from the bottle before wincing in pain and nearly dropping the jug, "And I doubt if she even remembers me this morning…"

Alfred smiled warmly as he stood and helped Steven back to the stool, "Would the young master be needing a doctor or breakfast this morning, or perhaps both."

"No, no… I'm fine, I'll have my side checked out on my way to the mall and probably eat breakfast when I get there," he sighed to some degree as his eyes misted over in remembrance.

"And perhaps I'll bump into that little Irish angel again… heh… like it would matter if I did…"

Alfred nodded lightly before leaving the kitchen to attend to his daily duties leaving Steven in silent contemplation before he too rose and wondered to the shower while favoring his right side. After he finished his shower, he considerably bandaged up his side and carefully got dressed so as not to provoke any further damage with the wound. Pulling his hair back and tying it neatly with a black silk cord, Steven headed out of the house saying good-bye to Alfred as he left. Steven shut of his security system and hopped into the Porsche turning the ignition making it hum like a kitten. A slight smile came to his lips at the sound as he pulled out of the long driveway and sped off toward the doctor's office on the way to the mall. He admired the scenery of old trees and the fall colors of the leaves as he drove, his thoughts on occasion turning to Sarah, and then he was there pulling in to park at the doctor's office. He took a space near the building's entrance before turning off the car and carefully exiting. His steps took him into the office where he approached the admittance window and signed a sheet to let the secretary and the doctor know he was there. A sharp intake of breath hissed into him as he sat down to wait patiently; it was apparent to him that this wasn't going to be a quick fix. Only a moment had passed before he was being called into a back room where the doctor was waiting for him.

Ernie, an older man with thick spectacles and a bushy white mustache in a white lab coat smiled in greeting as Steven entered the room, "Ah, Mr. Nightwolf, what seems to be ailing you this fine morning?"

Steven took off his shirt and gingerly removed the bandage he had applied earlier causing him to wince noticeably and the doctor to gasp in slight shock. Shaking his head, Ernie gently tested the sensitivity along the edges of the wound and then had one of the nurses fetched lidocaine, cleaning supplies, and needle and thread.

"So what the hell happened to you, boy?" The doc asked in genuinely concerned tone.

"You wouldn't believe me if I told you, Ernie," Steven answered with a sharp hiss as the doctor began to clean the injury.

"Well, I'd say try me... but, knowing you and all the odd stuff that life has put you through you may be right..." Ernie said with a heavy sigh as he injected the lidocaine to try and numb up the area before beginning to sew it up with the needle and thread, which only caused Steven to flinch in pain.

"Well, at least you have a high-pain tolerance." Ernie continued as he sewed, "But, I want you to avoid any strenuous or otherwise extra circular activities for at least a few weeks."

"Damn..." Steven said with an exasperated sigh as he carefully put his shirt on once the bandaging was done.

"Yes, that includes dancing and sex, young man," Ernie said with a knowing chuckle and teasing smile knowing that Steven would never listen, even if it was in his best interest.

"Thanks Ernie, I'll check back next Saturday and you can chew me out then, okay?" Steven said with a grin as he walked to the front desk and paid the bill.

Ernie only sighed with slight exasperation as he waived bye and watched Steven leave heading toward the mall.

"He's gone. Looks like he had a pretty rough time with whatever you sent after that old lady..." Ernie said in hushed tones.

A soft dark chuckle echoed some in the room before a deep foreboding voice reached the doctor, "Good, then things are going according to my plan. You did well doctor... now I'll show mercy to your family... by executing them quickly!"

Ernie turned toward the shadows in the room and glared angrily as he nearly yelled at them, "You said you would let them go if I helped you! You filthy bastard! Give me my family back!"

Laughter filled the room once more before the voice echoed out again just as a scalpel flew off of the procedure tray and landed itself deep into Ernie's chest causing him to collapse to the floor gasping for air, "Oh just shut up and die you old fool... I never really had your family."

Sarah awoke at about ten thirty that Saturday morning and instinctively reached for her head, "Ugh..."

"Well, glad to see that you've returned to the world of the living with the rest of us," her mother said handing her two aspirins and a glass of water, "Did you at least enjoy yourself last night?"

Sarah sat up and took the aspirins with a gulp of water and then snapped fully awake realizing that she was on her living room couch and that her mother was sitting on the coffee table giving her a stern look.

Ughh! She moaned as she fell back into the pillows of the couch wishing she were dead.

"Well?" her mother asked sternly.

Sarah grudgingly sat up once again and replied in a near whisper of a voice, "Yes ma'am."

"Well, that's good dear," her tone changed to a lighter bit, "So tell me about this tall handsome gentleman who brought you home last night? Oh, what was his name…?"

"Sebastian?" Sarah said quizzically perking up a bit, "Er… well, he's a good dancer, and very polite."

Her face suddenly flushed as she realized that she had broken into a wide grin while speaking about him.

"Well, he was very kind to bring you home last night instead of taking advantage of your condition. You should be more careful and count yourself lucky to have found such a young man." Sarah's mother stated smiling tenderly, "So, do you have any plans for today?"

Sarah's face turned bright red with embarrassment for a moment as she answered, "No, I passed out in his car… probably made an absolute fool of myself and won't ever see him again…"

"Oh, I wouldn't be too sure of that, glum angel, I'm fairly certain that he goes to your school…" her mother trailed off with a slight grin.

"Really think so, mom?" Sarah inquired, hope sparkling in her eyes, "Maybe he works at the local mall or something then…"

Mrs. Roanoak smiled and nodded as she stood up from the coffee table, "Why don't you get ready and I'll take you over to the mall, at the very least you can do a little shopping for yourself and perhaps even get your own job."

Sarah stood nodding and made her way to the shower and to get ready for the day. After she was dressed, she and her mother went out to the family car and began the drive to the local mall. On the way there, they passed one of the local doctors' offices and Sarah noted the green Porsche parked there pointing it out to her mother, "See that Porsche, Mom?"

"Uh-huh, what about it?" her mother asked, noting that it was the same car which dropped Sarah off the night before.

"Well, I sit beside the guy who owns it at school. I mean, he's kinda cute, but he's always mean to everyone and I dunno why." Sarah continued on watching as they passed by the building and the car.

"I'm sure he has his reasons dear, people always act a certain way for a certain purpose." Her mother responded in an old wizened tone.

Sarah thought about her mother's words and surmised that she would have to learn why Steven was such a prick to everyone, *well*, she thought, *everyone except Devin*.

Sarah browsed the shops in the mall, leisurely looking into windows and comparing prices on this thing or that as she walked. She put in applications for employment, but she just couldn't seem to get the image of Sebastian out of her mind as she strolled along. Soon she made her way to a fountain at the center of the mall and sat down looking into the coin filled water. As she sat there, she pulled out a penny and tossed it into the water making a whisper of a wish, "I wish that I could just bump into him here today so that I could get his phone number… oh, Sebastian… where are you?"

She stood up and walked away from the fountain. As she made her way in front of the radio shack, Steven was walking out, arms full of parts, and they collided together as gracefully as a head on collision.

Crash!

Steven dropped everything he was carrying and began to apologize as he helped her up, "Sorry, I wasn't watching where I was going. Guess we're even now for the chair."

She looked at him with surprise and slight anger as he helped her up and dusted her off before bending over with a noticeable wince to retrieve his merchandise. Sarah paused in concern for a moment giving him a long look over before the memory of his attitude at school drifted into her mind. She yelled after him as he quickly walked off, "Ohhh! *Jerk*!"

She quickly turned and began walking in the opposite direction when something struck her and made her pause to turn watching him walk off, "Did he just apologize to me?"

She shook her head as she watched him disappear into the crowded mall and thought to herself, *He has beautiful long hair, just like Sebastian*, then began scolding herself silently for comparing the two of them. She continued her leisurely walk through the mall thinking about the recent encounter and began to believe her mother's earlier words did ring true after all. *Maybe*, she thought to herself, *there IS a reason why he's such a prick at school.*

Steven continued walking through the mall and stopped for a moment to look at jewelry through one of the display windows, silently he thought of how it would look on Sarah before he caught himself and swore under his breath.

"I must be losing my mind," he mumbled to himself as he turned away from the display and continued walking, "She'd never accept me for who I really am…"

Steven continued to browse through the mall finally stopping at the bookstore where he entered and began browsing through the endless rows of literature. He noted that there were more and more witches coming forward and sharing their magical secrets with the world, a fact that in itself caused him to smile a little bit. He continued to browse when a leather bound volume caught his eye, giving him a moment to pause as he cautiously picked it up. Turning the book in his hands, he noted that it was a journal, the front of it was embossed with a wolf howling up at a full moon, and the leather was a smooth dark-brown color. It was blank with parchment for pages and golden Celtic knot work along the edges. It even had a silver locking mechanism which he noted was quite strong and effective for something found in a common bookstore. Only one silver word graced the cover above the picture; it simply said "Wolf." His mind reeled with the idea of coincidence and strange similarity but quickly dismissed it as he approached the counter and paid for it quickly. He turned and began to make his way out of the store nearly running into Sarah again, though this time he caught himself in time and paused in step. She looked at the book curiously and then at him noting that a card had fallen out of his back pocket before speaking, "Buying a journal?"

Steven looked around quickly to see if anyone was watching before leaning in and whispering a reply, "Yes, why are you following me?"

She raised an inquisitive brow for a moment a bit surprised that he was actually being somewhat polite if not direct, "I just wanted to apologize for the other day in class…"

"Don't worry about it," He said before grabbing his side wincing noticeably once again as he tried to manage a smile, "I'm an asshole in school anyway…"

Sarah turned, watching him walk away, debating if to follow when she noted that he seemed to vanish into thin air as he entered the crowds. Turning with a sigh, she looked down and picked up the dropped card and silently read it to herself.

> Steven Janarah Nightwolf
> 555-465-0608
> Private Tutor

Steven wove his way through the crowds of the mall trying to ditch his fiery red-headed follower. Ducking into the bathroom, he entered a stall and lit a cigarette taking a deep drag with an exasperated sigh. Breathing out in relief he mumbled to himself, "Finally, I've never had so much trouble trying to ditch someone my whole life."

The sound of a broom sweeping across the floor caught his attention quickly as it was followed by an old deep gruff voice, "You know lad, when I was young I had a pretty lass that wouldn't leave me alone…"

Steven smiled to himself as Sarah popped instantly into his mind and he took another drag before speaking once more, "Really? Whatever became of it?"

"Well," the old voice chuckled, "She eventually caught me and we were married"—sigh—"Sometimes I still miss her and the games we use to play…"

"Well, I dun plan on getting married for some time yet to come," Steven replied thoughtfully for a moment, "Though I do suppose a family would be nice someday…"

"Ah… but you have a family already, or have you forgotten the vows you made that night to that young girl?" The old voice chuckled as it seemed to fade away.

Steven bolted out of the stall looking around the empty bathroom wildly. He sighed as he tossed the cigarette in the toilet and flushed it, his tone turning suspicious as he took another quick look around, "Damn if life isn't getting weirder by the day… maybe I really am just losing my mind."

He left the bathroom reemerging with the crowds as he made his way to an embroidery booth near the fountain at the center of the mall. He handed the man the book he had recently purchased and gave him instructions on certain adjustments to be made so that it could be picked up the following day.

Love and Hate

Watching, watching, as I may…
Tis all I can do anyway…
Tempted I may be, tempted I may stay…
Yet you seem so far away…
How I long to touch your skin,
How I wish for love that would never end…
Gentle embrace abandoned be…
By the gods how you beckon me…
Oh, is this how we should live…
Separated by space, yet so close we could kiss…
For death may come to take thee from me…
And then the past would just repeat in solidarity…

October 2008
Week 2, Monday

STEVEN ENTERED LITERATURE still thinking on the weekend's events which had taken up residence within his mind. He was so preoccupied that he actually smiled at Sarah rather than scowling when she took up the seat beside him. Sarah stared at him for a moment in slight surprise and shock before quickly pulling out her notepad and pen. She quickly made a note about his change in attitude and mood and leaving it open to questions as to why. As class went on, she also made note that Steven seemed to return to his calm and collected demeanor. Figuring that his attitude had probably changed as well back to the prick she had met the week before, she decided to test her theory, "Good morning."

He raised a slight brow in her direction, but remained silent and focused on class in every other regard. Silently he thought to himself while catching a sideways glance at her, *What? What is it that you want from me? Don't you realize that I just want to be left alone ?*

Sarah suppressed a slight smile as she made a note to herself as being correct on the change in his moods. She just couldn't reason why he was polite at the mall, but so cruel while in school. She sighed in mild agitation as she returned her attention to the class at hand. Steven quietly noted her sigh and wondered if it were possible to get her to leave him alone during school by agitating or ignoring her. The bell rang and everyone left for their next class. He noted that as he traversed through the halls that she was hot on his heels close behind him. As he entered calculus class and took his usual seat and he pulled out his notepad and pen. Sarah came in right behind him and sat in the desk just to his right which caused the other students within the class to glance at them and then each other nervously for a moment nervously. She frowned at their reaction, but held her tongue as she pulled out her own notebook and pencil. Coach A entered the room as the bell rang.

"Morning class!" he stated with a large grin, "I was wondering if one of you could verify a rumor that I've heard this morning? Hmmm, any takers?"

The class perked up at the mention of gossip over a lengthy discussion of math in the morning.

"It seems, according to rumor of course, that someone underage at this school had a little run in with alcohol and made some poor decisions…" he trailed off, "I was only wondering if any of you could perhaps clarify or shed some light on the rumors at hand?"

Sarah raised her hand and began to speak up above the whispers which were being spoken by the other students in the classroom, "Yes sir, she had too much to drink and had to get a ride home from the club."

The classroom buzzed with talk as Steven frowned at the answer given, knowing that it was only partially the truth. Thus, he stood up and cleared his throat causing the room to fall into a deathly silent atmosphere, "That is only part of it I am afraid, the person in question, Angela, had so much to drink that she passed out on the dance floor with her rear in the air waiving around like an advertisement sign before someone picked her up and took her home so that nothing would happen to her in her wasted state."

He sat back down trying not to grin with satisfaction as the facts, for the most part, were revealed to take their course. Sarah's eyes widened as she looked over at him in anger and utter disbelief as she hissed to him in a whisper, "How could you tell everyone that? Or even know about that? You weren't even there!"

Steven looked at her, barely keeping a straight face as he calmly replied to her in his icy tone, "I know."

Sarah stood up grabbing her things and stormed out of the class without even asking to be excused. Steven chuckled to himself as he leaned back in his chair relaxing, quite satisfied at his success. The room filled with rumors about Angela as class went on and soon the bell rang. Steven grabbed up his things and headed straight to the bathroom, his movements taking him to his usual seat on the counter where he lit up a cigarette. Taking a long drag he breathed out several *o*'s with a sigh of satisfaction. As he sat there smoking, he thought about what might happen to Angela and her reputation.

"Oh well," he sighed to himself, "What's done is done."

Finishing his cigarette, he put it out on the counter and headed off to business class. As he entered the classroom, he groaned quietly in annoyance seeing Sarah once more sitting in the chair beside his. He rolled his eyes heavenward asking for forgiveness for whatever he had done wrong in a previous life as he walked to his seat and sat down quietly. Mr. Fergus began class as usual with his back to the students as he lectured on about laws and concepts of business all the while writing on the board. A paper airplane flew across the room catching Sarah's attention away from her notes and was soon followed by a paper ball from the opposite side of the room.

Steven slid his chair away from her before he began to lounge back in it as if everything were perfectly normal. Rumors floated back and forth across the classroom almost as often as the paper instruments of war. Sarah turned her attention back to her notes sighing in irritation at the immature behavior being presented. Soon a paper ball flew just a hair from her nose causing her to look up to see the students engaged in world war three of their own design with paper instruments of doom as the teacher continued to lecture completely oblivious to what was transpiring behind his back. Though she was still highly upset with Steven for what he had said in calculus she decided to glance over and see if he too was participating in this immature display of aggression. As she looked over she saw that he had distanced himself far enough away so as not to be caught off guard by her foot should she decide to go for his chair legs again while he lounged back.

He doesn't even really seem to care too much if at all about what's going on around him, Sarah thought to herself as she now stared at him curiously. Steven glanced over at her and raised a brow in a peculiar manner, which caught her off-guard and made her wonder what to think. Then, with a slight smile tracing his lips for the briefest moment Steven raised one finger and all of the paper instruments of war froze in the air suspended by some unknown force before bombarding Mr. Fegus as he turned around with mouth agape. Sarah sat there gawking at what she had just witnessed, not truly willing to believe it possible while trying to convince herself that it was merely her eyes playing tricks on her. Mr. Fergus was however turning a bright shade of red as the classroom fell silent, "All of you have detention right after school today with the exception of Mr. Nightwolf, is that understood?"

The students nodded dumbly with all of their heads down and Sarah's heart sank as she tried to think of what she would tell her mother when she got home late from school.

"Ah… Mr. Fergus?" Steven spoke up in clam tones.

The teacher turned and looked at him curiously, though anger still flashed in his eyes, "Yes Steven?"

"The young lady beside me here," he gestured to Sarah as she gulped nervously and watched as the teachers eyes fell upon her, "Was not involved with the paper ball massacre of third period business, she has been taking notes and paying attention to you this whole time."

Sarah registered surprise and confusion at Steven's remark and once again wondered why he was kind at one point while a total jackass at another.

"Thank you Steven, Miss Roanoak you are also excused from the classes punishment," Mr. Fergus stated managing a smile and trying to sound cheerful and upbeat once more.

Sarah turned looking at Steven once again as if trying to puzzle him out. He turned suddenly whispering to her, "Stop it! All that staring is starting to creep me out!"

Sarah quickly turned back to her notes trying to think of what to say considering that he had just caught her off guard again. The bell rang and everyone began to shuffle out of the room, most of them with their heads still down. Steven packed away his notebook and stood leaving to lunch, Sarah stealthily followed after him in curiosity. She waited until he sat down at an empty table before moving to it and sitting directly across from him and eyed a book which he seemed to be writing in. Steven looked up from the book with a growingly more annoyed expression crossing his features before frowning, "Yes?"

She considered him for a moment before speaking in low tones, "Why did you tell everyone in calculus about Angela?"

Steven looked at her, his eyes narrowing in irritation as he flatly responded, "Why should you care?"

Sarah flushed noticeably at his response, "As a matter of fact I do care, and Angela is my friend, so I want to know."

Steven sighed lightly and then looked her over for a moment before nodding thoughtfully as he put his book away in his bag, "I see… well she's not my friend and it's a long story that I don't have time for right now…" the last bit coming out a bit more scornfully than he had intended.

She backed away from him at his tone before finding her own boldness, "Well, maybe if you weren't such a prick to everyone you'd have more friends!"

Steven's eyes misted for a moment as her words hit him like a brick wall before he blinked them clear and responded in a tone that could freeze hell, "You don't know anything about me girl…"

Sarah sat frozen in place as Steven rose from the table and left the lunchroom quickly, his face now starting to turn red. After he was gone, she felt a great pain and loss fill her heart as she couldn't put his troubled stormy blue eyes out of her mind. She put her head down in her hand and cried silently for a time all the while wondering why she felt this way.

Steven left the lunchroom barely holding the raging emotions within himself under control. His steps took him to the court-yard at the center of the school ad he walked over to a bench in the shadows and sat down to weep quietly where none would see him.

"Damn!"

He cursed silently to himself, "Damn her for getting to me!"

Sarah rubbed her eyes dry and noticed that Steven had left his bag on the floor in his haste to leave. She leaned over and picked it up causing the leather bound journal she had seen him buy over the weekend to fall out onto the table and pop open. Sarah's eyes went to the page and she gasped in surprise to see that the page was actually a loose paper which had the sketch on it which he was working on the previous week. What surprised her more was that the sketch was of her, though that only served to cause her to smile to herself. She turned the page to view a note about her eyes and smile as well as an explanation of his slight crush on her, but also of his uncertainty of what to do about it. As she continued to read on, she learned that he acted the way he did to try and keep people away, yet somehow Devin and him had a very strong friendship which was kept as a secret from nearly all. There was no explanation of why however, and she was left puzzling over it until she came across a poem which struck her as vaguely familiar, though she couldn't figure out why. She read the title aloud to herself as she thought on it, "Irish Angel."

Sarah closed the journal and heard the lock click audibly. Curiously, she tried to re-open the journal, but found that it was securely closed now. Sighing softly, she placed it back into his bag and headed to art class as the bell began to ring.

Steven heard the bell ring and left the courtyard to go to class while still trying to calm himself down at the same time. As he entered the art class he cursed to himself quietly realizing that he had left his pack somewhere. Shaking his head he sat at his usual table to look down and see that his bag was sitting there beside his chair. Sarah watched as Steven entered the classroom and noted that his face was flushed and that he was cursing under his breath to himself until he sat down and a peculiar look akin to surprise and confusion spread across his face. She turned away just in time, as he snapped his head up and in her direction with an inquisitive look.

Devin entered the room chatting with a friend about the past weekend, but as he reached Sarah's table he noticed Steven's look and followed it right to her. He sat down beside her and suppressed a slight smile. Sarah remained engrossed with her blank notebook, staring blankly at the page as Devin leaned over and whispered to her, "Ahhh… yes, quite the work of art if I might say so myself."

Sarah looked up at Devin finally realizing that he was there, "Huh? Oh, it's nothing, just artists block…"

Devin noted the look of a mind elsewhere in thought portrayed in her eyes and frowned realizing that he was wasting his sarcasm to an empty audience.

"Devin," a voice whispered near his ear causing him to jump before he saw Steven looking at him, "see if you can find out if she went through my stuff please."

He nodded just barely in Steven's direction before returning his attention to Sarah who was now watching him curiously.

"What's he doing over there? Is he still looking at me?" she asked him as her eyes seemed to be gauging his reaction.

"Uh… I dunno, but me thinks he likes you a bit," Devin replied trying to figure out if she had heard Steven as well.

Sarah continued to look at him curiously, "That's nice, but I already guessed that much."

A far off look entered her eyes once more as she continued, "Besides, I've got my sights set on Sebastian…"

Devin snorted laughter and quieted himself quickly as Sarah gave him a penetrating glance, "Gawd girl, you honestly think you'll see him again?"

"Of course I will," she said as a matter of fact, "He goes to this school after all doesn't he?"

Devin smiled broadly, "Uh… yeah, he's here, but I doubt you'll ever see him. He's not who you think he is…"

Sarah shook her head defiantly, "Really? Well I think he's the perfect gentleman and an amazing dancer. Hell, he could have taken advantage of me Friday night but took me home instead..."

Devin simply stared at her as if trying to figure something out. Sarah stared back at him calmly and then suddenly burst out loudly so that everyone could hear her, "And at least he acknowledges my existence and is polite to me instead of being cruel all the time while harboring a secret crush that he's afraid to admit."

Devin's mouth stood agape as he tried to find something to say to change the subject, but as he glanced over at Steven, he realized that it was a bit too late as his face was already changing from its tan complexion to a bright red. He quickly put his hand over Sarah's mouth to try and stop the now escalating situation from getting worse as she tried to speak again, "And another thing mmmmmmmm..."

Devin hissed to her in her ear as Steven began to rise from his chair, "Shut up! Are you crazy or just stupid? Even I know better than to really push his buttons and piss him off!"

Sarah looked at Devin and then to Steven, their eyes meeting. She went completely pale realizing that she really had hit the wrong nerve on him this time. Devin quickly let go of her and stepped between the two while thinking to himself, *Damn, this is really gonna hurt.*

Then, just as he braced himself for the worst he was caught by surprise as Steven, practically glowing with energy, simply grabbed up his bag and left the room. Devin sighed in relief as he gratefully sank back down into the chair beside Sarah who's voice came out trembling like the squeaking of a mouse, "W-why didn't he do anything Devin? I know he could have... I could feel that electricity in the air..."

He looked over at her still trembling form and spoke, noticing that his voice was but a hoarse whisper, "I dunno... I guess he really does like you otherwise he would have let his temper snap and we'd both be in a world of hurt you can't even imagine."

He cleared his throat as he continued regaining some of his voice back, "Why are you trying to get to him anyway? Don't you know he's only mean to everyone so that they leave him alone? His life hasn't exactly been a bed of roses like everyone else here."

Sarah only mutely nodded as color started to return to her face.

Crash! The sound echoed through the class door from the hall.

Devin ran to the door and poked his head out to see vending machines flying down the hall and crumpling up like paper cups. He slowly returned to his seat with a look of shock on his face, "I think he finally snapped while walking by the vending machines…"

Sarah looked at him a bit nervously and thought it best just to remain silent for the time being.

Steven walked out of the classroom as calmly as he could manage, despite the growing inferno inside him. As he passed down the hall and walked by the vending machines something inside him just snapped, and he waived his hands furiously in their direction causing them to fly down the hall and to crumple up as if they were nothing more than an empty soda can. His eyes narrowed as he abruptly turned and stormed out of the school to his car.

The bell rang and Sarah grabbed up her bag when something near Steven's table caught her eye. She abruptly walked over picking up the piece of paper noticing that it was the same one she had seen during lunch. The sketch was perfect, with even more detail than she had seen earlier giving it a life-like quality. She also noticed that is was now signed, *For Sarah, a beauty on earth. Steven J. Nightwolf*

Sarah stood there feeling very foolish and stupid now about her earlier outburst. Leaving the art room, she went to go sit in the school's courtyard for a moment to try and reason things out in her head. She sat on a bench in the shade when an old voice caught her attention, "You know, he's really not that bad once you get to know him and get past all of those barriers he puts up… he's just overly cautious about his emotions and letting people get too close… comes from not having a family I'd bet…"

Sarah looked up to see the old school janitor leaning on his broom and smiling softly as she tried to find her voice, "W-what do you mean?"

"Well, you see, Steven is a great deal more sensitive and caring than he would ever let anyone know… or even admit to himself I'd imagine. Hell, I'd say you got his clock all wound up pretty good there missy," the old janitor chuckled knowingly, "He really does like you, but I imagine he's just too damn proud to admit it, maybe even to himself."

Sarah stared at the old man for a moment thinking on what he told her before she spoke again, "He was out here during lunch wasn't he? Was he crying?"

The old janitor nodded silently and continued on sweeping the cobblestone path which wound through the beautiful courtyard. Sarah stood up nodding to the janitor before heading off to class. As she went through the rest of the day, she asked around about Sebastian, but the only guy with long hair that anyone knew of who went to the school was Steven. By the end of the day, she realized that he wasn't coming back to class and that she probably wouldn't see him.

Steven sat on his car in the parking lot of the high school smoking a cigarette and thinking on what Sarah had said in art class, his thoughts led him to the conclusion that she might actually be right. Just maybe he was too cruel to the people around him and didn't want to admit that he liked her because of what it might mean. As the busses began pulling away, he noticed Devin standing outside his window and lazily rolled it down eyeing him curiously.

"You know after you left she was asking about Sebastian all around the school until the end of class right?" Devin asked in moderate tones still uncertain of his mood.

Steven thought for a moment and then waived his hands across his hair and face changing his appearance back to the one he used at the club, "I think it's time to put an end to this Sebastian thing."

Steven exited his car and Devin walked with him to where the remaining busses were about to leave from. As they reached the sidewalk, they could see Sarah running over to the two of them with a wide smile. Steven whispered lowly to Devin before she reached them, "Well, here goes nothing. I hope I'm doing the right thing here."

Devin nodded silently as Sarah reached them and had to catch her breath before speaking, "I-I've been looking for you…"

Steven looked her up and down and began to hate himself for what he was about to say, "Sarah," he started gently, "I'm married…"

Her jaw dropped in disbelief as she slapped him before running to her bus in tears. Steven sighed heavily as he watched it drive away and then turned to Devin instantly assuming his true form, "God I hated doing that…"

Devin looked at him oddly for a long moment as he watched Steven gently rub his face before he exclaimed to him, "You do like her don't you? And there I thought you were just trying to get her to leave you alone…"

They stood there for a long moment in silence, both knowing the truth of the matter, yet neither really willing to say it. Soon Steven turned and went back to his car hopping into the driver's seat. Devin just stood there and watched him leave, but somewhere in the back of his mind he was genuinely worried about his friend and his change in attitude, he just couldn't put his finger on why. Still, Devin knew that this change in Steven's character would dramatically affect things in one fashion or another.

Getting to Know You

A breeze, a touch,
Your gentle caress which I crave…
Eyes of jade, made to entice…
Hair of fire, more than suffice…
Beauty to amaze, meant for no man alive or in the grave…
Oh how they must hound thee,
Simply for a glance, yet your smile is rarer still,
Hope for a glimmer, and to gain your hand at will…
It's like a thick morning mist,
The haze you put into my mind…
Then all my worries and struggles become benign…
How I love to hear you sigh,
The sweet sound of your breath makes me believe to heaven I've gone and died…
A crush, mayhap a simple term…
Or is it a touch of the love i crave and constantly yearn…

October 2008
Week 2, Tuesday

The figure cloaked in black walked down the dark alleyway quietly. His face was hidden save for a pair of glowing golden eyes which seem to tell a story of concern for those less fortunate and of power unknown to most. His boots made no sound as he approached the police tape. Had anyone, save for the drunk bum, been there to see him, they would have either gasped in awe or ran in fear at the sight of him walking through the tape as if his very being was made up of nothing but an illusion. The figure approached the wall surrounded by the tape and examined it closely. His senses were tingling all over, but he still couldn't place the uneasy feeling which was welling up inside him.

"Yes," the figure mumbled to himself as he passed his hand through the wall and then pulled it back out and waived it across the front of the surface of it for a few moments.

He tested the wall once more and found that he was right; he was able to repair the walls, for it was now solid once more.

"Shadow magic?" he continued mumbling to himself, "This will have to be dealt with quickly."

With that the figure vanished into nothingness.

Steven awoke to the beep of his alarm clock and silently compared its sound to that of a wailing banshee as he gradually got out of bed and walked to the bathroom to shower. His mind swirled with memories of the dreams from the night before of black cloaks and transparent walls. Then his mind wandered back to the glowing sword from the dream he had had before the weekend.

"Well, better to dream about being some weird superhero than to dream about school I guess," he remarked to himself while shaving in the shower.

He cleaned his wound wincing in noticeable agony before stepping out of the shower still feeling rather tired, but shook it off as he grabbed a towel to dry off. Looking into the mirror, he pulled back his hair with a black silk cord and ventured over to his closet to pick out the clothes for the day. Yawning with a stretch that nearly caused him to double over in pain, he paused and picked out a long-sleeved button up green silk shirt and a pair of loose fitting but expensive black leather pants. Sighing as he dressed, he slipped on his black leather riding boots and went down to the kitchen to grab something to eat. The fridge was full of both health and junk food Steven noted as he browsed with boredom. Eventually after several minutes, he gave up on breakfast and went to the living room and turned on the TV to watch the local news. The forecast called for partly cloudy with a chance of rain, as the other newscasters went on about some delinquent youth whose identity remained unknown was vandalizing local businesses around town. Steven chuckled softly to himself as he listened and commented offhandedly to himself, "I'll bet Devin will get a kick out of this one."

Sighing in boredom he turned off the TV and headed out to his car for the drive to school.

Sarah's mind continuously drifted to Steven as she got dressed for the day. She was beginning to believe that he might not actually be that bad of a guy after Sebastian had told her that he was married the previous afternoon. Soon she found herself at the bus stop and watching the passing cars go by. Suddenly Steven's Porsche flew by blasting Metallica causing her to shake her head in disbelief and amazement as she thought to herself, *He's going to get himself killed driving like that.*

Then her bus pulled up and she was off to school herself.

Steven pulled into the parking lot and resumed the spot marked for his car. As he exited the vehicle, he noted that the busses were arriving and decided to head to class before he ran into Sarah, whom he wasn't quite sure of what to think, but certainly knew that he was growing very fond of. Sarah exited the bus and scanned the parking lot for a brief moment. Seeing Steven's Porsche already parked, she decided to chance curiosity and began walking toward it. As she reached out to touch the car, an old voice startled her into jumping back startled.

"Wouldn't do that if I were you lass… the last young'un that touched that boy's car nearly got himself killed, what with convulsing on the ground and all…"

Sarah turned to see the old school janitor leaning on his broom once more. Smiling innocently, she started to ask him a question, "And who was this kid and what exactly happened to him?"

The old janitor's gaze shifted as if recalling some distant memory from the depths of his mind, "Yes, that would have been Devin, Devin Noirlion. At the beginning of last school year, he took a bet with some of the freshmen and upperclassmen that he would steal something from the school witch's car. Yes... it was actually rather funny afterwards. He reached over and no sooner had he touched that car when a bolt of fiery blue lightning came down from the skies and struck him down, and on a clear day too. All the students scattered like cockroaches, too afraid to offer him any help as the boy lay there twitching like a dying prisoner in an electric chair. Then, not but twenty minutes later, Devin got back up right as rain and ran back into school cussing up a storm and rubbing his hands like they had been burned."

The old janitor's soft chuckle and mannerisms seemed somehow familiar to Sarah, though she couldn't quite place it. Then the bell rang and she turned running off to the school calling back to him, "Bye."

Steven entered literature class and took his seat, pulling out the leather bound journal he had purchased over the weekend and skimmed through the pages noticing that the sketch he had done of Sarah was missing. Softly he cursed to himself, "Damn, I must have lost it yesterday."

Flipping to a blank page, he began to write about the previous day's events, leaving out entirely that he was Sebastian and only writing about what he did and how he had felt. Sarah entered the class, just before the late bell rang and sat a seat away from him. She noticed that the corners of his mouth twitched just a fraction but otherwise he continued to write in the journal she had seen him buy at the mall. Sarah quickly got up and moved over to the seat beside him knowing that it might agitate him, but decided to chance it anyways. Steven frowned noticeably, wrote one last line, and then closed the journal with a resounding click of the lock.

"What cha' got?" Sarah asked trying to play innocent while batting her eyes in a rather ditzy manner.

Steven looked at her silently for a moment and she could see the storm beginning to brew in his eyes as he spoke, "Must you?"

Sarah only smiled back at him charmingly causing his face to quickly turn three shades redder before he took a long deep breath and applied his attention to the class at hand. She pouted to herself trying to think of a way to get past his barriers to his inner emotions, so that he might open up to her, but nothing was coming to mind. Sighing heavily she resigned to paying attention to the class as well. Soon the bell rang and Steven grabbed his bag and bolted out of class, leaving Sarah still sitting in her chair. He walked down the hall casually when the sound of a freshmen snickering at him caught his attention, and he was already starting out the day on a bad note. Stopping abruptly he turned and looked down at the group of freshmen, his eyes seeming to flash like lightning. In a voice similar to the growl of a timber wolf, he snarled at them, "What's so amusing you twits?"

The group of freshmen backed up against the wall while turning as white as a ghost from fear. Eventually one of them found their voice and meekly spoke, "Sorry sir, we didn't mean to laugh… it's just that Angela has been telling everyone that worst lay she has ever had last Friday…"

"*What*?" he roared turning beet red and causing the group to begin trembling, "I'll kill the lying bitch!"

One of the freshmen lost it completely and dropped to the floor out cold as the others cringed more against the wall together as Steven went storming down the hall, every single person seeming to try and scramble out of his way quickly.

Sarah emerged from the classroom to see everyone nearly pressed flat against the wall as they all tried to get out of Steven's way as he stormed down the hall all red in the face. Looking around to try and get a grasp of what might be going on, she noticed the group of freshmen all huddled together trying to revive their passed out companion and made her way over to them calmly asking them what had happened. The one meek freshmen spoke up once more answering her question telling her the whole story of what had just transpired while still looking around nervously.

So, she thought to herself, *Angela's been spreading rumors about him because he told everyone about what she did Friday night, but why sex?*

Sarah resolved to speak to Coach A about the situation and headed down the hall quickly to calculus. She entered the classroom and noticed that Steven was already sitting in the back of the room in his normal seat; only his face was a mask of anger and hostility and not the usual calm and collected appearance which was usually there. She quietly sat down beside him and pulled out her notebook and pencil. Steven sat quietly; his mind swam with so much rage and frustration that he could barely contain it. His thoughts bent only to the rumor which he had just heard that he didn't even notice Sarah sitting down beside him until she gently nudged him and passed him a note. Distracted momentarily from his brooding and caught off guard by the gesture he carefully unfolded it and read through its contents silently to himself.

"I know you're angry right now, but please trust me and let me talk to her first before you do anything. Sarah"

He glanced over at her uncertainly for a long moment as if trying to determine her motives and then nodded once while whispering to her, "She's your friend, but don't betray my trust."

Sarah gave him a small nervous smile and then turned to think about what she was going to say to Angela. She knew she had just gotten through his barriers and that this might be the only chance she got to do so. She prayed silently that she just didn't screw it up; for she figured that he might really get pissed at her if she did. Soon the bell ran and the class emptied save for Sarah, who remained to approach Coach A, "Um… Coach A?"

"Yes, Miss Roanoak?" he responded cheerfully.

"Well sir, it's about Angela, she got really messed up last weekend and because Steven told you, she's been spreading these rumors about him to the whole school," she answered a bit nervously.

Coach A's expression turned serious for a brief moment, "Don't worry Miss Roanoak. Angela is going to be taken cared of today, as a matter of fact she is probably going to receive some unsettling news due to her recent behavior," then he raised a brow with a slight grin, "Besides, why should rumors about Mr. Nightwolf bother you? Not going soft on him or is it the other way around?"

Sarah blushed feverishly for a moment before quickly replying, "No! I just don't like seeing my fellow students abused so horribly behind their back…"

He chuckled heartily shaking his head, "Maybe that's the truth of it, Miss Roanoak, but you're the only student that Steven has ever allowed to sit beside him without scaring half to death in the past three years. The only other person who has done that was Mr. Lion, and even that only lasted for a few days. Now you don't even see the two of them even hang out together anymore."

Sarah suppressed her surprise as Devin's words rang through her head from the previous day, *I guess he really does like you, otherwise he'd have let his temper snap and we'd both be in a world of hurt…*

She gave her thanks to Coach A and said good bye before heading out of the room to business class.

Steven sat on the bathroom counter smoking a cigarette, blowing out puffs of smoke on occasion as he tapped the faucet off and on irritably. The sound of the door opening caught his eye as he watched the principal, Mr. Schaffer, walk into the bathroom and moved over to sit beside him on the opposite side of the sink before speaking, "I thought I'd find you here."

Steven offered him a cigarette and his lighter which he gratefully took before lighting up one himself. The two of them both took a long drag and exhaled before the principal spoke again, "Look Steven… I'm sorry about the rumors, I just heard and I can assure you that the matter is being handled…"

Steven took another drag and blew out several *o*'s before interrupting in a calm tone, "No… I'll take care of the situation myself…"

"Now Steven," the principal started again, "D-don't do anything rash okay? Especially after what happened last year to that new student…"

Steven lazily ground his cigarette out on the counter as he looked at the principal coolly, "That was an isolated incident, and you know as well as I do that it wasn't my fault… even though everyone blames me for it… I'm not going to hurt anyone…"

The last part almost came out in a whisper as his expression took to a saddened one, as if remembering some dark part of the previous year. Sighing, Steven got up and left the principal standing there with a worried and concerned look spread across his face.

Sarah walked into the business class and took her seat pulling out her notebook and pencil. The bell rang and Mr. Fergus began his lecture as usual. Her eyes scanned the room and then watched the door, concerned and curious, noticing that Steven hadn't shown up to class and couldn't help but to wonder where he might be.

Steven walked down the hall and out the door into the school courtyard where he abruptly took a seat at its center in the shade on the ground behind some trees. He thought silently while wrestling with emotions that turned inside him like a tornado, "What am I to do now? Trust her, but I don't trust people… they always betray me… except Devin…"

After a moment he crossed his les and closed his eyes, his breathing lengthened and he began to meditate to calm his mind and the turmoil inside his heart.

Sarah sat in business class as her thoughts tumbled between Steven and Angela. She soon found herself thinking about Steven and Sebastian, comparing the two in her own mind. She noted how similar they were in stature and appearance, save for a few minor features like hair and eye color and the handsome goatee that Sebastian had. She sighed heavily as she thought to herself that Steven wasn't as much of an asshole but still needed to lighten up a lot. Then a curious thought struck her, I wonder if Steven is a good dancer? and she found herself smiling at the prospect of dancing with him some time. The bell rang and she left class for lunch only to be distracted by the beauty of the courtyard on a sunny day through the doors and windows.

She exited the school into the courtyard and strolled down the cobblestone path through the beautiful garden. Her steps only paused to allow her to bend over to smell some of the roses which were in full bloom. As she looked up from where she had knelt, she gasped in awe at the sight before her. Sarah sat down as she looked through the slit in the trees to see Steven sitting cross-legged and humming softly, but he was about a foot in the air with leaves spinning around him in clockwise motion. She didn't know how long she sat there watching him; but found that as he lowered to the ground and opened his eyes and stood with cat-like grace, her mind swam with hundreds of questions which she was determined to have answers for.

Steven looked around the courtyard, now calm and completely relaxed when his eyes fell upon Sarah staring at him through the trees. He froze in midmotion as a cat which had been startled while trying to sneak upon its prey. They both remained there frozen for a long moment, frozen in time, staring into each other's eyes in fascination and perhaps something more; when Steven finally moved breaking the moment and headed toward the door back into the school. Sarah moved quickly to cut him off before he could reach it and stood between him and the entrance looking at him almost in longing. Steven approached her and stopped just in front of her looking down into her eyes. Seeing through walls and barriers that he had always kept up Sarah smiled knowing that he really did like her and had finally let her in. Steven smiled as well as the thought crossed his mind, *Maybe it really could work...*

Sarah started to speak, her voice stammering nervously, "I-I li..."

Steven simply held up one finger gently to her lips, "Shhh... you don't know what you're asking for dear angel..."

She looked at him almost pleadingly as he started to pass by her opening the door with a grace only known to the wind.

"Please..." she started softly, "Steven?"

He paused looking at her for a long moment before replying in a whisper, "Maybe..."

Steven then proceeded to the lunchroom from the courtyard to see a crying Angela running down the hall and a teacher holding her cheerleading jersey. He deliberately approached the teacher and then spoke in low tones which were frigid and numbing, "What is this?"

The teacher jumped and turned toward him as if startled by a ghost, "It's... ah... well... Angela's been removed from the... cheerleading squad... that is..."

"Why?" he growled menacingly more akin to a wolf about to kill its prey than any person.

The teacher began to pale and stutter, "B-b-because… M-mr. Shaffter… s-said to…"

"Well put her back on it and give her back her jersey because I said so!" he nearly roared causing the teacher to flinch and cringe at his tone.

"Y-yes, s-sir!" the teacher stammered as he ran down the hall after Angela faster than he had probably run his entire life.

Sarah watched the display from the courtyard doors and couldn't help but to smile, she thought that she might be gaining a good idea why he acted the way he did now. Steven waved his hand in frustration causing the lunchroom doors to slam open as he walked in and sat at his empty table. He sighed heavily as he pulled out a packed lunch from his bag and set it on the table. Sarah entered the lunchroom just a moment behind him and walked over to his table moving to the opposite side across from where he was sitting. She stood there for a moment looking down at him with curiosity still burning in her eyes, "May I?"

Steven looked up at her as he considered his answer before finally giving in, "Mmmm… yeah, go ahead…"

She sat down calmly while still staring at him. Steven looked up at her once more, "Honestly, I hate it when people stare at me so much, it just gives me the creeps…"

Sarah blushed lightly as she diverted her eyes to the table, "I'm sorry… and I'm sorry about what I said yesterday too… I was wrong…"

Steven studied her for a moment before he responded in his normal deep and rich voice, "It's okay… d-don't worry about it…"

He then turned his attention to his food to try and hide a nervousness that he didn't want to admit. Sarah watched him eat and a smile unknowingly crept across her face as she thought, *Ya know, he really is kinda cute.*

After a moment, he pushed a sandwich across the table to her while looking at her to gauge her reaction silently. Sarah studied the sandwich for a moment before taking it and realizing that she was actually quite hungry. He smiled as he whispered across the table to her, "Don't tell anyone, okay?"

Sarah studied him for a moment before a smile crept across her face as well.

"Deal." She replied trying not to laugh as she realized he was talking about the sandwich and not about him floating in midair.

The bell rang and the two of them walked to class hand in hand, though neither of them seemed to notice that they were doing it. Steven entered art class first and moved to his usual seat with Sarah right behind him and took hers. Soon Devin came in with a scowl on his face shortly followed by Angela. The two of them both sat down at Sarah's table quietly. Then Angela suddenly turned to Steven and with a look of anger and malice shouted at him, "You lousy fuck! You ruined my life!"

Steven's expression changed instantly from a cheerful smile to a flat icy stare as he looked into Angela's eyes. She began to stutter and tried to speak as her expression quickly changed to that of pure terror. Her face drained of color as she squeaked and the room seemed to drop in temperature by at least ten degrees causing everyone to shiver and skirt away from the two tables.

"Tramp! I have never entertained the idea of sex with you in my worst nightmares, nor have I ever or would ever have sex with you!" Steven hissed as he rose from his chair and began walking toward her, his eyes flashing dangerously like the lightning in a hurricane, "Now you will speak the truth or I will punish you and I guarantee that it will be far worse than anything the teachers at this school can do to you!"

Angela fell out of her chair to her knees, mumbling and begging, her usually tan features now a ghostly pale. Steven continued his approach and Sarah stood up moving between him and Angela. She thought quickly and hugged him in a close embrace as she looked into his eyes and pleaded with him, "Please… Steven. Let me deal with this… please…"

Steven met her gaze as the anger drained noticeably away with her tightening embrace. His tone softened back to normal as he returned the embrace and from her to the now crying Angela before he spoke in a half-whisper, "As you wish…"

Angela mumbled in a barely audible squeak as she curled up into a ball on the floor under the table, "I-I'm sorry…"

Devin just sat there in total awe and shock at the situation, not because Steven had lost his temper with Angela, for he knew that he would never truly hurt her, but because of his reaction to Sarah. They were hugging, and even more, she had gotten Steven to calm down almost instantly.

"Ahem… Steven," Devin coughed trying to break whatever moment was transpiring.

Devin resolved that he would have to talk to Steven about all of this later. The rest of class seemed to follow Devin's reaction of shock and awe, for they all had a certain type of fear and respect for him which came from his I-won't–take-shit–from-anyone attitude and to see this type of reaction from him with a female, no matter who she was, caught them all off guard. Steve released his embrace, but kept hold of her hand gently as the two of them made their way to the door of the classroom. As they entered the hall, he closed the door behind them before looking into her eyes once more, "Why… did you stop me?"

"Because…" Sarah started, looking deeply into his eyes, "I car…"

He turned away and closed his eyes briefly before putting a gentle finger to her lips to silence her word, "Don't… people always end up dead around me…"

He turned and left the school quickly leaving Sarah standing in the hall looking after him. After Steven had exited the building, Devin emerged from the classroom into the hall with a very worried expression across his face. As soon as he saw Sarah just standing there alone, he just burst out at her, "What the hell did you do to him?"

She turned with a look of confusion etched on her face as she responded to him, "What are you talking about Devin?"

"What do you think I am talking about?" his voice raised in a few octaves frantically, "Steven... what did you do to him?"

"I-i... didn't do anything to him," she answered still not quite grasping what Devin was getting at.

"If you hurt him..."he started, "Well, let's just say that you'll regret it. Because he's a better person than anyone gives him credit for and I won't see him used if that's what you intend on doing."

Sarah stared back at him, surprise registering on her face as she realized what he was saying, "I-I'm not going to use him... I just want to get close to him..."

Devin examined her closely before speaking once more in a more relaxed tone, "I hope so, Sarah, he's already lost too much in his life..."

Sarah watched him as he began to walk down the hall before speaking out of impulse, "Can you get him to come to the club, Friday night?"

Devin stopped and looked back at her with a sly grin, "I can try."

With that the bell rang and students began to pile out into the halls on their way between classes. Devin and Sarah walked to history quietly together, both wondering if Steven would be there when they arrived.

Steven exited the school with a calm outward expression, but his insides were flopping around like a fish out of water. Silently he stood in the sunlight with his eyes closed as he listened to the wind. Whispering, his voice sounded like a light breeze on a warm summer's day, "What do you think of her, Kari?"

The wind picked up in a flurry of leaves and hissed its response back through the leaves in the trees, "She is stronger than you give her credit for... and is with you now as she was always meant to be..."

"Meant to be? What are you talking about Kari? She's just some normal girl like everyone else... she's not like me and Devin... is she?" he hissed back to the wind in slight confusion.

The wind only picked up once more to fill the air with its musical laughter before going silent. Steven mumbled to himself sarcastically as he reentered the school and proceeded to history class, "Sometimes I think talking to a tree might be more informative, Kari..."

As he entered the school, the bell rang and the halls filled with students, but as he walked he noticed something he hadn't before. Everyone was moving out of his way to the point that he thought they were actually cringing. Then Steven began to realize that maybe he really was being too cruel to everyone and decided to make a resolution with himself to try and be more compassionate and understanding of others. Entering History class, he assumed his usual seat and pulled out his notebook and pen. Moments later Sarah and Devin entered the room and both seemed to smile in relief at seeing him there, before moving to sit on either side of him calmly. Soon the bell rang and Miss Callum began her lectures. As she droned on about dead civilizations and fallen empires, Steven began to tap his pencil impatiently on his desk, completely oblivious of the lecture and bored with the topics at hand. True, he loved history and discovering the past, but he already knew this and it seemed to be the same thing, over and over again.

"Mr. Nightwolf!" The teacher blurted pulling him out of his thoughts, "Could you please quit that tapping?"

Steven stared back at her, as a smile charmingly crept across his face and he stopped tapping his pencil, "Sorry..."

Devin raised a slight brow in surprise, for he had never really heard Steven apologize to anyone save for once, and that was a very bad night. The class also looked on curiously trying to figure out why the sudden change in his attitude. Yawning in boredom, he began to balance the pencil on its tip and let go of it leaving it to stand and rotate on its own on top of his desk.

"*Ring*!"

The pencil fell as the bell rang, breaking his concentration and signaling the end of the day. Grabbing up his bag Steven prepared to leave when Miss Callum called him over to her desk, "Mr. Nightwolf?"

"Yes Miss Callum?" he inquired as he approached her desk with a charming smile that caused her to blush just a bit.

She looked him over for a long moment as if considering something before noticing Sarah still standing over near the classroom door and watching her very closely.

"Steven, I realize from what the other teachers in the school have told me that you are a very talented and smart student and already studied most if not all of the course materials lined out in this class, but please try not to distract the other students…"

Steven nodded once as he looked at her calmly, "I'll do my best not to, miss."

"What I mean is…" she began again searching for the right words, "When you get bored… well… odd things just seem to happen, and I think that it makes the other students nervous…"

"Mmmmm…" Steven considered the fact for a moment before continuing, "Then make me a student aid, let me help teach the subject so that I am not just sitting there getting so bored all the time and it can also give you time to give individual help to the students who need it most."

"A student aid… alright, I'll give you the chance, but if you mess it up then I'll have something for you deal?" she said with a coy smile.

"Okay," he answered with a shrug of indifference as he turned and headed to leave the room.

As he reached the door, he paused beside Sarah and noted the scowl on her lips as she was staring at the teacher.

"Something wrong?" he inquired curiously.

"No..." she said turning and leaning in giving him a kiss so that Miss Callum could see them.

He blinked a few times then raised an even more curious brow and considered the touch of her lips on his as he wrapped an arm around her. He walked with her down the halls and out of the school when he was struck by impulse and a slight grin trailed his lips, "Wanna ride?"

Sarah's eyes brightened like stars had replaced them as she hugged him once more and exclaimed in excitement, "Yeah!"

He grinned noticeably as they walked across the parking lot to his car. When they reached it, he mumbled something she couldn't quite hear and she looked at him curiously until the surface of the car seemed to shimmer with electricity before returning to normal.

"What is that?" she asked backing away a bit.

"Nothing," he responded opening the door for her.

Sarah raised a brow this time as she climbed into the Porsche and admired the fine leather interior. Steven entered a moment later on the driver's side and started the engine with a smile. She looked at him nervously for a moment remembering the two-wheeled stunt he had pulled earlier that morning. He only winked at her reassuringly as he pulled out of the parking lot and began to speed down the road causing her to grip her pants tightly. Steven looked over at her and began to slow down until she relaxed again, "Don't like going fast, eh?"

"No..." Sarah answered softly as she was silently relieved that he had noticed and slowed down to a comfortable speed.

"So..." he started, trying to make some sort of small talk, "Where's your house... or should I take you to mine?"

"1323, Wicca circle," she answered turning a little pink at his teasing though she still smiled as she glanced over at him.

He nodded silently and continued driving at a comfortable speed so that he didn't make her nervous. Soon they were pulling into her driveway and Steven was turning off the engine.

"Nice place," Steven remarked honestly as Sarah stepped out of the car.

"Thanks," she said popping her head back in, "Um… you can come in if you want… for a little bit…"

Steven smiled as he stepped out of the car following her to the door, his tone teasing, "Parents not home, I take it?"

Sarah grinned giving him a devilish look, "Yeah, but that's ok."

He grinned to himself as he followed her inside and proceeded to the couch and took a seat as she closed the door behind them. He looked her up and down for a long moment noticing once more how beautiful she was and couldn't help but to find himself staring at her. Sarah turned from the door and met his gaze as she thought to herself, *What if I just kissed him and went for it, what then?*

She walked over to where he was sitting on the couch and sat down on his legs, straddling him as he stared up into her eyes and warmly wrapped his arms around her just before their lips met. Their eyes closed just briefly as the thought, *I can't believe this is really happening*, ran through both their minds at the same time. Just as they felt the fire spark, the sound of a car pulling into the drive broke the moment and Sarah looked over toward the door with a quite panicked expression, "Damn! My mom's home early!"

Steven looked at her before calmly speaking, "Relax, breath, and then go get me a drink… I'll tutor you in history, ok?"

Sarah looked at him for a moment briefly baffled then it dawned on her to what he was hinting at. She grinned as she went into the kitchen and came back with two sodas just as her mother walked into the door trying to hide a slight smile with a fake frown.

"Hi mom," Sarah said cheerfully as she set the drinks down on the coffee table and then sat down beside Steven.

Mrs. Roanoak looked at the two of them with a raised brow before speaking, "Well? Aren't you going to introduce me to your new boyfriend, Sarah?"

Sarah blushed a deep red, "Mom!"

Her mother smiled at her daughter still waiting.

"This is Steven, Mom, Steven this is my mom. He's my history tutor, Mom," she answered still blushing fervently.

Steven stood up and shook her hand politely, "It's a pleasure to meet you, Mrs. Roanoak."

They smiled to each other as they shook hands, and Mrs. Roanoak went into the kitchen before her daughter could notice the silent exchange. Steven then turned to Sarah with a smile and leaned down kissing her gently, "Well, I should be getting home myself, see you tomorrow?"

Sarah grinned as she responded back, "You bet."

"Oh, one more thing," he took her hand and kissed it gently while looking into her eyes causing her heart to skip a beat, "Miss me…"

Sarah almost laughed as she followed him out the door watching him get in his car and started driving off, calling after him, "Rogue!"

She watched from the porch as his car drove away while her mother came out to stand beside her, "History tutor, eh?"

Sarah turned looking at her mother and couldn't help but to smile, "Yeah, he's… well… really good at school stuff."

Her mother smiled back at her warmly, "So when's your first date?"

"Huh?" Sarah exclaimed surprised by her mother's question, "eh… well, hopefully this weekend if I can drag him to the club…"

Her mother nodded, still bearing a slight grin, "I like this one Sarah, I think he'll be loyal just as if you two were married, unlike the last one..."

Sarah scowled briefly remembering how a girl named Valerie had stolen her last boy friend at her previous school, Kevin, from her, "Steven's not an easy catch mom, besides... everyone else is too afraid... ah, I mean nervous around him to bother."

Sarah's mom looked at her knowingly before speaking again, "I'm sure the school witch would be avoided by most girls, after all he does have a reputation to keep up..."

Sarah's mouth fell open in surprise and disbelief at her mother's words, "You knew? And you never said anything?"

Mrs. Roanoak laughed softly, "Dear, he was the one who drove you home from the club last Friday night, besides, the Nightwolf's have always been associated with the occult. It keeps people away from them, or should I say... him... now..."

Sarah just stared at her mother for a long moment and blinked several times, it rather made a little sense now that's why he didn't like the mention of Sebastian, then she paused and quirked a brow in thought, "What do you mean 'him' now?"

Her mom sighed softly and looked at her seriously with a tone to match, "That is something you'll have to ask him when you two trust each other enough dear."

Sarah only nodded, her mind growing ever more curious with questions about Steven and what he was really all about.

Romantic Unions

A sudden smile across your face,
The sweet tenderness of your embrace…
The fragrance of you fills the air,
As if soft velvet pedals of a rose scattered everywhere…
I feel your touch, even your stare…
All focused on me, I would know them anywhere…
It confuses my senses to have you near…
For then it is only my heart which I hear…
What should I do?
Where shall this go?
As we embrace and not think of the 'marrow…
Let me take you with me,
Forever and a day…
Let our love lead the way…

October 2008
Week 2, Wednesday

Steven awoke to his alarm clock and waived his hand absently, sending it flying across the room into the wall where it became several pieces. Sitting up he sighed while cursing under his breath realizing that it was totally destroyed. Dragging himself out of bed, he went to the shower to get ready for the day. As he showered, he wondered what it must be like to have grown up like everyone else, normal, with a family, and no strange abilities. *Perhaps then*, he reasoned in his head, *I'd be like everyone else with lots of friends and a normal life without all of this weird stuff happening to me all the time.*

He sighed once more in resignation as he dried himself off and dressed. Leaving his house to his car he called back to Alfred his butler, "Al, could you pick me up a new alarm clock today?"

"Of course, Master Steven," the old butler's voice could be heard from the kitchen.

"Thanks," Steven yelled back as he climbed into his car and started the engine.

As he drove to school, he noticed Sarah standing at the bus stop near her house and he pulled over to her and rolled down the window, "Wanna ride?"

Sarah smiled sweetly as she climbed into the passenger side and closed the door, "Yeah, sure."

He smiled as he pulled back onto the road, "Hungry?"

Sarah looked at him curiously for a moment, "No, I don't have any money."

"So?" he stated as he began driving toward Micky D's with a slight chuckle, "I asked if you were hungry, not if you had any money, angel."

She blushed at the last word as she looked down a bit, "Yes, I'm hungry, but you don't have to get me anything."

"Ahhh..." he smiled and glanced over at her, "Don't worry about it."

Looking over at her on occasion as he drove, Steven noted that her long red hair was pulled back in the same fashion as his and that the hunter green silk shirt she was wearing was short-sleeved and tailored to show off her features without revealing too much. Her skirt was knee high and cotton, with colors to match her shirt. She had a light jacket folded across her lap, black and which he certainly thought completed the outfit. Her whole outfit only seemed to bring out her stunning jade green eyes, which Steven found absolutely breathtaking.

"I like your outfit," he said in a near whisper before clearing his throat, "It brings out your eyes."

Sarah blushed deeply at his compliment before returning the compliment. He pulled to a stop at a red light waiting for it to turn. His eyes continued trailing over, still admiring her appearance, he didn't even notice that the light had changed until she gently let him know. Blushing furiously now, he resolved to keep his mind on the road while pulling through the intersection. At about halfway through the intersection a Mercedes came barreling at him in his lane. Steven reacted with cat-like reflexes as he cut the wheel hard and then reversed it while alternating between break and gas causing his car to spin around the Mercedes in a perfect 360 and end up on its rear side still in the right lane. Honking his horn, he cursed under his breath and continued to the restaurant. After another few moments he pulled into the parking lot and turned off the engine with a slight sigh of relief, "Are you alright, Sarah?"

Steven turned and looked at her when she didn't answer right away. He noted that she was now as white as a ghost and trembling all over with her hands clenched tightly in her lap. Leaning over he wrapped his arms around her in a gentle embrace, "Hey… we're okay now, alive and unhurt. It's alright…"

Sarah soon came back to herself and noticed that she was clinging onto him for dear life and tried to speak, "W-we could have been killed back there by that maniac!"

Steven patted her back gently, "Yes, but we weren't…"

She took a deep breath trying to regain her composure, "Where did you learn to drive like that?"

He smiled as he released his embrace of her, "Ah… well, funny thing… Alfred wouldn't let me get my license until I took this stunt driving class about a year and a half ago, never really thought it would come in handy. Are you sure you're ok?"

"Y-yes, I'm fine," she answered managing a smile.

"Good, how about some breakfast then?" he said continuing to smile as he helped her out of the car.

As they walked to the entrance of Mickey-D's, Steven paused and turned toward his car, "boucliers vers le bas."

The air around his car shimmered as they entered the building and Sarah regarded him quizzically for a moment.

"Alright, what would you like my little Irish Angel?" he asked her teasingly.

"Oh, I'm your little Angel now is it?" Sarah exclaimed trying not to smile, "Who missed who then?"

Steven made a gesture of being wounded in the heart as he chuckled. Sarah smacked him playfully in the side causing him to wince a bit, "Ass."

"Ow. Only kidding angel, now really, what would you like?" he asked grabbing his side reflexively trying to hide the pain he was in.

Sarah looked at him inquiringly until her stomach reminded her that she was quite hungry despite their near death encounter earlier, "Oh anything, just no coffee please."

"Alright, find us a table and I'll get us some food," he said smiling but still noticeably testing his side some.

She looked at him once more as if trying to figure out what was wrong before turning and walking off to secure them a table. Steven approached the counter and placed his order with the cashier, "Two steaks, egg, and cheese biscuits, double hash-browns… ah, one coffee, and one orange juice please."

As he waited patiently for the food, he could have sworn he saw someone out of the corner of his eye wearing a green cloak, but as he snapped his head around, it was only empty air. Grabbing the tray of food he shook his head and mumbled to himself, "I really need to start getting more sleep…"

As he reached the table, he placed the tray down and set the coffee in front of Sarah. She took a sip and spit it out giving him a look of pure malice.

"Oh! Sorry, wrong cup angel," Steven said switching the drink and trying to suppress a grin.

"You know, I'm really starting to think you're evil," she said jokingly as she continued to glare at him.

Putting on an innocent face he looked at her with a smile, "I'm not evil, just a little mischievous on occasion."

"Hrmph," she grumbled taking a bite of her biscuit.

Valerie awoke suddenly, her heart racing like a freight train. Her hair was a mess and her night shirt completely soaked with sweat. She ached all over as if she had been tossed around like a rag doll as she slept. Deliberately she wiped her brow, her mind going back to the dream which had her so worked up. The only thing she could remember however was the sight of a dark green Porsche racing straight at her, and she could only sit there and watch it coming. Shaking her head clear of the memory of the dream and squinting she peered at the old oaken grandfather clock which stood near her dresser across the room. It was still early, only four in the morning she realized, as she stared on at the clock. Sighing heavily, she fell back into the covers of her light-blue bed spread. Staring at the intricate patterns of flowers carved into the ceiling she moaned audibly while stretching.

Devin dashed through the streets of the industrial side of town followed closely by two overweight cops. Sighting an opening in a fence, he merely turned sideways and slipped through it as the two began to close in. Passing through to the other side with ease, he bolted around the next corner as the overweight officers struggled with the fence. Devin nearly ran into another cop after rounding another corner, but used his momentum to shove him into the brick wall of the alley breaking his nose. His steps picked up more as he left the man cussing behind him. Upon reaching the end of the alley, he stepped out onto Main Street and began casually walking along the side walk without looking back.

"Hey! There he is!" a voice from behind him yelled.

Devin took off once more, the sound of the voice and heavy jogging echoing in his ears from behind him now. As the two officers radioed for backup, he vanished into a crowd of people crossing the street. The officers looked through the crowd cussing as they scratched their heads finding not a trace of the boy.

"Mike, did ya see where he went?" the first one said confused at how someone could just up and vanish.

"Nope Jim, but I found something odd here in this alley way. Com'ere and check this out," the other replied from a nearby side alley.

Jim halted traffic for a moment as he ran across the street to where Mike was standing near a brick wall, "Well?"

Mike put his hand through the wall a bit nervously before pulling it back out quickly, "Do you see this shit?"

Jim backed away from the wall as he dropped his radio, "D-don't do that again Mike! Something's really wrong here… I'm gonna radio it back up to HQ and get someone down here."

Valerie stepped out of the shower and dried off as she walked to her closet to pick out the days clothes. She wanted to make a good impression on her first day even though the idea of transferring schools made her stomach fill with butterflies. She had no idea why her grandmother put in for the transfer, but she wasn't going to question it. She pulled back her raven black hair with a blue cord before putting on a tight Tommy girl tee and Tommy girl jeans which showed off her slender figure. She then grabbed her Gucci school bag and her keys before heading downstairs to say goodbye to her grandmother.

"Bye Mammy, love you!" she said as she began out the door giving her grandmother a kiss on the cheek.

"Valerie?" Tiara started, but it was too late as she was already out the door skipping to her Mercedes 320.

The metallic silver paint and tinted windows shined brightly in the morning sunlight. Valerie smiled as she opened the car door and tossed her bag into the back seat. Getting in she checked her lipstick in the mirror and buckled her seatbelt. As she adjusted her mirrors, she thought she saw a man standing near the wood line in a green cloak watching her. She snapped her head around looking out the window only to see trees and morning fog lining the ground. Becoming a bit freaked out she began to back out of the drive and onto the road. Suddenly she felt something hit her car and she slammed on the breaks to see Devin running into the passenger side of her car. Their eyes met and both noted a slight bit of surprise from the other. Devin's deep brown eyes seemed to mesmerize Valerie until the moment was over, and he rolled over the hood of her car quickly and then ran down the street rounding a corner. His face seemed to stick in her mind until two overweight cops ran by in hot pursuit.

Already beginning to have second thoughts about going to school, she sighed as she pulled out and continued on her way down the road. The day was shaping out to be stranger than she was used to, so she decided to turn on the radio to try and get her mind off of the morning's curious course of events.

"Skies partly cloudy with a small chance of rain, temperatures in the high eighties… and here's Janet with the news… Thank you John, we bring you a special bulletin this morning. Earlier a young adolescent male was seen vandalizing an electronics store and is currently being pursued by the police. He is about five foot eight and has short auburn red hair. Authorities say that he may be armed and should be considered extremely dangerous…"—click—"addy mack 'ole make ya… JUMP! JUMP!…"—click

Valerie opened her glove box and pulled out her Madonna CD popping it in. She turned up the volume and began tapping the steering wheel and nodding her head to the tune.

"Oh whoa, girls just wanna have fu-un!"

No sooner has she sung the lines and looked up from the radio when she saw a dark green Porsche coming straight at her honking its horn.

"*Crap*!" she screamed as she pumped the breaks with no reaction and raised her hands to cover her face. Hitting a patch of grease, her car began to fish tail uncontrollably sending her back into the right lane. Her car came to a halt, finally on the other side of the intersection just before a mother crossing the street with her infant. Valerie closed her eyes and placed her head on the steering wheel as she burst into tears while her body began to shake.

Tap, tap, tap!

Her head shot up to see Devin standing beside her door tapping on her window to get her attention. She stared at him for a moment in disbelief until he spoke through the partially opened window, "Are you okay?"

She shook her head yes as confusion dawned from trying to figure out where he had come from.

"Is your car damaged?" he continued as a concerned look crossed his face.

Valerie blinked away the last of her tears before replying shakily, "N-no, I don't think so… where did you come from?"

Devin held up his wrist and pointed to his watch, "On my way to school, had to take a detour, you?"

Now completely confused Valerie looked at him blankly, "Are you walking? You'll be late if you go from here…"

He shrugged with a slight grin, "That's okay, I'm always late or not there at all anyways…"

Valerie's jaw dropped in exclamation at his words, "Not there? That's ridiculous!"

Devin chuckled as his grin broadened at her reaction, "So… are you gonna roll down your window or should I just keep walking, beautiful?"

She hesitated a moment as her cheeks flushed a little before rolling down her window cautiously allowing her raven black hair to shine bright in the morning sun.

"Thanks," he said as he leaned on the door, "Not often I get to meet a princess on my way to school."

Valerie looked at him once more meeting his eyes, her cheeks flushing a bit red, though more at the compliment than anything else. She nodded and then spoke as a smile spread across her face, "Get in… I'm on my way to school anyway and just maybe we can make it on time…"

Devin walked around to the passenger side of the car and opened the door hopping into the seat smoothly, "Nice ride!"

Steven and Sarah left the Micky Ds out to his car happy with their little morning meal. As she reached for the door handle, he grabbed her hand back quickly and pulled her away from the car gently, "Hold on now, angel, don't want you to get hurt…"

"Huh?" Sarah started with a confused expression, "What could possibly hurt me by touching your car door?"

"Watch," he said pulling out a quarter and tossing it at his car.

As the coin came within half an inch of the surface of the car and abrupt bluish lighting storm rippled across the entire length of its surface. Sarah gasped in surprise as she watched the charred lump of metal that was the quarter hit the ground smoking like a molten rain drop.

"Degré de sécurité de voiture," he said and the air around the car shimmered notably.

"Alright, now it's safe, angel," he said opening the door for her.

Sarah got in the car and looked over at him as he entered, curiosity and nervous surprise still showing on her face, "What kind of security system is on this car? I've never even heard of something that can do what I just saw."

Steven chuckled as he started the car and pulled out of the parking lot and onto the road heading to school, "Oh… well, it's something of my own design. It's rigged up like a tazer for the surface of the car, so it should only stun a person for an hour or so in theory without hurting them, but I'd rather not test it."

Sarah nodded as they continued down the road and into the school parking lot. Pulling into his space, Steven turned off the car and they exited the vehicle. As they began walking toward the school, he called back to his car causing her to pause and watch the shimmering around it for a moment with fascination. As she turned back around she noticed that he had kept walking and she jogged to catch up to him. When she reached him she unconsciously slipped an arm around him causing Steven to wince noticeably and jump with a slight surprise.

"Are you alright?" she asked with concern in her voice.

Steven smiled back trying to hide the pain as she continued to hold onto him gently, "I-I'm fine, why?"

"You're not fine, otherwise you wouldn't be flinching every other step," she said in a matter of fact tones.

"It's nothing…" he flinched again as she tightened her grip nearly dropping him to the ground, "Okay… okay, I get your point. It's only a small cut, it just hurts a little."

She looked at him doubtfully as they entered the school, "You're going to let me have a look at that little cut after school."

Valerie and Devin pulled into the school parking lot. As she looked for an open space her eyes widened seeing the same green Porsche that she had nearly hit that morning. Devin looked at her curiously as she eyes the car, "So what's your name anyway, I dun' think I've seen you around here before."

"Valerie, and you?" she answered not really paying him much attention as she took one of the empty spaces by Steven's Porsche and turned off her engine.

"Devin. Hey, nice car eh?" he replied as they exited the car.

Shaking her head she read the name on the space to herself, "Steven Nightwolf, how does a kid get his name put on a parking space anyway?"

"You know him?" Devin asked her as she grabbed her bag out of the back seat of the car.

"No," she stated, anger briefly flashing through her eyes, "he almost hit me head on back at that intersection I picked you up at."

Devin nodded, faking a frown, "Well, I'll have to introduce you then."

She looked at him with a serious sort of curiosity, "You know him then?"

He snickered lightly before answering her, "It's a joke! You really should stay away from him, after all everyone says he's a…" he paused as if considering something.

"What? What do they say?" Valerie insisted on knowing, her curiosity now getting the better of her.

"Well, he's terribly rich for one, but only 'coz his family died or something… some people say he killed them himself just for the money…" he began making his tone a bit foreboding.

"Hold on!" Valerie interrupted, "He killed his family?"

"I dunno…" Devin continued, "There's lots of rumors about him, if you really want to know, you should probably ask him yourself…"

He started walking off toward the school as they continued talking.

"Everyone thinks he's strange, so they're all too afraid to ask him anything themselves…" he continued on as they walked.

"But, if he's so rich why doesn't he go to a private school or something?" Valerie asked a bit baffled.

Devin almost started laughing at her question, "He's a witch… what kind of private school is going to take a witch?"

Valerie turned a bit red as the continued into the school and stopped in front of the poetry lit class.

"Well, this is my first class," he said with a smile.

She raised a curious brow as she pulled out her schedule and looked it over for a moment, "That's funny, I have the same class."

"Think you're a poet then eh?" Devin asked, a wide grin spreading across his lips.

Valerie blushed. "Well, I enjoy writing and I think that poetry is a good way to improve my skill."

He held open the door for her and gestured her to go in first, "Makes sense, after you princess."

She raised a slight brow once more as her blush deepened and walked in, "You seem to have good manners, what's that all about?"

Devin shrugged indifferently, "Let's sit down," and diverted to a pair of desks.

She smiled and pranced over to one of the desks sitting down gracefully. Devin took the one beside her and unceremoniously dropped his leather satchel on the floor before opening it and pulling out a notebook and pencil.

Steven and Sarah walked into the school heading to literature class hand in hand. Neither of them really paying enough attention to everyone else to notice the stares and gawking of the other students as they went. As they entered the class they sat together, only this time they were both smiling noticeably and the class was whispering curiously trying to figure out if they really were a couple.

Valerie looked around the room trying to get an idea as to the type of people she was going to school with. Most of the students seemed to be dressed preppy and seemed to be rather well off financially judging by their clothing. She also noticed that they all wore darker colors than she was at that time. Devin looked to the front of the room hearing the bell ring and watched as the last few stragglers ran inside hoping to beat the teacher to the room for roll call. Valerie looked up to notice some guy eyeing her from across the room. He had coke bottle glasses with a pimple filled face and picked his nose as he watched her with a butter ball grin. She suddenly felt ill and looked down holding her stomach.

"You alright?" Devin asked looking over at her in some concern.

Valerie nodded once regaining her composure, "That guy across the room, he looks like a pizza on crack and keeps eyeing me."

Devin looked over and had to suppress a laugh as he spoke, "Ohhhh, heh, heh… that's T.P. Timmy. He tried hitting on the prom queen last year and ended up getting his house rolled to the point you couldn't even see the front door. Of course, that was after the wrestling team and the star quarter back beat him into the week prior. Thank the gods his face healed otherwise he'd really look messed up."

The door opened cutting off any further conversation as a tall leggy woman with long brown hair and dressed in a dark blue business suit entered the room causing most of the guys to turn their head and gawk in silent awe. Devin's jaw dropped in awe as he watched her step across the room and behind the desk while picking up the attendance roster.

"Jacob Adams?" her voice flowed like music across the classroom.

A guy in the back raised his hand quickly while stuttering, "H-here m-am!"

"Please call me Miss Jones, now… Martha Jackson," the teacher continued on down the rows until she reached Devin's name.

"Devin Nor, uh… nor…" she struggled with the pronunciation.

"Noirlion, miss," Devin said smoothly in his slight French accent.

"Mmmm, I'll just call you by your first name Devin," she said smiling as she winked at him.

Devin felt his stomach drop as he gulped, "Cool..."

Miss Jones finished the roll call, completely oblivious to the male students which currently resembled drooling puppies, "And last but not least, Valerie Swordfish... Ah, our new student. Welcome, Miss Swordfish."

Valerie only nodded as she nervously fidgeted with her pen. Devin smiled turning to her, "Teacher's pet."

She smacked him in the back of the head as he looked away. The teacher noticed the action and looked over at the two of them as Devin rubbed his head tenderly, "Is there a problem, Miss Swordfish?"

Valerie smiled as she answered, "Uh... no, just a bug. I think I got it."

Devin snickered as he continued to rub his head, "Suck up..."

Whapp!

"Ow!" he exclaimed in surprise, cringing from the second blow.

"Guess, I missed it the first time," Valerie commented smugly.

Miss Jones tried not to laugh at the two of them, "Just try not to hurt the guy please, it'd be a shame for him to have to see Helga the school nurse in only the second week of school."

Devin shuddered at the thought as he mumbled to himself, "Too true..."

Miss Jones then turned to the board and wrote Poetry in large letters."Now, who can tell me what poetry is?" she asked and a few hands went up in the class, "Mr. Thomas?"

A scraggly looking guy wearing a Megadeth tee shirt, torn jeans, and combat boots stood up, "It's like a really good joint after pounding yer little brother's face into the sand box and yelling 'Get some!'"

"Uhh... anyone else?" the teacher asked, now looking for a girl to answer, "Miss Swordfish?"

Valerie stood up gracefully before clearing her throat and speaking, "It's like a warm waterfall that cascades around you while caressing your skin..."

Thomas stood up again, "That's a sissy answer! Poetry is like a brutal headbutt at a Metallica concert, man!"

"Mr. Thomas! Please sit down... Thank you. Now, poetry is actually both brutal and gentle. It is sweet and harsh; it all depends on what kind of feeling you want to place behind it and portray to your audience. So, your homework for tonight will be to write an essay, in poetic form, on what poetry means to you," Miss Jones stated as she started going over poetic forms in class.

Steven and Sarah exited calculus class together when he suddenly paused and looked at her sheepishly, "Excuse me, angel, gotta go to the toilet real quick. Why don't you go on ahead and I'll catch up?"

Sarah smiled at him slyly, "Alright, but don't be late like you usually are."

He grinned back, "Me, nah! I'm never late, remember?"

She gave him a *yeah right* look and went ahead to business class. Steven made his way down the hall to the bathroom and entered it still wearing a smile. He made his way over to the sink counter and took a seat in his usual spot as he pulled out his cigarettes. He lit one up just as one of the freshmen from the other day came out of a stall and froze while staring at him nervously. Steven chuckled softly as he took a drag, "I'm not gonna bite you kid, so relax."

The freshman's look tentatively turned to surprise, "B-but you're t-the w..."

"Yes, yes," Steven cut him off, "I'm the school witch and I do apologize for snapping at you and your friends the other day. I wasn't mad at you… It's just that false rumors kinda piss me off."

The freshman's nervous fear subsided and quickly replaced with curiosity as he continued to stare at Steven, "I'm Matt, are you really a witch?"

Steven chuckled more as he blew out a smoke ring, "Some people believe that, yes. But no, I can just do things that other people can't, that's all."

"Wow!" the freshman exclaimed.

Steven smiled as he waived toward the door causing it to open on its own, "Go on and get out of here before you're late to class. Oh, and keep our little conversation to yourself, ok?"

"You bet man!" Matt said as he dashed out of the bathroom with a look of awe on his face as he went to class.

Valerie followed Devin out of poetry class and turned to him as they walked, "So, how am I…"

She was suddenly interrupted by a guy running down the hall screaming, "Come'ere punk!"

Devin turned and his eyes widened, "Uh oh…"

He bolted down the hall and out the door ducking behind a corner. The guy ran out behind him and kept going, totally oblivious to Devin as he stood quietly in the shadows. After a moment he walked back in sighing heavily in relief. Valerie looked at him with her arms crossed, "What was that all about?"

Devin picked up his bag and dusted it off with a bit of a grin, "Just a jealous basketball player. I was talking to his girl over the summer and he thought we were doing a lot more, what a moron…"

She shook her head in disbelief and looked at her class schedule, "Ugh… Pre-Cal… I hate math."

He pointed down the hall trying not to laugh, "Second door on the left."

"What about you?" she asked curiously.

"Driver's ed," he chuckled.

Valerie rolled her eyes at him as she sighed, "God save the queen... Good luck."

Devin nodded, "See ya."

He walked down the hall and into the classroom yawning at the prospect of another boring class as he took a seat in the back. As the class went on, he couldn't shake the feeling that there was something very familiar about his new female friend. Then as the bell rang, it hit him, "Oh hell, Valerie is Tiara's granddaughter, that's why her last name seemed so familiar!"

He hurried out of the class and down the hall to the bathroom where he saw Steven sitting on the sink smoking a cigarette. Devin shook his head laughing, "What are you doing? Don't you know that that shit's bad for you?"

Steven took a long drag and blew out a few smoke circles casually before responding, "Well, I'd say by all appearances my good chap, that I am smoking a fag. Care for one? And yes, I do know."

Devin shook his head no as he tried not to laugh at Steven's fake British accent, "Have you met that new girl yet?"

Steven smiled as a far off look entered his eyes, "Yes, Sarah is quite something else..."

Devin raised a slight brow, "No lover boy, not that girl that has you drooling all over yourself as if you were her little puppy dog... I'm talking about Valerie, Tiara's granddaughter..."

Steven then came back to himself as he looked at Devin, "Is she cute?"

Devin seemed to think for a second before answering with his french flare, "Oh yes, she is very nice."

Steven chuckled to himself, "Ah! Seems like you've taken a fancy for her."

"Well, she does have nice… uh, well anyway she's cute," he stated turning a bit red in the face.

"Oh! It's all so clear to me now!" Steven exclaimed sarcastically with a grin.

"Oh get over yourself," Devin shot back turning even redder.

"Hmm? What?" Steven asked pretending he was deaf.

At that, the bell rang and they both exclaimed at the same time, "Shit!"

Steven turned to Devin putting his cigarette out on the counter, "Sarah's gonna kill me, see ya in art."

Devin smirked as he shook his head, "You've got it bad, later man."

The two parted ways, Devin heading toward the auditorium as Steven headed down the hall to business. As Devin rounded a corner he bumped into the vice principal, Mr. Carter.

"Mr. Lion, what are you doing out of class? Taken to roaming the halls have we?" he demanded grabbing the back of Devin's shirt.

"I'm sorry Mr. Cartman, uh Carter. I had an upset stomach and had to take a nasty…" Devin began trying to sound meek.

"Uh… uh that's ok son. Just try to keep your schedule this year. We don't want another failed semester now, do we?" Mr. Carter interrupted turning noticeably green.

Devin shook his head deliberately as the vice principal noted a cloud of smoke coming out of the bathroom from down the hall. Letting Devin go, he ran down to the bathroom with a determined look on his face as Devin continued on to class.

Steven walked into business class late and moved over to his seat sitting beside Sarah with a sheepish grin.

"You're late…" she started whispering to him with a disapproving glance, "Where have you been? And why do you smell like a cigarette?"

"Er… I was talking to Devin, yeah…" he answered still looking a little sheepish.

"Uh huh," she replied back trying not to grin at his discomfort.

As Devin opened the auditorium doors, a short middle-aged man looked up from passing out papers.

"Hrmph, you're late," the little man stated with obvious hostility in his voice.

"Yes, I sincerely apologize, sir," Devin replied as he looked around for a seat.

The little man shrugged, mild surprise showing on his face at Devin's words before he spoke again to try and reinforce his position, "Well… don't make a habit of it."

"Yes sir," Devin said as he closed the door and walked down the aisle toward the stage causing a few heads to turn, one of which had a familiar face with it.

He smiled seeing Valerie's deep blue eyes and began heading in her direction. Sitting down next to her, he opened his bag and pulled out a pad and pen.

"Now, before we were *blessed* by this young man's delayed entrance we were going over the basic principles of drama…" the little teacher began as he pointed at Devin with a stabbing motion, "You! Tell us what you, as an actor, would do if you were on stage during a live performance and suddenly forgot your lines."

The man peered at Devin awaiting a response while Devin began to consider how much he looked like a little bald penguin.

"Well," Devin began with a smile creeping across his face, "it would be no problem to simply improvise the next line, so long as you have a good understanding of the scene taking place and the plot line of the play of course…"

The little teacher's eyes widened as his head pulled back and he raised his finger in a *but you are wrong* gesture, "Aha! However, if you, for some unknown reason have forgotten the very basis for the scene. What then?"

Devin put his hand to his chin as a mocking gesture of thinking hard as the class snickered softly under their breath before he answered, "I would imagine that if one took in the scene, costumes, scenery, props, then you would simply pretend that you are indeed that person and would try to respond as they would in accordance to the situation."

The teacher seemed to think for a moment before he pointed to the stage, "Then allow me to test your theory, sir. Let's see if you really know what you're talking about."

Devin shrugged as he stood up from his seat and moved down the aisle toward the stage. Upon stepping up onto the stage, he turned toward the teacher to observe an obtrusive smirk.

"Now, imagine that you are standing at a bus stop," the man began as Devin closed his eyes to try and visualize the scene, "There's a steel frame and glass stand with four attached seats... sit in one."

Devin turned with his eyes still closed and moved a few steps forward before turning once more and sitting in the air as if there were actually a chair there.

"As you sit there," the man continued picking up a card, "Read from these cards and I'll fill in the rest. When I don't pick up a card, then we'll see if your idea pans out and you can guess the next line."

Devin nodded in understanding as the teacher chuckled to himself. He remained sitting on his imaginary chair as the first cue card was held up.

"Oh, hey Cindy!" Devin began cheerfully as if he were greeting an old friend, "Do you know what time the bus comes by here?"

The teacher cleared his throat and gave a very poor imitation of a feminine voice, "Oh, I think somewhere around five thirty or so..."

"What time is it now?" Devin continued reading from the cue card.

"Umm, about five ten..." the teacher attempted the voice again before signaling for Valerie to come down and read for him from the cue cards as he cleared his throat again with some difficulty.

"So where are you heading today, Cindy?" Devin continued, a smile trailing his lips as he noted that Valerie was taking over for the voice.

"To the mall to do some shopping. Why don't you come along, it'll be fun," Valerie read from the card and batted her eyes at Devin as the teacher put the other cards face down.

"Well, I would Cindy, but I'm outta cash," Devin replied as he pulled his pockets inside out and smiled foolishly at her.

Valerie giggled audibly at his improv as the teacher shot her a sharp look while reading over the cue card that Devin couldn't see.

"Holy shh..." the teacher began to cover his mouth in disbelief, "You just said that line exactly?"

"Good stuff, eh?" Devin snickered as he grinned devilishly.

"Alright smart arse," the teacher began as he pulled a small stack of index cards from his pocket, divided through them, and then placed half of them facing him and the other half he handed to Valerie, "I'm going to have Miss Swordfish here speak off of the cards and you are going to try to guess what the next line will be."

"Bring it on," Devin remarked with a boastful grin.

The teacher shook his head dubiously and nodded for Valerie to begin.

Valerie looked at Devin with a sly smile as she began to speak, "My Jack, that's an awfully nice jacket you're wearing today."

Devin watched as Valerie mouthed off his line from behind the teacher as she read over his shoulder before he responded, "Oh, you like it?"

"Lucky guess," the teacher said as he nodded to Valerie to continue, who promptly read her next line before mouthing to

Devin his along with the rest of what was on the card, "Yeah, where'd you get it?"

Devin smiled as he realized she was mouthing off the next few lines to him and decided to just flow with it to make the teacher look like a fool, "I bought it downtown, at that little leather shop in the back alley."

He continued on changing his voice to a mock imitation of a feminine one, "How much did you pay for it?"

Clearing his throat, he continued to roll with it as the teacher was frantically looking over the cards in disbelief, "It only cost me a hundred dollars and it has this neat little secret pocket with a zipper on the inside here…"

The teacher's eyes grew wide and round as he looked between the cue cards and Devin in utter astonishment, "What the? How did you?"

He then turned around and looked to Valerie and the other students in the front row who all only shrugged dumbly at the whole situation.

"I told you, given the environment, the props, and so forth, did I not?" Devin remarked in a childish tone which he hoped got to the man since he had put him up on stage just to try and embarrass Devin in the first place.

The teacher quickly removed his name tag and stuffed it in his pocket with his watch while grinning almost manically, "What's my name then Mr. Obvious?"

Valerie mouthed the answer to Devin as her eyes fell upon the man's journal sitting open on the podium.

Devin grinned delightfully as he responded, "Mr. Hembree."

"How old am I?" The teacher continued questioning as Devin acted as if he were looking off into the distance of some unknown horizon for the answer so as to give Valerie the time to read.

As soon as she mouthed him the answer and a few lines in Mr. Hembree's journal Devin seemed to come back to himself and answered quickly, "Thirty-eight."

"What kind of watch was I wearing?" Mr. Hembree asked as he began to turn a little red in the face and panic fill his voice.

Valerie grinned devilishly to Devin as she mouthed to him the watch which the teacher had slipped in his pocket. Devin's tone turned dubiously mocking as he answered, "It's a Timex, Ironman Triathlon, and it's in your left pant's pocket. And, your face is turning red because you're afraid of what else I could know!"

Mr. Hembree began to gasp as he grabbed his chest dramatically and panted out while staring at Devin, "W-what else do you know?"

Devin thought back to what Valerie had mouthed to him and hoped that she was right as he crossed his fingers, "You hate your father because any time you call him you can never get a word in edge wise and you blame him as well as drugs for all the failures in your past rather than taking the blame yourself—"

"Stop it!" the teacher yelled as he grabbed his chest more noticeably and began wheezing heavily dramatically falling to his knees, "Stop… it…"

Devin blinked in surprise looking at him with genuine concern now, "Sir? Are you okay?"

Mr. Hembree's face was now beginning to turn purple as he collapsed fully to the floor with white foam trailing out of his mouth as his body convulsed a few times.

"Sir!" Devin shouted as he jumped off the stage and ran over to the fallen teacher.

As he checked his pulse, Devin yelled at the other student who were just gawking at the situation at hand, "Someone go get the nurse and call an ambulance!"

Almost all of the students, save Valerie, ran out of the auditorium in a near panic. Devin noted the bubbly saliva coming out of Mr. Hembree's mouth and quickly grabbed a pen from the desk to keep the man from biting his tongue. He then turned the teacher onto his side and tried checking the pulse again only to find that it had stopped, "Mr. Hembree! C'mon, man, wake up, help is on the way!"

Valerie gently put her hands on Devin's shoulders trying to calm him down as she realized he was beginning to panic now. Then a strange tingly sensation passed through her and into Devin to Mr. Hembree. The three of them sat there for a long moment as a look of déjà vu crossed Devin's features followed by confusion, though it was only to be forgotten as the teacher twitched once more and began to breathe again. Devin also noted that the pulse had started once more as he looked back at Valerie oddly as if trying to ask a question he didn't have the words for. Suddenly a short fat lady burst into the auditorium yelling and panting, "Veer iz hee?"

Seeing Mr. Hembree on the floor Helga ran down the aisle panting and adjusting her nurse's cap, "Oh! Zer hee iz!"

Helga nearly fell while trying to kneel down beside the fallen teacher. She opened a black bag and took his vitals. Mr. Hembree opened his eyes weakly as he reached up and forcefully grabbed Devin's shirt, "W-what… did you do?"

Devin merely looked down at the man in complete bewilderment and for once had nothing to say.

"How'd you?" the man started as he attempted to sit up.

Devin gently pushed him back down as he finally spoke, "Rest sir, you need it," he then turned to Helga nodding, "He's all yours."

Some of the students had made their way back into the auditorium now as Devin stood up and walked over to his bag grabbing it up. One guy in the back wearing baggy jeans and a Nike tee shirt grabbed his crotch with his left hand as he pointed with his right before speaking to break the awkward silence which had descended across the area, "Yo! Dat was some ill shit dog!"

Devin managed a smile as he walked by Valerie and winked, "Hungry?"

Valerie shook her head in disbelief as she looked from Devin to the nurse who was pulling out a thermometer and telling Mr.

Hembree that she had to take a rectal temperature to make sure it was accurate. He continued walking, leaving the auditorium toward the lunchroom without saying another word.

Steven and Sarah sat side by side together at lunch while he absently flipped through his History book checking for anything that he might have forgotten. Sighing softly, she looked at him as she wrapped the end of his long hair around one of her fingers, "Steven? How do you do all those strange things?"

He looked up from his book at her surprised by the question, "Well, honestly, luv, I don't know. It's just that when I get angry, bored, or really want something to happen it just does."

He shrugged, then as if it didn't really matter, "Guess that's why everyone here thinks I'm a witch."

Sarah laughed in mirth before apologizing, "I'm sorry, but if I hadn't seen some of the stuff you can do, then I'd just say that people were overly superstitious."

Steven smiled warmly at her as he balanced his pencil on its tip before letting go of it and they watched it draw a heart on the table, "Maybe they are, but that still doesn't explain anything."

Sarah gasped as she watched the pencil before hugging him tightly which served to only cause him to wince and turn a few shades paler, "I'm starting to think that your little cut is more serious than you're letting on."

She let go of him quickly, though her eyes were watching him closely now. Steven inhaled sharply as he looked at her, "It's nothing, really…"

"Well I don't believe you," she stated rather flatly as she stood dragging him up with her, "We're going to my house, so I can have a look at it, or the doctor's office right now and you can worry about your stupid student aid position tomorrow."

Steven sighed as he allowed her to drag him out of the school and into the parking lot to his car. She hesitated as they reached it and looked at him sternly for a moment, "Well? Turn off that security system or whatever it is…"

Steven chuckled to himself until she nudged him gently in the side, "Owe! Alright, alright, you win, luv. *Degré de sécurité de voiture.*"

The air around the car shimmered for a brief moment and they got in buckling their seat belts. Steven started up the engine and they pulled out of the parking lot heading to her house.

Devin strolled into the lunchroom, high fiving one of his friends, Joe, a resident jock with the foot ball team.

"So what's up man?" Joe started as they sat down at the table with some preps and other jocks.

"Oh, same 'ole, same 'ole," Devin responded as he picked up an orange and tossed it at him jokingly.

"Ha!" Joe returned, catching the orange and pointing at Devin knowingly, "If I know anything man, it's that you always have some new type of trouble going on to talk about… so c'mon, spill the beans."

Devin smiled as he tried not to laugh at the implication.

"Well, there is this new girl I met on the way to school, she gave me a lift and…" he paused as he noted Steven being dragged out of the lunchroom by Sarah, though he seemed paler than normal and was clutching his side in what appeared to be pain, but before he could let his curiosity get to him the paging system sounded.

"Would Devin No-no… Mr. Lion, please report to the main office…" click!

"Whoa," Joe smirked sarcastically, "Looks like things are more interesting than usual. Wha'dya do? kill somebody?"

Devin shot Joe a warning glance sharply as he snapped back at him, "Hey! Don't go there man!"

"Sorry man, my bad,"Joe quickly replied remembering Devin's run-in with the school witch and some other kid named Marcus the previous year.

"It's alright," Devin replied lightly as he playfully smacked him in the shoulder, "Well, I'm outta here."

Devin turned and began to walk out of the cafeteria when a short preppy brunette with braces and pigtails cut him off at the doors. She smiled at him with a silvery head bobbing grin as she spoke nervously, "H-hey Devin, someone said that you saved the new drama teacher's life… Is that true?"

"Uhh…" Devin started as he glanced around to see that everyone was now watching him waiting for an answer, "Look, I gotta go."

He quickly walked around her trying to avoid anyone else as he moved down the hall to the office. He sighed to himself as he opened the door to the office and stepped in. He was immediately attacked by words.

"That's him!" Mr. Hembree shouted as the paramedics forced him back down onto the gurney.

Devin's eyes widened, as he looked around to see police and paramedics all crowded in the tiny little office room. One officer had a pad and pen and was noticeably scribbling down something down as another stepped toward Devin. The second officer stood well over six feet tall with broad shoulders and a muscular build. He paused as he stood in front of Devin and looked down at him with his hands loosely hanging off his belt.

"We'd like to ask you a few questions, Mr. Noirlion," the tall officer said with a perfect New Orleans accent while he gestured to the door leading out of the office.

Devin nodded, thankfully recognizing the tall officer and followed him out into the hall. The first officer remained in the office still jotting down people's statements with a look of exasperation on his face. The tall officer looked at Devin as he closed the door and faked an authoritative pose before whispering to him, "Dev, you've gotta keep your nose clean this year or you'll be right back in juvy"—snapping his fingers— "just like that! That little fat man in there says that you attacked him, and though everyone else says you saved his life, he swears by it."

The officer said, poking his finger lightly on Devin's chest, "You better get your head out of your ass because someone that looks an awful lot like you has been running around town causing all sorts of problems for my boys and vandalizing all of your old hangouts. All of this weird shit is starting to point back to last year when you and that witch were around and that kid was killed or whatever happened… what was his name? Mark? or Marcus? or something…"

"Marcus…" Devin answered looking down for a moment in memory.

Devin stood there gritting his teeth trying his best not to lose his composure as the officer continued, "Prove them wrong by explaining to me what exactly happened today and be smart about it. I don't usually give you trouble Dev, but your name is starting to get tossed around the precinct like a hacky sack and the mayor's on vacation leaving that prick of a commissioner in charge."

Devin nodded soberly as he took the words to heart and then a slow deliberate breath to steady himself before he spoke, "Mr. Hembree had a heart attack, I did what I could to keep him alive. But what's this about causing issues in town? You know I work at the clubhouse now DJing, I dun run the streets anymore. I'm just trying to get my life straight now—"

The officer raised a hand and cut him off in mid speech, "All I know is that this morning two of my boys chased down a guy matching your description, only they lost him in a crowd of pedestrians like he vanished into thin air. They claimed to have found an intangible wall near the area of this person's disappearance. It was two new recruits from the third precinct, Mike and Jim."

Devin's eyes widened at what he was hearing and he frowned noticeably at what it might mean, "I don't know what to tell you, Frank, I was getting a ride from Valerie Swordfish this morning, the new girl."

He shrugged shaking his head in confusion, "All I really know is that I can't change anyone else, but I can change myself, and I have. I'm trying to start this year off right, it's just hard to get a break when rumors like this come up and I get blindsided by them."

Frank sighed heavily as he ran his hand through his hair, "Just work with me, Dev, I'll do what I can for you, but I can't bend any rules for anyone right now. Not even you, okay?"

Devin nodded a few times. "Alright Frank."

Steven's Porsche pulled into Sarah's driveway, and he turned off the ignition before they both exited the vehicle. They walked hand in hand to her front door, and she unlocked it, motioning him to enter first as she followed in behind. Steven abruptly made his way to the couch where he sat down watching Sarah lock the front door with a click. She deliberately moved over to stand in front of him looking down with a concerned expression etched across her face, "Off with the shirt."

Steven couldn't help but to grin up at her as he began to unbutton his shirt, "Not using this opportunity to take advantage of me, are you?"

Sarah tried to hide a smile while barely keeping her voice in a serious tone, "No, I'm just making sure you're not causing yourself an undue injury."

Steven pulled his shirt off carefully revealing muscular arms, abs, and chest which only caused her smile to widen a bit in a hungry fashion until the large bandage on his side distracted her attention.

"My god! What happened?" she exclaimed as she leaned forward to try and get a better look at the injury.

Steven caught her hands quickly and looked deeply into her jade green eyes fondly, "I told you, it's only a little cut…"

Sarah looked back into his eyes feeling a warm tingly sensation fill her body as she whispered leaning in closer to him, "But…"

Steven leaned forward kissing her tenderly as she tenderly wrapped her arms around his neck leaning into the passionate moment and sat on his legs moving ever closer to him. He methodically moved from her lips to the underside of her neck, kissing gently as he went to ensure that he touched every delicate part of her skin there with his soft breath. The movement caused her to tilt her head back as she sighed, the fire was rising within her and a heavy sigh escaped her lips as it completely took her over. He continued to kiss around her neck and then down unto the v line in her shirt before he carefully began to unbutton it with his skilled tongue and teeth.

Her breathing became heavier as she leaned closer against his lips, the sigh becoming a soft moan as he tentatively pulled her shirt off and continued trailing soft kisses along her breasts. Steven's hands trailed gently across Sarah's lower back and trailed up her spine until they met with resistance with her bra, which, he surprisingly snapped open with great ease of experience. With a soft touch he pulled off the wayward garment with his free hand as his lips continued to trail further down, teasing along her skin with gentle kisses. Sarah leaned her head back further and arched her back as she ran her nails along his shoulders, a sigh of anticipation escaping her lips.

Steven pulled her ever closer to him, bringing her legs to rest around his waist as she leaned in and kissed him passionately. Their touch seemed to cause a steam of longing as their bare chests nestled against one another, their eyes locked for a long moment echoing to each other the desire which was welling up within both of them. His lips turned into a wide smile as he easily lifted her into a standing position and gently trailed a hand along her thigh and up her skirt, his fingers gentle and teasing in a fashion that only love could manage. Sarah bit her lip just barely as she looked down at him watching and feeling his delicate motions across her skin, she could feel a heat welling up inside her that made her want to just pin him down and take all that he had, yet there was something in his touch which restrained her and kept everything building inside her. Carefully he stood and laid her down on the couch, his gentle caress undoing the skirt and slipping it down her legs as his fingers trailed along the outside of her thighs with just a subtle hint of a touch. Sarah's lip quivered in anticipation as she watched him kneel down and take one of her feet in his hands as he softly started kissing along the inside of her leg. Her hands moved up to his head, fingers intertwining in his hair as she bit her lip and looked down at his slow movement up the inside of her thigh with his subtle kisses and gentle trailing of his tongue, her body beginning to ache it seemed, screaming at her to tell him to take her.

Still, Steven moved slow and deliberate, each motion one of caring and quiet tenderness as he moved ever closer to the den of honey which rested between her legs. Sarah's hands clenched in his hair pulling him closer as he teased her with the tip of his tongue, all the while he looked up smiling at her, almost as if waiting for her to lose control. Her back arched as he dove into her and struck her sensitive areas with calm precision that made it feel like her blood was boiling and a soft moan escaped her lips. Steven continued his delicate massage for a moment before pausing and looking up at her, the smile still present on his lips. Sarah looked down at him almost pleadingly, her hand grasping still in his hair, her breath a bit labored and panting, "P-please… don't stop…"

He looked up into her eyes, his lips pressed against her skin as he began to kiss up across her stomach, his hands the whole time gently caressing the inside of her thighs as he made his ascent along her body. It was only a small moment before his tongue cascaded across her breasts causing her to intake a sharp breath as his fingers steadily pressed into her and began to massage her interior causing her body to start trembling and arching against his touch. Her hands moved down from his head and trailed across his back, nails digging into his skin as her breath labored against his continued movements inside her. Sarah bit her lip as he slowly came to a halt, their eyes meeting once more as she narrowed hers playfully, "Tease…"

Steven's grin widened in excitement at her words as her hands moved along his back to trail along the edges of his pants and graced to their front, unbuttoning them.

"Oh, tired of waiting?" he teased her as she slipped his pants down along with his boxers her breath catching in her throat as she saw what was about to ravage her.

"Careful please… I've never…" Sarah cautioned as Steven pressed against her gently and then nodded to her words before kissing her passionately.

Devin wandered the halls of the school for what seemed like an eternity trying to wrap his mind around what was transpiring when it occurred to him that Sarah had dragged Steven out of the school rather quickly and he seemed to be in pain.

"What was that all about," he mused to himself as he nearly ran into Valerie who was turning a corner.

"Hey! I was looking for you, lunch is almost over and I heard them call your name over the intercom system. Everything alright?" she asked as she noted the bewildered expression on his face.

Devin came back to himself and a broad grin spread across his lips, "Yeah, everything's great! Say, you wanna get out of here?"

Valerie blinked several times before just gawking at him, "You mean ditch? Are you serious?"

Devin's grin widened more as he nodded once, "Yeah, let's go somewhere else and just chill. I know a great spot near the lake."

She shook her head for a moment as she followed him out of the school, "I'm gonna regret this, I just know it."

"Awe, come on. It'll be fine, not like I'm gonna eat you or anything." He teased.

Steven lay on the couch with Sarah resting on top of him, his hand trailing gently through her long hair as he looked down at her with a soft smile upon his lips, "I hope that was alright…"

Sarah nestled against him more, her hand resting lightly on his chest as she nodded, "Mhm…"

Steven chuckled and soon they both found themselves laughing happily at the situation. She soon leaned up and kissed him tenderly before she looked at her watch and a panicked expression registered on her face, "Oh shit! My mom will be home any minute!"

Steven sat up and began putting on his clothes, Sarah following his example as they looked at each other nervously with the sound of a car pulling into the driveway. He finished buttoning up his shirt and tying his hair back as she ran into the kitchen to seem like she was grabbing some drinks. As Sarah returned to the living room her mother was opening the front door and walked in with a smile, "Hello Steven, Sarah, how was your day at school kids?"

Steven smiled back cheerfully, his eyes shining like starlight, "Oh it was fine Mrs. Roanoak, and yours?"

Sarah sat down beside him while setting the drinks on the coffee table beside an open history book which she was thankful he had the foresight to quickly grab out of her bag beside the couch.

"My day was alright. It's good to see you two getting along so well," Mrs. Roanoak remarked as she went into the kitchen.

"Oh, we're getting along like a hand and glove..." Sarah said absently as she stared at Steven with a slight glow about her.

He chuckled some as he put an arm around her and took one of the drinks with his free hand taking a sip.

"Really now?" Mrs. Roanoak asked as she returned to the living room with a smile and a bit of a curious look on her face.

"Er... I mean really well mom," Sarah answered turning three different shades of red before leaning against Steven.

Steven only smiled as he tried not to laugh, "I think she means that I might actually be teaching her something, mum."

Sarah blushed even more at his comment taking it entirely the wrong way. Her mom only raised a curious brow before returning back to the kitchen. Steven carefully stood up with a noticeable wince as he made his way to the door, Sarah in tow right behind him. As they left the house, they stood on the front porch for a long moment before he wrapped her into a loving embrace, "So where's your mind still at, hmmm?"

"Tease," she returned before leaning up and kissing him, "You had better let me see that little cut tomorrow after school though."

"Alright, luv," he answered as he let her go and moved to his car getting in the driver's seat.

Sarah waived bye and blew him a kiss as he pulled out of the drive and drove away.

SAVE ME FROM MYSELF

Here is that which I give...
To take away sorrow and help thee live...
True, it may only be a rose,
But it carries happiness and health as it goes...
There is that other which you may also receive,
My promise of love and friendship that shall never leave...
Perhaps tis how one carries out the day...
Yet still, as it rests in thy window ceil,
Tis a constant reminder that I am here until you heal...
As a friend, as a companion, as a lover...
So keep in mind...
I shall never leave you behind...
And n'ere fear, for truth and love are always near...

OLATH WATCHED AS the drama class erupted into chaos as the teacher collapsed clutching his chest. His eyes turned narrowly to the shadows behind him as he mumbled something inaudible. His features were pale and thin, his hair a matted mess of brown and black, though his face registered a sense of calculated calm malice to it. His clothing was anything but in fashion as the pants he wore were old brown leather riding pants, his shirt a black French style long sleeved with ruffles on the sleeves and in the front around the collar, the boots obviously old and well worn typically used for riding as well were laced from the ankle up. Still, none had seemed to notice the out of place young man as he sat in the upper levels of the auditorium sitting quietly, observing everything around him. He watched as Devin screamed for people to get help and tried in vain desperation to try and revive the fallen man. As he leaned forward, some of his matted hair fell unkempt in front of his face, obscuring his features as he mumbled once more toward the shadows behind him. Soon the only people in the room were himself, Devin, Valerie, and the dying man on the floor.

Olath turned his attention to the fallen teacher and the two who were desperately trying to revive him, his eyes picked out the opposing colors in their auras and he compared the bright red of Devin to the soft blue of Valerie with muted interest. He could tell that there was something abnormal about them by the vibrancy and solidity of the colors around them, but he wasn't quite sure what it was just yet. Grumbling inaudibly, he turned once more to the shadows behind him as a spectral figure emerged looking at him for guidance, yet as he spoke, his voice had a slight pitch to it that grated on the ears, "Should we help them?"

"Why?" the spirit hissed coldly as it glanced over the situation at the bottom of the auditorium.

"Because that man might die if we just observe..." Olath answered as he eyed the spirit some.

The apparition half-heartedly pointed down to the unveiling scene before them as Valerie touched Devin's shoulders and their two auras seemed to mix for a brief moment, sending some type of force into the fallen teacher which caused him to sputter and recover back to life.

"Mmm... I see... they aren't always going to be that lucky... but I wonder who they are, watch them for me... I am willing to bet that they are the ones who killed Marcus..." Olath hissed to the spirit as he begrudgingly stood up and left the auditorium without so much as a sound.

Steven pulled into his driveway and weakly exited his car grabbing his side reflexively as he nearly passed out from the pain which jolted through him with the motion. After a moment of him leaning on the car breathing heavily, his butler Alfred came out to see what was taking him so long to enter the house.

"Master Steven! What happened?" Alfred inquired as he made his way to Steven and looped an arm over his shoulder and began to help him to the front door.

"I-I'm not entirely sure Alfred, but... you might want to call the doctor..." Steven answered as the pain over came him and he passed out at the door.

October 2008
Week 2, Thursday

Sarah waited at the bus stop and was more than a little surprised when the bus actually arrived before Steven. Tucking down the ill feeling, she got on the bus and assured herself that she would see him at school and that he was just running late.

Devin pulled up alongside Valerie's Benz on his Harley and honked his horn while winking at her slyly. Her face instantly turned a little red with blush as she rolled down her window and yelled out to him while trying not to laugh, "Show off!"

He only smiled as the light turned green and he sped off toward the school leaving Valerie to shake her head and continue grinning. She sped after him an instant later which caused them to pull into the school parking lot at about the same time. Devin parked his bike beside her car and was about to make some comment when he noticed Steven's car wasn't there and it struck him as peculiar. Valerie moved over in front of him and waived her hand in front of his face, "Hello, earth to Devin? You okay?"

"Huh? Yeah! Just mesmerized by your beauty is all," he chuckled as he winked and gave her a smile.

She grinned at the compliment before turning toward the school with a brisk walk calling back to him, "You're a rogue, Devin, a pure and simple rogue."

He caught himself laughing at her remark as he caught up and they went to their first class together.

Sarah entered literature class and noted that Steven wasn't there and she began to wonder what was keeping him. Pushing down the gnawing feeling in her stomach again, she decided to wait and see if he showed up throughout the day.

Devin entered drama class and moved down the aisle taking his seat next to Valerie while looking around curiously for a teacher, but there was none to be seen by the time the late bell rang. Chatter buzzed throughout the room that Mr. Hembree was dead, though it was pure speculation. The room fell silent as the doors to the auditorium swung open and Sebastian walked in and down the aisle.

"Good day class, I am Sebastian. I shall be conducting your drama class for the duration of this school year," he spoke as he approached the stage.

Devin stared at their new teacher, his mouth wide open in surprise as he wondered how the hell Steven had managed this one. Valerie looked over and closed his mouth gently with one hand before making a teasing off handed comment, "You know Devin, I never knew you went that way."

He turned to her, a surprised look still showing on his features before coming back to himself and commenting back to her in a lispy voice, "Oh, that's sssso typical."

She laughed audibly before a loud crack sounded echoing throughout the auditorium causing everyone to fall silent and turn their attention to Sebastian. He smiled as he sat on the stage with what looked like a broken pencil in-between his two hands.

"Now that I have everyone's attention I shall start the lesson," Sebastian stated as he stood up and retrieved a book which rested beside him on the stage.

Raising his voice so that it echoed from the stage across the auditorium Sebastian began his lecture, "William Shakespeare was one of the greatest playwrights of his time and thus I shall teach you true theatre and not this insensible crap your previous teacher was attempting to pawn off on you while he was piddling over his personal problems…"

He took a long breath as he winced and began walking up the aisle continuing his speech, "Romeo and Juliet is one of the most well known classic tragedies, however, we are not going to do Romeo and Juliet, we will be doing Macbeth. It is also a classic tragedy, be it a little less well known."

Sebastian stopped walking as he reached Devin and Valerie's seats, his eyes glaring down at them with just a subtle hint of a smile as he leaned forward and whispered to Devin, "You're right, Dev, she's a real knock out."

He turned just as Devin began to turn a few shades of red in the face and proceeded back down the aisle while instructing the class to retrieve their books from under the seats. Valerie looked at Devin as the teacher walked away and smiled sweetly as she spoke in a calm you're-in-trouble tone, "Dev… you know him? A real knock out?"

Devin chuckled nervously as his face turned a bit redder, "Er… yeah, yeah, we go way back. I didn't say anything bad about you, promise."

A surprised look registered on her face as her cheeks began to turn red as well before stammering out, "H-he's talking about me?"

Olath watch the exchange from the back of the auditorium with only slight interest. His eyes traveled over Sebastian for a long moment as he wondered about the purely yellow aura with only a few discolorations, but he could also tell there was something not quite right about the man's appearance. It was as if a veil were masking what he really looked like. His eyes narrowed as he remained focused on Sebastian until he pierced the glamour and saw him for what he really was, Steven Nightwolf. His tone hissed as he spoke to the spectral figure beside him, "So, it seems that not all the rumors about this school witch are entirely false. He might be able to fool everyone else with that little spell, but not me. Now, to find out who the others are."

A guttural chuckle came the spirit as it replied, "Perhaps… it's all three of them."

Olath's expression became a scowl as he contemplated this development and what he might have to set in place as time continued on.

Bells rang, time passed, and soon lunch had made its way into the hour. Sarah was becoming more concerned as she hadn't seen Steven all morning. Her steps hastened as she made her way to the cafeteria and paused seeing Steven sitting in his usual spot at the empty lunch table, but what gave her pause was the fact that Devin and Valerie were sitting there with him. Her temper flared at the sight of Valerie and before she knew it, she was standing beside Steven and reached across the table and slapped Valerie with all her might. Devin and Steven sat there with mouths agape in slight shock before Steven came to his senses and stood up quickly grabbing Sarah's hand and leading her out of the cafeteria still fuming.

Devin paused blinking before he turned as the two left and stared at Valerie for a moment before speaking, "What the hell was all that about?"

Valerie gently rubbed the side of her face while trying to suppress tears as she replied, "That's Sarah, we were at the same school last… and there was this really cute guy who was kind of hitting on me… I didn't know that she had been dating him at the time, so I went out with him. Call it dumb luck, or fate, or whatever, but she was having dinner with her mother at the same restaurant he took me out to. I guess she still thinks that I stole him away from her. I've never had the chance to explain it all to her, so I don't blame her for still being angry about it all…"

Devin stood from his seat and took her hand leading her out of the cafeteria quickly, much to her surprise and confusion.

Steven partially dragged Sarah out of the school and to where he had parked his car, shutting off its security system before leaning against it heavily and looking at her, "What the hell was that?"

Sarah still fuming looked at him with tears in her eyes giving him a sobbing response. "Valerie, s-she's the one who stole my boy friend away at my last high school, I… I just…"

Steven gently put his arms around her and pulled her into a loving embrace while whispering to her in an assuring fashion, "Luv, no one is going to steal me away from you… especially not Devin's new girlfriend."

She nodded softly against his chest before pulling her head back a little and looking up at him, "Devin's new girlfriend? Oh gods, I just made a fool of myself, didn't I?"

Steven chuckled in amusement as he spied Devin dragging Valerie across the parking lot toward them, "Be that as it may, luv, I think there will be a chance to clear it all up shortly."

Sarah turned around in Steven's arms and began turning red as she noted the two's approach, all the while her gaze lowering to the ground. As Devin and Valerie approached, he spoke first in a matter-of-fact tone, "I think there's something that needs to get out in the open here, hopefully without any more blows."

Steven nodded and looked between the two girls for a moment when they both spoke at the same time.

"I'm sorry!"

The two girls looked at each other in bewilderment for a long moment before Valerie spoke again, "Look, Sarah, I'm really sorry about that guy from our last school. If I had known you were seeing him I would have never agreed to go out on a date with him."

Sarah stared at her a moment in consideration before responding, "I'm sorry for slapping you and thinking the worst… I feel really foolish now that I know what happened."

They smiled at each other for a moment before Valerie spoke again, "Friends, then?"

Sarah nodded as their smiles widened, "Friends."

Steven and Devin looked at each other knowingly for a moment before Steven spoke, "Let's get out of here… Today's just been a pain for everyone all around and I think we could all use a breather. Devin, show your girl where my place is, alright?"

Devin nodded with a wide grin, "See you there man."

Valerie just looked between the two incredulously, "Leave? It's the middle of the day; we'll get in trouble for sure!"

Steven smirked as he opened the passengers' side door for Sarah, "We'll be just fine, now come on."

He walked around and hopped into the driver's seat and called out before driving off, "You two don't get lost on any detours now."

Devin just shook his head as he watched Steven and Sarah speed away before turning his attention to Valerie who was fidgeting with the buttons on her shirt.

"What's wrong?" he asked as he looked her over.

She looked up from her fidgeting and answered him nervously, "Is this really okay? I mean we skipped yesterday and I've never skipped classes my whole life, let alone half a day. Won't they call our parents or something?"

Devin smirked and laughed as he replied, "No worries, Steven will handle all of that… he is the school witch after all."

He gave her a knowing wink before leading her to his bike and pulling out an extra helmet from the saddle bags and handing it to her as he climbed on, "Just hold on tight and we'll be there in a minute."

Valerie nodded as she slipped on the helmet and climbed on behind him and held on for dear life as he sped out of the parking lot.

Steven drove down the road quietly for a long moment before smiling and looking at Sarah, "Guess I get to show you my home now. I hope you like it…"

She looked at him quizzically as he left off the road down a long drive which dove into an old thick forest of oak. Her eyes soon darted to the windows as she watched the massive old trees that they were passing and then her breath caught as the forest gave way to clearing. Before them stood the Nightwolf estate, a massive Victorian style chateau with a crystal clear lake resting in front of it. Her eyes went back to him and then the estate in disbelief until she found her voice again, "This is where you live?"

Steven nodded chuckling softly, "Yeah, I know it's… ah… a bit much, but its home for me."

She just gawked at him as he pulled up in front of the house and parked the car. He gracefully stepped out and moved around to the passenger side opening the door for her. Sarah took his hand as she exited the car, her eyes still taking in the view around her in astonishment, "You live here all by yourself?"

He smirked. "Well, with my butler Alfred, but yes… my parents died when I was very young in a car accident in the mountains."

She shook her head in disbelief once more as he led her to the front door and into the house.

Olath watched the four leave the parking lot of the school and sighed irritably while mumbling to the spectral figure to his side, "Those four make a volatile combination… follow them; I need to know how bad the one was wounded by the shadow, so that I can begin my plans…"

A soft chuckle came from the spirit as it wisped after the four. Olath's eyes trailed after, his face seemingly etched into a permanent scowl as he grumbled to himself, "I'll pay you back… it's only a matter of time."

Devin sped down the road with a wide grin on his lips beneath the helmet as Valerie clung to him for dear life; his heart was pounding and he couldn't shake that ecstatic feeling whenever she was around him. The closeness of her leaning against him with her arms around his waist only seemed to make his pulse race more and he wondered to himself, *Is this love?* He chuckled as he took the turn into the thick woods of Steven's estate which caused Valerie to nearly scream as she squeezed against him tighter. Soon his speed slowed and she relaxed against his back, though he still heard her gasp as they exited the woods into the clearing which revealed the large chateau.

"That's his house?" Valerie exclaimed.

Devin laughed heartily as he replied, "Yep, that's the Nightwolf estate."

"Holy shit! He must be really loaded!" She said with disbelief still in her voice.

Still snickering, he spoke once more as he pulled up to park beside Steven's Porsche, "Told you he was rich."

Valerie slipped off the helmet and stared at the mansion in awe before playfully slugging Devin in the shoulder, "Rich doesn't even begin to cover this, you ass."

He laughed once more as he packed up the helmets and led her to the front door where he knocked gingerly. Sarah opened the door, tears streaming down her face, as she rushed the two inside and led them to the study with confusion etched upon their faces. Her steps were nearly a sprint as she went to sit beside a sweating and feverish Steven who was laid out on the floor as if he had collapsed. Devin blinked, taking a moment to comprehend the situation when he noted the blood seeping through the side of Steven's shirt, "You idiot, what type of stupid heroic thing have you done now?"

Steven glanced at Devin and then past him as he coughed while trying to chuckle and smile, "You know, Dev, I'm really not sure… call Tiara… I'm fairly certain she's the only one who can help right now given that my doctor seems to have ended up dead somehow."

Devin frowned noticeably with his brow furrowing as Alfred entered the room and cleared his throat before speaking, "Don't worry, Master Devin, I have already placed the appropriate calls and each of your families will be along shortly."

Valerie looked between them all as her features paled to the point of her looking like a corpse in the morgue, "M-my grandmother is coming? Oh gods, she's going to kill me."

Alfred smiled kindly to her, "I am sure she will be quite forgiving Miss Valerie, given the current circumstances."

Devin nodded some at Alfred's words as he managed a small smile, "Besides, if this is an injury caused by something that Steven was actually fighting then we're gonna need Tiara to fix him."

"I don't understand; he needs a doctor, maybe even a hospital! Not my grandmother!" Valerie nearly shouted at Devin, the confusion and stress of the situation beginning to show on her face and in her voice.

"Oh relax, dear, I figured this might happen when he helped me against the shadow the other night," Tiara's wizened voice entered the room as she walked in, followed by Devin and Sarah's mothers.

Mrs. Noirlion sighed in exasperation as she surveyed the scene before speaking, "You lot really need to learn how to help him, because we're not going to be around forever."

Devin nodded at his mother's words while the two girls stared at her blankly in confusion. Mrs. Roanoak went and stood near her daughter and chuckled softly as she looked down at the two, "Looks like the old wolf has you in quite an uproar dear. Don't worry, by the morn he'll be right as rain and everything will make much more sense. Still, the three of you will have to help us tonight."

Sarah nodded numbly as she wiped her eyes with her sleeve, "Okay... I-I'll do my best, mom."

Steven's eyes began to glaze over in a glassy manner as incoherent mumblings trailed from his lips. The three youths simply stared at him in muted horror. Mrs. Noirlion frowned deeply as she looked to her son, "Devin, you and Sarah take him up to bed. We'll do what needs to be done down here. Valerie, go with Tiara and help her with the medicine in the kitchen."

Valerie just nodded dumbly as she stood and followed her grandmother from the room and into the kitchen down the hall. Devin and Sarah stood hoisting Steven up onto their shoulders and carried him up the stairs to his room. Mrs. Roanoak sighed as she looked at Mrs. Noirlion and shook her head a bit, "Well, this is a fine mess, Mira. He's just like his father, and just as reckless."

Mira just smirked as she began to move furniture around and clear out the center of the room, "Be that as it may Lila, he is most likely the reincarnation we have been waiting for. From what Tiara has told me, it was no ordinary shade he was fighting, but one of the seven deadly ones."

Lila looked at Mira dubiously then frowned noticeably, "If that's true then the fact that he beat it and survived a wound from its blade is a miracle in itself."

The two continued talking in hushed tones as they prepared the room for the ritual to come.

Sarah and Devin made their way up the stairs into Steven's room and then across it to the four post canopy bed. Once they laid him in it, Devin couldn't help but to whistle in amazement at the room. Sarah looked at him a moment scowling, tears still in her eyes, "How can you admire things when he's like this?"

Devin steadily turned facing her with a juvenile grin, his voice light and relaxed, "No worries Sarah. They said he would be all right by morning and I trust them. So, you stay here and watch over him and I'll go check how things are going downstairs."

She looked at him doubtfully as she sat beside the bed taking Steven's hand into her own. Devin grinned once more before darting out of the room, calling back as he left, "Trust me, everything's going to work out just fine. You'll see!"

Valerie stood in mute silence watching her grandmother sift through a root cellar pantry to retrieve the herbs she needed. Tiara paused smiling at her granddaughter as she placed an assortment of plants on the kitchen counter and called over to her, "Come here dear, it's time you finally learned something worthwhile."

Valerie nodded as she moved over to stand beside her grandmother and looked over the plants curiously before blinking some and exclaiming, "I know these plants!"

Tiara's smile widened at the reaction, "Yes, we use to go over these when you were much younger dear. Can you remember what each of them is for?"

Valerie took a moment to examine each plant and then began to recite their medicinal properties with what seemed to be uncanny intuition. Tiara nodded and smiled warmly once more at her granddaughter as she set some of the herbs in a specific order, "Well, let's go over drawing out the poison of fiends and make up a remedy for young Master Nightwolf."

Valerie looked to her for a moment in curiosity before asking, "Poison of fiends?"

Tiara nodded once as she instructed her to begin cutting up some of the herbs and grinding up others with the mortar and pestle, "Yes, you see he is so ill right now because he protected me from a demon of sorts the other night. He really is an amazing boy…"

Valerie did as she was instructed to do even though she was looking at her grandmother in slight disbelief, "A demon? But that stuff only exists in fairy tales, doesn't it?"

"Oh, you'd be surprised what's really out there, dear. I blame myself for not continuing to teach you after your parent's deaths, but I promise to start again now. It's never good to be left in the dark and unaware of the dangers which are out there," Tiara answered with a weary smile as they continued working on the medicine.

Sarah sat beside Steven's bed, gently dabbing his feverish brow with a damp cloth as she watched him toss and turn as if fighting with some unseen enemy. Her own brow was knitted with concern as he cried out on occasion, whether in pain or anguish she couldn't tell. Each time the sound broke her heart. Heartfelt tears flowed down her cheeks as she continued to care for him, for despite what the others had said, she felt as if she was going to lose him and that there was nothing she could do. Minutes passed though they seemed like hours, and finally footsteps turned Sarah's head to see Valerie entering the room with a steaming bowl and spoon. Valerie's eyes searched Sarah's face as she came to sit down beside her speaking in a soft whisper, "I'm sorry, Sarah, but this broth should help to ease the fever and draw out the poison. Grandmother says that you both have to remember something, but I don't know what she means by that. So please take care of him and give him this medicine. I have to go back downstairs and help out the others now."

Sarah took the bowl and spoon only nodding as she returned her attention to Steven. Valerie rose and left the two of them, hoping that somehow her words managed to give some comfort in the saddening situation. Sarah began to feed Steven the medicinal broth while at the same time dabbing his head gently with the cloth. As the night grew late, she laid her head on his chest, their two hands interlocked and drifted off into sleep.

Steven and Sarah's Dream

Quiet footsteps echoed in the darkness, softly treading the forest floor and taking the two who would be on toward the oaken grove, a hallowed out center amongst a circle of trees where the moon might look down and see the work of whoever wished to worship there. The night was calm, a rarity in the time and place where the family of Nightwolf resided. Gentle clouds drifted across the moon that illuminated the old standing grove of Oak, which served as their meeting place. Delicate hands prepared the kindling for a bonfire at the center of the circle, showing cautious practice and skill when placing the sticks and logs in their proper place. Still, the soft echoing of footsteps came, alerting those who stood within the circle of two people approaching. The first sound as the two entered came from Sarah; her hair was as red as fire and her eyes glittered like jade, a soft sigh escaped her lips followed by a slight smile. The two who entered the circle of Oak looked almost identical, save that one was noticeably younger than the other. It was obvious that they were brothers. Long black hair was carefully pulled back by a red ribbon; their eyes seemed to shine like emeralds in the moonlight, resonating the power that they held within.

"All is prepared?" Mick, the older of the two asked as they came to stand in front of the girl.

"Yes, Mick, all is ready. The others are all patrolling the forest to ensure that the hunters don't stumble upon us this night." She answered him with quiet tones as her gaze drifted to Steven; the younger brother, a soft smile tracing her lips for a moment.

Mick nodded once and began moving to the northern quadrant of the circle of Oak trees where a simple marble altar rested; it was adorned with various items for the upcoming ritual which was to be performed. The young girl watched Mick quietly for a long moment before speaking once again.

"You are certain that this ascension will work without any complications? It is the rule that only one per generation is allowed, you know?"

Mick turned looking back at her with a concerned look for a moment and then nodded, "Yes, I am aware of the tenets, but this is something that must be done to help try and preserve us. There are too many hunters about for us to be so utterly alone now."

She nodded once, her eyes drifting back to Steven for a long moment, settling on his with what could only be interpreted as a look of love. He seemed to return her look, his eyes tracing over her for a short moment before turning to focus on his brother, who was now staring at them both.

"Is it time, brother?" Steven asked, slight nervousness in his voice.

Mick nodded silently for a moment before responding, "It is. Are you ready?"

"I am. Let us begin." Steven answered affirmatively.

Steven moved to the eastern section of the circle of Oak and waited patiently, then Sarah followed him to stand by his side and took his hand for a moment while whispering softly to him, "You better remember me..."

He smiled briefly for a moment as Mick began walking around the circle, chanting and casting out salts and water around its edges. The light of the moon shone down brightly, perhaps as a sign of acceptance of their ritual, and the clouds seemed to part as Mick moved to the center of the circle and lit the bonfire. The flames illuminated the scene in an almost eerie light, however, causing shadows to dance along the edges of the trees and between them. The soft chanting echoed out from Mick, seeming to drift through the air like a warm summer's breeze, dancing among the leaves of the trees around them and then finally settling upon them. His movements took him around the circle once more before stopping in front of the two, his eyes tracing over them for a long moment before he spoke, his tone deep and somber, "Bride, is it true that you come of your own free will and accord?"

"I do." Sarah answered with a wide smile upon her lips.

"Groom, is it true that you come of your own free will and accord?"

"I do." Steven answered looking at Sarah with an equally wide smile.

"Above, you are the stars; below, you are the stones, as time doth pass, remember... Like a stone should your love be firm, like a star should your love be constant. Let the powers of the mind and of the intellect guide you in your marriage, let the strength of your wills bind you together, let the power of love and desire make you happy, and the strength of your dedication make you inseparable. Be close, but not too close. Possess one another, yet be understanding. Have patience with one another, for storms will come, but they will pass quickly. Be free in giving affection and warmth. Have no fear and let not the ways of the unenlightened give you unease, for the Gods are with you always. Once you kiss, know that you shall always be bound, no matter time or place, no matter life or death you shall be eternally linked. Do you both understand this?" Mick intoned as he continued the first part of the ritual, to marry them, knowing that the second part was the dangerous one.

The two nodded once, intoning together, "We do."

Mick nodded once more to them and laid a delicate green and gold sash across their hands, tying them both together, "You may now kiss and seal the pact."

The two looked at each other a long moment in silence, their breathing heavy and hearts pounding in their chests, the only sounds for that time, and then, they kissed, sealing the pact to be bound together. They held the moment for a long time, not seeming to want to leave that perfect time, but then the kiss ended and they turned looking at Mick once more.

"Now, it is time for you to assume your mantles of power, are you both ready for the tasks that lie ahead?"

The two nodded once and Mick continued the ritual, "Two who are bound from the four families shall bring salvation to the world, protect it from darkness, and lead people back from damnation. Two, who bear the marks of the families shall join in union as has never been done before and usher in a new era for the families and the powers we hold. You two have been chosen and wed. Now, as is written, you shall receive the mantles of power which has been passed down from your forefathers and mothers unto you."

The two embraced each other closely for a moment and then turned toward the altar in the northern section of the circle, calmly walking toward it hand in hand, still bound by the green and gold sash.

Mick continued speaking as he intuitively moved to the center of the circle, "As the passing of time so must we pass the power of the ancestors to the children, may they now accept their power and their blood cleanse the future to come!"

The two stopped in front of the altar and stood there in muted silence for a moment, Sarah took the athame from the stone surface with a graceful gesture and then turned to look at Steven. Her voice was soft and caring as she spoke to him, "Hold out your hand for me, husband, I shall draw your blood to bind us further and bring us into our power."

He nodded quietly as he held out his hand and with one fluid motion she cut across his palm with the ceremonial knife, a shallow cut, but deep enough to draw out a large amount of blood. She then turned the blade hilt toward him, and he took it in his free hand. His voice was just as caring as he spoke, his accent filled with British formality, "Hold out your hand for me, wife, I shall draw your blood to bind us further and bring us into our power."

She smiled faintly and held out her hand to him, his own motion was as graceful as the wind, cutting her palm and then placing the athame back on the altar. They both looked up to the moon, then they joined their bloody hands and held them up while still bound in the green and gold sash, speaking clearly and with purpose, "We now accept our mantle of power and our responsibility to the families; as husband and wife we shall do our sworn duties!"

They paused, almost hesitantly at the end of their words as the sky seemed to cloud, blocking out the moons light from the circle of Oak, darkening the area to nothing but the light of the now dying bonfire and the shadows dancing amongst the trees. The wind hissed wispily through the leaves, giving warning as howls erupted in the woods and the sounds of a hunting party filled the glade with shouts of anger and puritan prayers to cast out demons. The two watched the edges of the grove fearfully as the night darkened ever more and the wind picked up, brewing a storm, the sounds of witch hunters drawing ever closer. Mick cursed quietly under his breath and cast a glance back at them, his voice low and stern, “Flee, I shall distract them while you escape… let them not catch you or we shall all be doomed to darkness.”

The two nodded and looked back up to the sky, attempting to finish the ritual hurriedly, “Hear us! We call for the power of our ancestors, as is our right on the night of our marriage and ascension! We call for the blessings of the gods and the four corners for which our houses represent! Hear us!”

The sky flashed with lightning striking the altar and illuminating the circle in a horrifying sight. Mick turned, looking back at the two, his eyes widening as he witnessed the surge of electricity around them both, their faces etched with pain and agony, and then all was dark and silent. The sounds of hunting dogs filled the night with the sounds of the storm, and Mick knew that the worst was yet to come…

Sarah cried out as the two of them vanished, her voice echoing within the grove and in Mick’s ears, “*Steven*!”

The altar was gone as were his brother and his wife, naught but ash and rising smoke remained, barely illuminated in the dying bonfire’s light. He stared at the spot for a moment longer before drawing a horn from his sash and blowing hard on it to sound the retreat for the families which patrolled the forest, trying to hide the circle of Oak with spells and illusions. Then, Mick fled, turning toward the darkness and ran for his life.

Valerie stepped off the stairs and made her way into the study where all the others had moved all of the furniture out of the way to reveal an intricate pattern of lines and symbols which were engraved into the hard wood floor. Her eyes examined the floor for a long moment before she finally crossed the room making her way to her grandmother’s side. Tiara smiled at her granddaughter’s approach before handing her an ancient looking blue satin cloak and an intricately carved willow wand while speaking reassuringly, "First, we'll pass on our families powers to you dear, then we'll work on helping young Nightwolf with his injury."

Valerie nodded just a bit as she took the items and looked around the room until her eyes settled upon Devin. He smiled warmly as he clasped on a red shimmering cloak and an ancient looking long sword, whose hilt bore a crest, which had a black lion at its center. Valerie shook her head as she looked back to her grandmother, "I don't really understand what's happening, Mammy. Are you trying to tell me that we're all witches or some secret society or something weird like that?"

Tiara smiled warmly before replying, "Yes dear, each one of us here represents one of four families with ancient traditions and ancient roots to the old world. Our task, as it was handed down to us each generation, is to help protect this world from the darkness that lies in wait trying to destroy all that is, was, or ever will be."

Valerie blinked a few times as if a weight has just been added onto her very soul is fine as the end of the sentence without shoulders. She didn't know if she fully believed the answer she had been given, but she did know that everything which was going on now was very important somehow. She also knew that whatever responsibility she was about to accept was going to change her life forever.

Steven and Sarah's Dream

Steven and Sarah were drifting surrounded in darkness, bound by the sash and the blood that they now shared, their backs against each other while their hands clasped together in what seemed like an eternal emptiness when he spoke, "Do you remember me? From back then?"

Sarah nodded a bit, squeezing his hand gently. "I do… I can't believe we forgot all that."

"Would you still stay with me, even after I caused us so much pain?" His voice hushed and heavy with emotion as he asked.

She smiled, though he could not see, "I will, I love you after all and we made the choice together."

He seemed to nod as he sighed heavily, "I never want to lose you again… no matter what."

"Nor I, you my love," she answered.

"I love you Sarah." He said as a smile began to trail his own lips, his hands squeezing hers gently.

Valerie felt beside herself as her grandmother prepared her for the rituals to come, maybe even a little self-conscious. Tiara had been going over how things were to proceed and what she was to say, yet she still felt more than a little nervous about it all. Tiara had ensured that her granddaughter was completely nude, save for the blue satin cloak, which had been passed down throughout the family lines and the delicately carved willow wand. Carefully the wizened woman took out a long blue silk cord and carefully bound Valerie's hands behind her back with a practiced care before blindfolding her.

"Don't worry about a thing dear, the families have been conducting this ritual for generations," Tiara whispered reassuringly to Valerie.

Valerie nodded a bit nervously, her steps cautious as she was led back into the study by her grandmother. It wasn't just the idea of the ritual, which had her nervous, but more so being laid bare in front of everyone. As she entered the room, the sound of someone being smacked in the back of the head followed by an audible *ow* from Devin caused her to blush deeply and smile even more nervously. She had completely forgotten that he was there in the room as part of the ritual as well, and the idea of him seeing her like this caused the heat in her body to rise and her skin to flush. Soon Valerie's steps came to a halt and Mira's voice filled the room, "Let there be none who suffer loneliness, none who are friendless and without family. For all may find love and protection within this circle."

It was then Devin's voice which echoed through the air next, serious and unfaltering, "With open arms, the gods and our ancestors welcome all."

The sound of movement met Valerie's ears then as people went around the room, as did the soft patter of salt hitting the floor between footsteps. Tiara's voice then drifted across the room causing Valerie to shift a bit nervously, "I bring one who has made her way to us seeking her inheritance."

Devin's voice filled the air once more, almost with a challenging authority, "Who has caused her to come here?"

Tiara then answered, her voice unflinching, "She has come of her own free will."

Mira's voice sounded then with an almost holy authority as she asked the next question, "Who among us will vouch for this girl?"

Tiara answered once more, "I shall, as her grandmother, I attest to her lineage and right to join us and assume her mantle of power."

For a moment the sounds of a small bell being rung three times drifted through the air to Valerie's ears, almost hanging in the air like a hummingbird. It was then that the sound of people moving about, some that greeted her ears and she wondered what exactly was going on beyond the thick blindfold which covered her eyes. It was then that Mira's voice filled her ears at a much closer distance than she formerly was, "What is your name, girl?"

Valerie cleared her throat before she answered with as much confidence as she could muster, "I am Valerie Swordfish, I beg for admittance."

It was then that Devin's voice, close at hand, filled her ears and caused her to blush once more and remembered her lack of clothing, "Valerie Swordfish, why have you come here?"

Valerie shuffled her feet just a little as she realized she was still bound by the blue cord and then calmly answered, "To worship the gods and our ancestors, to become one with them, and to claim my inheritance as is my right."

It's was then Mira's turn to pose the next question as her voice drifted to her ears, "What is it that you bring with you now?"

Valerie blushed a bit more as she felt a slight draft for the briefest moment before answering, "I bring nothing save my family's cloak and wand, my true self, naked before you."

Mira's voice then softened in response as she spoke again, "Then I bid you welcome to our circle as your rite shall now begin."

Steven tiredly opened his eyes halfway, his body felt sore and battered all over, his mind reeling, trying to figure out where he was and what might be transpiring. It was only a brief moment before he was aware that he was lying on his bed with Sarah next to him, her head resting on his chest. A soft smile trailed his lips as he carefully pulled her closer to him, wrapping his arms around her lovingly, "I will never let you go. my love."

His eyes then closed and soon he was back sound asleep, unaware of the shadowy figure which seemed to hover just outside his window watching with keen interest.

Valerie gratefully slipped on the blue satin robe, which had been given to her at the conclusion of her ritual, though her face was still flushed red as she remembered that Devin was able to see her with little to nothing on. Sighing softly, she began to make her way from the bathroom, back to the study, pausing as she nearly bumped into Devin in the hall, her face instantly turning red once more. Devin managed a devilish smile as he leaned forward and kissed her on the cheek, "No worries, I'm sure you'll get to see me in the buff sooner or later."

Valerie shook her head as she smacked him playfully, "You're still a rogue, and I think you would enjoy that more than I would."

Devin raised a hand to his heart and pretended to act wounded, "Oh, oh that hurts right here, it does!"

Valerie giggled and turned heading once more to the study calling back to him, "Dun take too long, I'd like to go for a swim in that lake out there after we're done in here."

Devin's grin widened noticeably, "Oh, you're on!"

Olath tapped his foot irritably, his matted hair willfully falling in front of his eyes as he stared down the long driveway that led into a thick forest. His eyes were irritably narrowed as he observed the spirit gliding through the woods toward him in the darkness, his voice less than pleased, "Well? What did you find out?"

The spirit seemed to hover for a moment before hissing a cold response, "The Nightwolf boy is the one who fought the shadow… his… friends are his coven, though they seem untrained and unskilled for the most part. You should have no issues dealing with them, master."

Olath eyed the spirit for a moment longer then nodded, "Then let's be off, we need to begin separating them soon."

Devin ran out of the old Victorian-style mansion stripping off his clothes as his path took him to the lake, his voice called back teasingly to Valerie, "Last one in is a rotten egg!"

Valerie bound after him, following suit in stripping down, her voice teasing as she went by him, "Mmmm, seems like you might be that egg."

Devin laughed as he jumped into the water just behind her, causing a large splash to cover her, "Oops."

She turned looking at him, her hair dripping now and splashed him playfully as the moon shone down upon them lighting the area in a soft white light. Devin grinned as he engaged her in an all-out water fight, the two of them laughing as the mock battle proceeded on. They went back and forth for long moments until they were both panting from the activity and from laughing, though smiles traced both their lips as they sat in the water beside one another. Devin traced the hair from Valerie's face as she leaned her head on his shoulder.

"Do you think my grandmother is right, it's going to take Steven a few weeks to fully recover?" She finally asked after a moment of listening to the sounds of crickets and other forest creatures in the night.

Devin shrugged, "He's a tough nut, I've seen him fight some pretty bad things that most people don't even believe is out there and win. But I also know that Tiara has always been right when it comes to treating injuries. I trust her."

Valerie nodded just as she nestled in closer to him, a soft sigh escaping her lips for a moment, "It would be nice if this could last forever."

Devin chuckled a bit, "It would, but nothing lasts forever. So we take the good things when they come."

All the Wrong Suspects

In times of life we find ourselves questioning
the truth of things...
When given a doubt which tears at the truth of living...
Are you fallen or are you awake?
Testing that point at which you might break...
Following a path stumbling and bare...
Left behind by those who do not care...
Would you try to test the waters of eternity?
When life pushes you down and death is but a memory?
Struggle now with me and question the truth of things...

November 2008
Saturday Night, Week Three

Devin sat in the booth ensuring that all the hottest songs of the time were playing for those who were out on the dance floor or just relaxing at the bar. His eyes drifted across those who were there, and he smiled seeing Steven escorting Sarah and Valerie into the club, though what did surprise him was the fact that Steven looked like himself and wasn't using any glamour. After watching the three for a moment, he couldn't help but to feel that things in life were complete and perfect, but he wasn't sure why. Shrugging to himself, he spoke over his microphone to the back and had someone relieve him for his break. Soon he was making his way across the dance floor to his friends who were lounging at the bar. Halfway across the floor however, Angela caught him and refused to let him continue on until he consented to a dance with her. Steven glanced over and chuckled to himself as he looked to Valerie his voice teasing, "Looks like you might have some competition."

"Huh?" Valerie looked around and began to scowl leaving her spot at the bar and made her way to Devin who was being held hostage in a dance with Angela.

It was one swift motion as Valerie slapped Angela and dragged Devin to where Steven and Sarah were laughing at the bar trying to conceal their grins. Devin moved obediently, partially surprised by the action, as he found himself beside a snickering Steven at the bar, "Hey, that's not funny man!"

Devin's response only seemed to fuel Steven as he burst out into guffaw, calming himself before speaking, "Well Dev, I think you have a keeper there. She'll most likely trounce any other female that gets near you."

Devin managed a sly smile as he wrapped an arm around Valerie's waist, "That's fine with me, saves me the trouble of telling all the other girls how unlucky they are not to have me."

Valerie playfully slugged him in the arm before leaning over and giving him a sensual kiss before she pulled back with a teasing tone, "Mmmm, or unlucky, were they to know how much of a rogue you are."

Devin made a motion to show that he was wounded, though the smile across his lips said otherwise. Steven turned to the bartender and ordered them each a drink before he returned to lounging against the bar and looking around at the crowd. Sarah lovingly slipped her arm around him which caused a smile to trail his lips before he looked over at her and gave her a gentle kiss. His tone was soft as he whispered into her ear, "So, would you like to dance, my little Irish angel?"

Sarah blushed just a little before nodding with a smile and the two went out onto the dance floor. Irritable, Angela made her way to the bar, a scowl upon her features as she spied on Devin and Valerie. She hated the idea of someone getting close to him, even though she was aware that Devin wanted nothing to do with her any more. She rubbed her face gently before she ordered a drink for herself and plopped down on a bar stool to brood over the situation before her eyes. It was only a moment before a young man sat beside her with matted brownish black hair and managed a smile before speaking to her, "Seems you have been slighted, though I cannot imagine why for someone so beautiful."

Angela barely suppressed a small giggle as she turned to him, "Well, do you dance?"

The young man nodded and the two proceeded to the dance floor. The night continued on with the couples dancing off and on in-between the times that Devin was called back to the booth on occasion. Soon it was late into the evening and Steven yawned before he smiled at Sarah, "Going to visit the toilet, love, be back."

Sarah nodded once as she smiled sipping on her drink and relaxing against the bar. Steven made his way down the stairs from the dance floor toward the restroom when a peculiar sight caught his eye. He turned to do a double take and then frowned to himself as he watched Devin leaving with a very drunk Angela. Thinking he would ask Valerie what happened he continued with his business.

Valerie and Devin danced over to where Sarah was sitting at the bar and moved to stand beside her. Devin grinned as he looked about some, "Where's your boy toy Sarah?"

Sarah smirked just a bit as she thumbed in the direction of the restrooms where Steven could be seen coming up the stairs back to the dance floor and the bar, though his expression seemed to be a mix of confusion and slight surprise. Devin noted the peculiar look upon his friend's face and waited for him to sit down beside Sarah before asking, "What's wrong man?"

Steven looked between Devin and Valerie for a long moment then gently rubbed his eyes, "Nothing, just tired I think. It's getting late and we should all be getting home. One thing though Devin… I have this odd feeling, why don't you stay at Valerie's tonight?"

Valerie turned three shades of red as she nearly spit out her drink coughing in shock at the suggestion. Devin merely grinned as he patted her on the back gently, "Alright man. Do you mind, Valerie?"

She shook her head then looked at him in a serious manner, "Don't try anything sneaky while I'm asleep, got it?"

Devin tried to put on a mock shocked expression, though failed miserably, "Me? Why I am an absolute angel and a gentleman!"

Steven only snickered as he began to lead Sarah out of the club calling back to them, "Yeah, and I'm the pope!"

November 2008
Week Four, Monday

Steven half-dozed in his chair during art class, all the while Sarah was giving him scolding glances which he coyly pretended not to see. Devin and Valerie sat across from Sarah, both with a slight smirk on their lips as they watched her waggling her finger at Steven. After a moment Devin looked around the room curiously before speaking, "You know, I'm no expert but shouldn't Angela be in here?"

The two girls looked at him and then shrugged as if they weren't overly concerned about it. Still, Devin couldn't shake this nagging feeling he had running along the back of his spine as if someone had just walked over his grave. Shuddering he returned his attention to the assignment in front of him, a still life of an apple. A long sigh left his lips as Valerie looked over remarking curiously, "That's a pretty big raisin, Dev."

"Uh… yeah, raisin, right…" he grumbled as he crumpled up the paper wishing he had the same artistic skill that Steven always demonstrated.

Soon the bell rang and everyone packed up their belongings and began to make their way out of the classroom. Steven quirked a brow as he noted the three officers outside the room quietly talking with the teacher and looking at Devin who was still packing up his things. He decided to wait and see what was transpiring before heading off, his curiosity getting the best of him as Sarah came over to his table and looked at him quizzically.

"What is it?" she leaned in whispering to him.

Steven gestured to the officers outside the classroom and then to Devin who was now starting out of the room with Valerie in tow. The two of them watched as the scene unfolded, Devin's face registering confusion as the cops spoke to him and then began to lead him down the hall and out of the school. Valerie's expression reflected both anger and confusion as Steven and Sarah made their way to her and the door to the class.

"What was that all about, Valerie?" Steven asked as he watched the cops escorting Devin out of the school.

"They asked him if he knew where Angela was, and then said they wanted him to go with them to the station to answer some questions," she answered still staring after Devin.

"Angela? Why would Devin know where she is?" Sarah asked off handedly.

Steven shrugged as he began after the group, calling back to the two, "I'll find out, you two continue on to class. I'll let you know as soon as I know something."

Valerie and Sarah both frowned but did as they were told while watching Steven half-trot down the hall and out of the school.

Steven exited the school and watched the police putting Devin in the back of a squad car and speeding off in the direction of the local police station. His eyes narrowed some as he wondered what all of this was about, yet he couldn't shake this feeling that something quite bad was happening, he just couldn't put his finger on what it was. Sighing irritably, he went to his car and turned off its security system before getting in and taking off after the police car.

Devin scowled to himself as he sat in the back of the cop cruiser, he wasn't sure what was going on or why the police wanted to ask him about Angela, but he did know this probably wasn't going to end well. He sighed heavily as he watched the scenery go by until they were pulling into the parking lot of the station and parking. The policemen opened the back door and led him into the station where they took him down a hall and placed him in an interrogation room. Devin's eyes scanned the area as he was left alone in the room and he found himself staring at the mirror wondering who would be listening to the conversation that would take place once the officer arrived to question him. After a moment, he went and sat down on one side of a desk, which was in the center of the room with a chair on either side of it. Devin hated waiting, and the longer he was there, the more he wondered what the hell was actually going on.

It was nearly half an hour later when Officer Frank entered the room to see Devin pacing back and forth anxiously, though he stopped when he saw the man enter the room.

"Frank, what the hell is going on?" Devin asked irritably.

"Listen, son, sit down. We have a lot that we have to go over," Frank answered as he moved to one of the chairs at the table and sat down with a serious and notably concerned expression on his face.

Devin nodded as he took the opposite chair and sat down looking at the officer evenly for a long moment, "Well? I figure this has to be something important to have me brought down here and put in this room for so long."

Frank took in a long breath and then let it out in an exaggerated expression before he began to speak, "Devin, your ex-girlfriend Angela has been reported missing. The only information we have right now is that people saw you dancing with her at the club you work at and then leaving with her. Now, I want to know what happened last Saturday night, and you better be straight with me."

Devin blinked in genuine surprise before he collected his thoughts and answered, "I did dance with her, but that's only because she refused to let me cross the dance floor without doing so. My current girl however saved me from her persistence only a moment into the dance thankfully, but I never left with Angela. I left with Valerie, and she can vouch for me on that, so can Tiara, her grandmother. I spent the night at their place. So, I can't honestly tell you much more."

Frank looked him over and nodded after a minute, "Alright, but I want you to stay in town. The district attorney thinks that you're a suspect with the eyewitness accounts. So, until we get to the bottom of this, keep your nose clean and expect to answer more questions as time goes on."

Devin nodded a few times though his expression still had a bit of disbelief on it, "I can't believe this, will you let me know whatever is found out? I may not like Angela anymore, but I do worry."

Frank deliberately stood and moved to the door opening it and gesturing him out of the room, "Be that as it may, I doubt I will be able to tell you much of anything until your name is cleared, if it is… these guys are trying to play hard ball, and the only lead we had were the witnesses saying that you left with Angela."

Devin shook his head once, "Unfortunately your witnesses are wrong. I wish I could tell you more, but I honestly don't know what would even be useful since I didn't even see her leave the club."

Frank nodded once more as he led Devin to the front of the station where Steven was arguing with the officer at the front desk. Both Devin and Frank stopped briefly as Steven paused in his yelling at a cop who was now shaking visibly in the chair behind the desk.

"Is everything alright, Devin?" Steven asked as his attention was diverted away from the officer.

Frank tried to suppress a grin as he patted Devin on the back before turning and heading back down the hall, "Just remember to stick around the area, Devin."

Devin sighed as he nodded and walked over to Steven, "We'll talk on the way back to school."

Steven nodded once and the two of them left the building.

November 2008
Week Four, Thursday

Steven tepidly took a bite out of a sandwich as Sarah leaned on his shoulder while they sat at the lunch table. On occasion, his eyes drifted up and looked over Devin who was sitting with Valerie, though he seemed lost in a brooding and dark mood. After a few more bites after several minutes can be removed, Steven finally spoke, "You know, if something has happened to her, it's not your fault. She does have a habit nowadays of going off with whichever guy who tickles her fancy and skipping school for more than a day at a time."

Devin's expression only seemed to darken at Steven's words as he sighed heavily, "I know that... I just don't like this twisting feeling I have in my gut about the whole situation. It's like I know there is something..."

Devin was cut off in mid sentence as four police officers entered the cafeteria and came over to their table with grim expressions on their faces, "Mr. Noirlion?"

Devin stood up and nodded once, "Yeah?"

"I'm afraid we have to take you into custody now, you are under arrest for the murder of Angela Lampit," the officer said as another one pulled out his cuffs.

All four of the youth stared at the officers in disbelief and astonishment as the officer began to put the cuffs on Devin and read him his rights. Soon they were leading Devin out of the cafeteria, though Steven was narrowing his eyes as he watched trying to surmise what was going on.

"Alright you two, let's go. I want to get to the bottom of this, and I think I am going to need both of your help in the matter," Steven stated as he deliberately rose from his seat and began walking toward the exit of the cafeteria.

Sarah and Valerie quickly followed suit and they left the school to his car. Steven quickly turned off the security system on his vehicle and opened the passenger door to allow them both entry before he sat in the driver's seat and pulled out of the school parking lot heading to the police station.

Devin was escorted into the police station and down a long hall to a solitary cell. The officer removed the handcuffs and opened the cell door before shoving him in, "You might want to get a lawyer, boy, because I doubt you're getting away with this murder."

Devin scowled as he eyes the officer, "Ever hear of innocent until proven guilty, asshole?"

The cop slammed the cell door shut and turned walking away, "We found her body, and tire marks matching your bike, so with the witnesses I'm betting it's only a matter of time till you finally get what's coming to you, punk."

Grumbling, Devin sat on the bench in the cell and looked at the ceiling offering up a silent prayer to the gods for help.

Steven pulled into the police station parking lot and turned off his engine before exiting the car and heading to the front doors with the girls in tow behind him. As he entered the station, his eyes went to the officer behind the desk who he had been yelling at a few days prior. The officer upon seeing Steven began turning pale before he spoke, "M-mr. Nightwolf… what can I d-do for you today?"

Steven nearly growled as he slammed his hands on the front of the desk causing it to rattle and causing the officer to jump a bit, "Where is Devin and what the hell is going on?"

It was then that Frank's familiar voice caused Steven's head to turn its attention away from the desk officer, "Steven, why don't you come in with me? Oh, and bring the girls, I want to ask you a few questions."

Steven's expression darkened as he nodded and motioned for the two girls to follow him while he walked beside Frank down the long hall to the interrogation room. Valerie and Sarah looked to each other with a slight frown as they followed, the details were sketchy at best as far as what any of them knew, so they had no clue what to expect. As they all entered the room, Steven went to lean on one of the walls as he eyed Frank sitting down at the table with a sigh.

"What the hell is going on, Frank? Does some moron really think that Devin did something to Angela?" Steven asked as he pulled out a pack of cigarettes.

Franks took a long breath before he began to speak, "Look Steven, we found Angela's body at the lake shore. She was hacked up pretty good with some type of long blade, most likely a machete, but we're still waiting on forensics to take a look at it all. We also found tire marks around and near the body that are from a motorcycle, which is also being examined. And there is the fact that we have multiple witnesses that say Devin left with Angela from the club Saturday night, which was the last time anyone saw her alive. So, if you have anything that might help

Devin out, you need to let me know now, because the evidence is pretty stacked against him right now."

Steven pulled a cigarette out and lit it taking a long drag for a moment before he spoke, totally missing the dirty look that Sarah was giving him now that she knew about his bad habit, "Well, I'll tell you what I saw. Devin danced with Angela for all of one minute before Valerie here went up and smacked the girl and dragged ole Dev back to the bar. The two of them danced and were by each other's side for the rest of the night. Now, I did see Angela leaving with someone who bore a remarkable resemblance to Devin while I was leaving the toilet, but it certainly wasn't Dev. As I returned from the privy, I saw that Devin was still dancing with Valerie. We all left at the same time, I took Sarah home with me, and Valerie took Devin home with her. I'm fairly certain that he spent the whole night with her; you just have to ask her."

Franks casually nodded as he looked to Sarah, "You confirm that everything said is accurate to your knowledge, miss?"

Sarah nodded. "Yes, everything is as Steven says."

Frank nodded as he looked to Valerie, "Well, did Devin stay with you the whole night?"

Valerie blushed deeply as she nodded, "Yeah. He never left my side the whole night. My grandmother can even verify that he stayed in my room with me."

Frank nodded once more, "Alright then, kids, I'll give Tiara a call and verify Valerie's story and we'll go from there. But for now, he's a suspect until everything is verified and even then it might take a day or two to get him released. This matter is a very serious one, and the D.A. is really looking to fry someone. If you could Steven, give a description to the sketch artist so that maybe we can try to find this other person who looks similar to Dev... and you might want to get your friend a lawyer."

Steven nodded some as he took a long drag off the cigarette, "Alright Frank, I'll give my family lawyer a call, so he can come in and help to represent Dev."

Frank nodded once more before standing and opening the door for them, "I dunno what's going on Steven, but it's got my guts twisting up something awful. Best be careful out there and all of you stick together."

Steven nodded once more as he turned and started walking down the hall with the two girls right beside him, his voice low as he whispered to them, "Something unnatural is going on... we might need to have you and your grandmother do a vision seeking to try and find out what's going on Valerie."

Valerie nodded once as she watched Steven put out his cigarette on the front desk as he passed it while leaving the police station, which caused both girls to begin to smile for the first time all day.

December 2008
Week 2, Monday

Steven leaned against his car as Devin walked out of the police station rubbing his wrists tenderly, his expression showed a great amount of relief but also concern. Steven nodded once as Devin came to stand in front of him and he offered Devin a cigarette which he gratefully took and lit up before taking a long drag and then speaking, "I have no idea what you did, but thanks."

Steven lit up a cigarette of his own and took a drag before smiling, "I told them the truth, nothing more, and it was verified. Still, it shouldn't have taken them so long to release you, stupid pigs."

Devin smirked before his tone turned somber, "Did you find out anything?"

Steven frowned and shook his head, "Valerie and Tiara tried to do a vision seeking, but they couldn't get past the shadows. Someone or something is blocking their sight and I think it means to get all of us. Right now everyone is living at my place, so, you should be prepared for that since you are going to be living there too from now on until this whole thing is resolved."

Devin took another slow drag as he nodded, "Understandably. What about the festival that's coming up?"

Steven frowned once more as he looked to the ground for a long moment, "I am going, I have to. You know that."

"Then I am sure you won't mind all of our company," Devin replied with a slight smirk which caused Steven to look up with a half-smile.

"Get in, let's get out of here before the cops change their minds and want to find some other evidence which doesn't link you to the crime," Steven said as he opened the door and hopped into the driver's seat.

The Wild Hunt

In the shallows we wade, letting the water
caress our skin like soft suede...
Perhaps it is in the sunset, or the rising of the tides, but
still we wait for some unforgettable ride...
What are you searching for, so cries the wind, what are
you here for, again, and again...
In these days where some may be lost and unbound,
we are constantly searching for something
we wish we have found...
Now in cool waters, let the waves caress...
Now as the sun falters, let the light drift...
Float amongst the waves and let the sea carry you out, it
is not oblivion, but you will find peace throughout...
As the day's light fades, we let the moon come to bear,
its light drifting over us and washing
away our worries and cares...
Here then, in the moonlight may we find
ourselves and our true meanings...
For here we may meditate and let her wash over us...
a sea of inspirations which is teeming...
Floating now amongst the sea, we may look
up and admire...
Floating now amongst the waves,
we can feel the caress and desire...
And so we float on... and on... awaiting our great wave...
let it rise up and consume us before the next day's rays...

December 20, 2008

FLYERS COVERED TELEPHONE poles and the sides of buildings as Steven and Sarah drove from his home toward the lake near the outskirts of town. They were advertisements for the winter festival celebration that the gypsies put on every year for Yule. Devin and Valerie were right behind Steven as they followed in her car. Despite recent events, Steven seemed more at ease and happier than he had over the previous days and as he drove, Sarah seemed to notice and smile at his more upbeat mood. She slipped a hand over to rest on his leg as he drove which caused him to smile a bit more as he partially glanced at her, "The gypsies are close friends of mine, something about us both being kind of outcasts pulled us together last year… well… that and… never mind."

Sarah looked over at him curiously for a long moment before deciding to pry a little, "What? What else happens?"

Steven took a slow breath as he focused on the road and then nodded before speaking, "I became really close to one of the gypsy's there last year, but she was killed by a kid named Marcus who wanted to… sacrifice her to try and become a god or something darker."

Sarah just stared at him for a moment in slight disbelief, "Wha-what happened?"

Steven's features dipped into a slight scowl, "I killed him…"

The rest of the drive was quiet as they made their way down the road through light forest on the way to the lake. Devin however was not so quiet as he and Valerie drove behind Steven; his voice was growing more cheerful the closer they came to the lake, "Did you know that me and Steven know the gypsies personally? We're kind of like adopted family to them, not to brag or anything. Hell, I'm willing to bet they'll let us take part in the hunt part of the festival."

Valerie simply looked over at Devin on occasion as he spoke while she drove, "What's the hunt part of the festival?"

Devin grinned wide as he leaned over whispering in her ear, "Well, the eligible guys have to hunt a white stag with nothing but a spear and a knife, and the victors get to go to a tent with the maiden of their choice and have a night of… ah… merriment."

Valerie nearly swerved a little at his explanation as she eyed him while paying attention to the road, "And who are these maidens?"

Devin grinned a bit more as he leaned back in his seat whistling innocently, "Oh, I dunno… Steven already talked to the head of the camp and told him who the two maidens were going to be for me and him."

Valerie scowled at the prospect of Devin with another girl and began to brood over the idea.

Steven pulled into the makeshift parking lot which had been set aside for those who were either going to be attending the festival or helping set it up. Only a short distance away stood several of the vardos which were the gypsy's wagon homes. Colorful and festive, the wagons seemed to give off a warm sort of feeling to the area in the cold season. The season was however warmer than usual this year, as the weather seemed to stay in the high forties. Off a short distance the lake also seemed to glisten in the early morning light, almost as if a shimmering veil of life welcoming all to its shores. As Steven exited his car, a man dressed in long cotton pants with a tan color, a lose fitting white shirt with a brown leather jerkin over top, came up and embraced him in a large bear like hug and then patted him on the back heartily. Steven chuckled and returned the gesture as Sarah just stared in surprise at the situation.

"Young master Nightwolf, it has been too long since we saw you last. We can never forget the justice you provided for our people and still mourn for your and our loss. But, this is no time for sadness, come, you must join us in setting up for the coming festivities. And who is…" the gypsy paused as he looked at Sarah, his words caught for a moment as his eyes traced over her for a long moment in surprise before he continued, "Ah my apologies, young miss, I am Grego, the caravan master for my little family here."

Grego gestured to the wagons at the end of his words which caused Sarah to turn and admire the beautiful colors and detailed art work which decorated them. Steven smiled and nodded to Grego as he spoke, "This is Sarah Roanoak. Ah… we are inseparable, Grego. It is wonderful to see you again!"

The old gypsy man nodded once and ushered them toward the circle of wagons near the lake, his voice jovial and merry as he began telling Sarah about the festivities and the good food which was to come.

Valerie pulled into the parking lot and parked beside Steven's car as she looked around at the area. The large trees and flittering sunrays, which came through their branches caught her breath until she saw the lake and almost squeaked with excitement. Devin only chuckled as he exited the car and looked about himself, his eyes settling fondly on the vardo wagons of the gypsies. Valerie climbed out from the driver's seat and walked over to stand beside him looking over at the brightly colored wagons, "You how did you and Steven get to know a bunch of gypsies anyway?"

Devin turned to her for a moment and then a smile erupted across his face, "*Welllllll…* Steven kinda had a fling with one of the girls last year… and yeah, now we're good friends with them."

Valerie looked at him dubiously for a moment and then shrugged briefly, "Alright, so what do we do now."

Devin thumbed toward where Steven and Sarah were sitting at a campfire with Grego, "We go say hi and later this afternoon we'll help them set up for the festival which will start tomorrow."

The four youths spent the rest of the day drinking tea and setting up tents and booths. To both Valerie and Sarah's surprise though, both Devin and Steven had no issue with using their powers among the gypsies and thus made the set up vastly faster and easier than they had first anticipated when they were told of all the work which had to be done. Sarah stood with Steven, never leaving his side, though she always gasped in awe when he would spread his arms with palms facing down causing a wind to lift up the massive tents to allow the gypsies to set up the poles with great ease. Though, what perhaps surprised her more was the fact that they viewed Steven as one of their own and perfectly normal in what he could do. Her eyes traveled about when one of the women of the camp paused and simply began to stare at Sarah in what appeared to be disbelief before catching herself and hustling along with several decorations that she handed to Steven.

Steven smiled and nodded as he took the decorations, "Thank you, Anya, I'll see that these are put up in the appropriate spots here. Oh, this is Sarah."

The gypsy woman looked Sarah over for a long moment before smiling warmly, "It's nice to meet you, dear; any friend of Steven's is always welcome among us."

Sarah smiled back in return, "Thank you, miss, it's a great honor to be here."

Steven chuckled as he began to toss decorations into the air and waive his hands about causing them to fly off in several different directions and land on prongs, poles, and hooks throughout the festival area with astonishing accuracy. Anya continued to look over Sarah for a long moment as he worked and then nodded as she spoke, "She looks just like her, seems fate has been kind to you, young Nightwolf."

Steven blinked as a startled look crossed his face and he missed one of the ornament locations which nearly sent it crashing down until he caught himself and steadied his concentration once more before responding with a deep breath, "I hadn't noticed that until now..."

Sarah looked between the two quizzically for a long moment as the gypsy woman nodded with a slight smile and trotted off chuckling at his near slip. Sighing softly, he finished placing the ornaments and then looked to Sarah who was staring at him waiting for an explanation, "I was involved with a young gypsy girl here last year... I never really considered the fact that you look like her. It never even crossed my mind until Anya pointed it out just now."

Sarah raised a slight brow as she placed her hands on her hips, "Oh? And will she be around for the festival then?"

Steven's expression darkened quickly as he turned to look for another work to do, "No..."

She was just a little surprised at the quick change in his mood now; it had been some time since he dropped his cold exterior around her and so it seemed a bit odd to her now that his defenses would rebound on this subject. She followed him as he walked amongst the tents and booths and began to reason to herself that something bad must have happened and that she might have to ask him about it later.

Devin walked with Valerie along the lake and gestured to her the several barrels which were set up to be filled with water. She looked at him a bit incredulously for a moment before speaking, "And what do you want me to do about it, grab a bucket and begin filling them?"

Devin snickered at her question before he answered her, a large grin still gracing his lips, "No, you're the one who's supposed to be good with water, so I imagine it's time for you to get some practice."

She frowned as she looked from the lake to the barrels for a moment, "And just what exactly am I suppose to do then?"

Devin shrugged as he tried to think on how to explain it, "Well, I'm not so good at explaining such things, but Steven says that it's like feeling the element and then telling it what to do, and I guess hand gestures help to. At least he's always doing them."

She looked at him with a *yeah, and I'm a fairy princess* type of look, though sighed when he gestured to the water once more with a serious look, "Alright, I'll try it."

Taking a slow deep breath, she closed her eyes and stretched her hands out toward the lake and tried to concentrate on the water. Devin began clapping which caused her to open her eyes and gasp in surprise as she saw the water rising up over the two of them; however, it was just that distraction which caused her to lose her concentration and the two of them were shortly covered and soaked with water. Devin began to cough and scowl as he looked at her for a moment, "Really now, you have to focus…"

Valerie only giggled and nodded as she began again and timidly began filling the barrels, the sensation she felt came with a strange elation. This was part of her heritage, and she found it amazing and inspiring all at the same time. She had always dreamt of being special in some way, but this was even beyond her imagining and her lips spread in an unmistakable smile.

Sarah wandered about the area curiously looking at everything coming up in quick timing and began to wonder what life might have been like growing up in such a culture. Her mind and eyes wandered as she nearly ran into Anya, though the pause made her flush as the older woman smiled warmly at her before speaking, "You're just like my daughter, always wandering and dreaming. So where are you at now, dear? Surprised that we are so accepting of you all here with what others would deem as odd or unusual abilities?"

Sarah nodded just a little as she smiled, "It really is wonderful. I was just wondering what it must be like to live like you all do, it seems so nice. Your daughter? Is she here?"

Anya shook her head gently for a moment as a sad look crossed her face, "I'm afraid not child, she died last summer. She was very close to Steven though. That's how we met him actually… and how he came to get this town to accept us when we travel through during different seasons. He really is a remarkable boy."

Sarah dipped her head. "I am sorry to hear of your loss. I guess that's why he doesn't seem to want to talk about it then."

Anya nodded just once, "Ah, but don't you worry about it dear. It's the future we must look forward to and not let the past keep us chained down."

Sarah smiled once more as she nodded, "Yes. Do you need any help with anything? I feel kind of useless just wandering around here."

Anya just smiled as she answered, "Of course, dear, there are many other little things for us to place about to help usher in the festival. Come with me and you can give me a hand with them."

Sarah grinned as she followed, happy to finally be of some assistance.

December 21, 2008

The day began with people arriving from all over town. To Sarah's surprise there were so many that she believed the whole city had come to join in the festival and it seemed a bit overwhelming. Steven had taken up residence at the entry gate with Grego and was wearing a traditional gypsy outfit to include the sash and loose fitting pants. Sarah watched the two at the entry gate and giggled thinking of how well Steven fit in with them and of how handsome he looked in the attire which he was wearing that was such a contrast to his usual expensive clothing. She even doubted that anyone would even recognized him in the outfit he was wearing as they seemed to be smiling and passing by him happily. It was only a moment before she began wondering about and bumped into Anya and Valerie; both greeted her with a smile before dragging her off to one of the personal tents to change into their own clothing for the festivities.

"You're a little older, but I imagine you'll still fit into some of my daughter's old clothing," Anya said as she picked out a thin yet elegant crimson and black dress with white frills around the cuffs and neck line before handing it to Sarah.

Sarah changed into the dress and moved over to a chair in front of a mirror and sat examining how she looked for a moment. Anya came up behind her and began combing her hair gently before beginning to braid some of it to look like a crown around the top of her head, "It's no wonder he fell in love with you; you really are very beautiful, dear."

Sarah blushed at the compliment and smiled, "Thank you."

She stared into the mirror watching Anya do her hair while Valerie changed into a brown dress with white frills in the background. Sighing softly, Sarah's eyes drifted down before she spoke, "Anya, did he love her?"

Anya smiled warmly as she responded, "I think so. It really tore him up when he wasn't able to save her from that dark magician."

Sarah blinked as she raised her gaze and stared back through the mirror at Anya, "A dark magician killed her?"

Anya nodded somberly for a moment, "Steven had arrived just a moment too late and the boy had already cut out her heart for some sort of dark ritual sacrifice, but he rained down thunder and lightning upon him. His sorrow and anger took such a form that nothing could have escaped and thus he destroyed the dark one. Still, vengeance didn't ease the pain and suffering he felt, I can still see it on his features at times when he visits us here."

Sarah looked down once more as Anya finished weaving her hair, "Oh gods, I never knew. He really has had a hard life this go."

Anya nodded as she helped Sarah up and smiled warmly at her, "Well, that's why they sent you to him dear. Maybe it's time he got to keep something nice for a change."

Valerie and Sarah wandered about the festival handing out flower woven wreathes to the local girls and women to wear on their heads. It was only when they neared the lake that they took a pause to watch Devin and a young gypsy girl near the shore seeming to be going at each other with half-staves. Valerie nearly took off running at the two, thinking that they were actually fighting when she felt a hand on her shoulder and turned to see Steven with a smile on his lips and Sarah hanging onto his arm.

"They're fine, Valerie; it's just a practice for the dance tonight. Devin does the fire dance with Tatiana during Yule and Beltane. So don't worry about either of them getting hurt. They have to practice now so that they don't make any mistakes during the actual dance," he said as he slowly let go of her shoulder.

She quirked a brow as she looked back to the two near the lake and then back to Steven, "What's a fire dance?"

Steven chuckled, "Go enjoy the day time festivities and you'll see tonight, alright. I don't want to spoil it for you."

She pouted almost in a child like manner but nodded as the three of them began walking the grounds and partaking in the games and food about.

As the day dwindled on, most of the people left, though there were still a host of the teenagers from the high school which had decided to stay for the night time festivities. Torches were lit to light the way throughout the tents and booths as well as candles placed behind stained glass holders to give the area a surreal warm lighting. Orange, red, yellow, and blues lit areas in-between booths. At the center of the camp was a large bonfire with log seats placed around it in rows at a distance to allow observers space to see the show which was about to take place. The only lighting came from the fire itself and the torches at the edge of the large circle of seating.

Anya gracefully danced around the fire with Grego as he tumbled a tambourine against his thigh. Soon drums from the north side of the circular seating began to beat in a slow rhythmic pattern followed by violins and guitars from the east. As the tempo began to pick up, several of the young gypsy girls danced into the circle around the bonfire and began to twirl about as Anya began to sing, "Ai da nú-da nú-da nái Da-rá da nú-da nai! Ai da nú-da nú-da ná Da-rá da nú-da nai!" Grego began picking up the tempo of his tambourine while Anya continued to sing, her voice increasing the speed of the dancing as well as the tempo of the playing, Ai da nú-da nú-da nái Da-rá da nú-da nai!... Ai da nú-da nú-da nái. Da-rá da nú-da nai!

Steven smiled as he watched Sarah's reaction to the display, she seemed quite taken by the whole affair. Valerie sat beside them as well, her mind seeming elsewhere as she wondered where Devin might be, as she hadn't seen him since earlier in the day when he was practicing down at the lake shore. The tempo continued to increase as Anya continued to sing, the song seeming to entrance the audience with the dancing display, "A me djáva pa d'erévnye, pa balshym xátkam, Syr yanáva balavás chavoré te xan!

It was then that the other girls and Grego joined in with a chorus, filling the night air with a melody that stuck within the minds of those watching as the speed of the dance and tempo of the music continued to increase, "Ai tu térnori-nie lamáisya... Syr pxenáva lavoró – sabiraisyá!"

The young gypsy girls continued to dance about, twirling and moving by the young boys at the edge of the circle closest to the fire teasing them with veils and smiles as they all continued to sing, "Ai da shátritsa rogozhytko... Ande shátritsa chai bidytko."

Steven began to clap along with the tempo of the music as did several of the others who were watching. Everyone who was there seemed to be enjoying the beginning of the show as well as the music as it continued on and Anya continued singing on for another iteration.

Soon the song and dance was over and the young girls danced out of the circle while Grego and Anya went and sat at the north end of the circle near the drum players from the camp. It was then that Devin and Tatiana gracefully walked into the circle from a nearby tent. Devin's garb consisted of what looked like loose fitting pants and no shirt, while his counterpart wore a slip of a skirt which came down covering her front and back leaving her legs bare save for the leather boots that she wore. On her upper torso she wore what looked like a partial bodice which was laced in the front leaving her stomach bear and in view. Valerie turned a bit red as she watched the two emerge together which caused Steven to chuckle before he leaned over and whispered to her, "I wouldn't worry too much dear, I'm pretty certain you have Dev wrapped around your finger. So there's no need to get jealous."

She huffed as she folded her arms and stared at the two as they began dancing around the bonfire as music began to play once more. It was only a moment before the two's dance turned into something more, as they seemed to be skillfully weaving balls of fire about one another in a display of building passion. As the tempo of the music steadily increased so did their theatrics of dancing with the fire which seemed to move in fluid with their motions. The flames cascaded across them in a constant play of shadows and light, showing off their forms and movements in key with the ever increasing music which caused the crowd to gasp and sigh. The passion displayed matched the heat of the fire as the dance continued in an extraordinary display of closeness, skill, and then distance. Even Valerie had to take a pause as she caught her breath watching Devin, for she had never seen such a display before.

His hands and body moved in harmonious sync with the beating of the drums, the fire which he brandished moved like water about him as he danced. She could feel the passion herself and had to catch herself from standing and swooning as she watched the sweat glisten on his bare chest. It was only Steven chuckling once more that pulled her back from her revelry of watching which caused her to blush deeply as she noticed how far forward she was leaning now. Sarah leaned against Steven heavily as she watched as well, unaware that her hands were tracing along him until he leaned over and kissed her gently which caused her to blush as well while whispering softly, "It's an amazing dance… it just… pulls you right in."

Steven nodded quietly as he smiled whispering back, "It used to be me out there last year during this time, but after last Yule, Devin seemed more fitted to it than I. He gets along with fire a lot more than I do."

December 30, 2008

The days went by and the crowd dwindled to just the gypsies and several select friends. Sarah and Valerie had taken to learning the songs and dances while Steven and Devin continued to perform for curious on lookers. All in all each of them knew that things were starting to wind down and talk of the wild hunt ceremony to come was cause for mixed feelings of excitement and nervousness for any involved. As the sun began to set, Valerie and Sarah whispered amongst each other speculations as to what exactly the ceremony entailed and what their part was going to be in it. They paused as Anya walked up to the two of them smiling widely, "Are you two ready to participate in the wild hunt, dears?"

Valerie and Sarah looked at one another for a moment and then to Anya before Valerie spoke, "What exactly are we going to be doing, Anya?"

"Well, we'll dress the two of you up as maidens and place you each in the tent of your hunter for the night. Should your hunter be successful then they will join you after the hunt and spend the evening with you. So you should have the night to do as you please with the one you care for, so long as they are successful in their hunting. I have great confidence in both Steven and Devin, so I do not foresee any problems with either of you spending the evening alone," Anya answered smiling once more.

The two looked at one another once more before following Anya to her wagon, only taking a moment to pause as they spied Steven and Devin changing into what looked like old fur hunting outfits that made them look like barbarians from an ancient cold world. The sight caused the two to giggle before entering the wagon and looking around. The interior of the wagon was warm feeling and lit by small lanterns, the fire light flickered against the burgundy and crimson walls giving the area a homely feel. The scents of jasmine and lavender filled the air rising up from several incent sticks which were lit throughout the wagon. Anya moved to the back of the wagon and opened a chest near her bed, her hands moved with careful precision ad she pulled out two fur skirts and two half-halter tops also made from fur. Both Valerie and Sarah stared at the clothing as it was handed to each of them, their faces flushing at the lack of modesty that would be provided from wearing such things.

"I can't wear this!" Valerie exclaimed as she examined how revealing the skirt would be.

Sarah was already changing and giggled at Valerie's reaction to the clothing. Anya sighed lightly and began to pretend to put the clothing away as she spoke in downcast tones to add to the effect of her words, "Well, I guess Devin will be quite surprised when it's Tatiana in his tent tonight then."

"*What*? Give me that!" Valerie screamed as she turned bright red and snatched back the outfit.

Anya chuckled as she winked knowingly at Sarah who was trying desperately not to laugh. Valerie grumbled as she changed while Sarah went to sit near Anya who had motioned her over to a chair in front of a tall standing mirror.

"It is my task to prepare the both of you for this night. Thus I shall be doing your hair and body paint once you are both changed, as well as explaining your roles and why they are important," Anya began as she started applying intricate designs to Sarah's naked arms.

Valerie's brow furrowed as she made her way over to Anya as well, though her face was still beet red due to the shortness of the skirt.

Steven and Devin changed into the ceremonial hunters garb within the tent and eyed the selection of weapons available for hunting the stag. Sighing softly Steven took up a bow and a quiver of arrows as well as a buck knife before looking to Devin who was picking out a short spear and knife.

"You think it will be harder this year than last?" Steven asked as he slung the quiver across his back.

"Nah, piece of cake man. After all, it's about time we had a break and enjoyed ourselves with all of the crap that's been going on," Devin answered as he gingerly tested the weight of the spear.

"You know that Tatiana was hoping to get your tent this year," Steven teased knowingly.

Devin turned noticeably red at the notion, "Yeah, I heard. I don't think Valerie would take too kindly to that though."

"Mmmmm, probably not. She's a bit feisty, a good match for you," Steven snickered as he pulled back the bow string testily.

Devin looked at him and grinned. "Yeah, she is isn't she?"

Steven chuckled as he headed toward the exit of the tent, "Well, I guess we'll see who's in your tent when you kill your stag."

Devin frowned as he followed. The beginning of the ceremony began with them and the other hunters drinking from the sacred drinking horn and listening to a tale of how the gods conducted the ancient hunt for the fabled white stag in order to reign in the New Year with prosperity and fertility. The tale itself brought to mind ancient warriors riding on horses hunting with spears, swords, and bows. Many hounds trailing in front of the mighty riders sniffing and baying as the night was illuminated by the full moon. Soon the hunting horn sounded, echoing out into the night and the hunters were off in search of their stag.

Sarah entered her tent and looked around at the furnishings. The bed which sat at the center of the tent was more like a grouping of large thick furs and pillows and thin silk curtains hung from the top of the tent giving the area a bit of a mystical look. Small lanterns hung from the tent poles illuminating the area in a soft glow, and incense filled the air with the smells of lavender and cinnamon. Her steps took her to the makeshift bed and she sat down amongst the furs with a soft sigh. It was all so warm and soft, and the scents in the air seemed to relax her. Her mind drifted to the explanations that Anya had given them. They were the maidens, the lovers for the huntsmen who succeeded. Their task was to welcome into the tent the huntsman whose tent they resided in and to lay them down and become one with them. Sarah had no objection to the matter; after all she was already spending the nights with Steven at his home. But she remembered Valerie's reaction to the explanation and giggled while remembering the shocked and embarrassed look which was on her face. Now all Sarah had to do was wait.

Devin moved through the forest, spear in hand as his eyes scanned the darkening forest for signs of the stag that he was to be hunting. Only a few stood out to him, broken branches from young trees and partially trampled brush. He was beginning to think that the hunt this year was going to be more difficult than the previous when the moonlight filtered through the branches and his eyes caught sight of the beautiful white stag. The sight of it made him catch his breath as it stared back at him with large brown eyes as if knowing what Devin's purpose was. He skillfully pulled back his arm and launched the spear toward the stag. A soft whooshing sound echoed through the air as the animal bolted, taking off with all haste through the thickening forest with Devin hot on its trail. His hand grabbed up the spear as he ran after the deer, his steps dodging him through brush and under branches. Soon he came to a halt at the edge of a glade as the stag stared at him from across the open space. It pawed at the ground with a hoof as it seemed determined to face its hunter with defiance. Devin pulled back once more as the stag charged and launched the spear. His aim was true and the spear hit home stopping the animal as it came crashing down just mere feet from goring Devin with its antlers which still glistened as if silver in the moonlight.

He panted heavily as he happily sat down and looked about the area in slight exhaustion. It seemed odd to him that his prey was so defiant and determined to become the hunter, it struck him as uncharacteristic. Leaning back against a tree as he caught his breath, his eyes spied another white stag across the glade, though its focus seemed to be on the tree line to the east. Devin's eyes turned in the direction which the animal was peering as it cautiously moved to the center of the glade and he was for a moment actually surprised to see Steven gracefully emerging from the wood line and walking toward the deer without his weapon drawn. He watched for a moment in absolute wonderment as Steven continued walking until he was less than an arm's length from the stag and reached out petting its nose gently while seeming to speak to it. Devin strained trying to hear what was said, but they were just too far away for him to hear. It was only a moment until the stag dipped its head and Steven drew his knife and took its life in a quick and efficient manner.

Devin simply shook his head as he stood up and made his way over to his friend, "I don't know how you do that but it amazes me every time I see it."

Steven turned and smiled, "It's merely explaining the reason, and then seeing if the stag accepts."

Devin continued to shake his head and then looked about. "Time to take the meal back to camp."

Steven nodded as he expertly tied the legs up on the stag and hefted it up onto his shoulders, "Slow going, these ones are larger than last year and… umf… a bit heavier."

Devin eyed his stag a moment and then nodded following suit, grunting as he hefted it up with effort, "Remind me to start working out with you more often."

Steven only chuckled as they slowly made their way back to camp.

Valerie paced around her tent nervously in anticipation of what might happen throughout the night. She didn't even notice as Devin quietly entered the tent until he was wrapping his arms around her gently from behind which nearly caused her to jump until she realized who it was. Taking a breath, she relaxed against his embrace and turned her head back some to look at him before turning around in his arms.

"You have returned from your great hunt successful, my love, and I am prepared to help ease away the worries of the fray," she said as she nervously smiled up at him.

Devin smiled down at her reassuringly as he spoke, "Aye, I have returned to find you my maiden. My hunt was successful and I give myself unto your arms and care."

Valerie's smile widened as she leaned forward and kissed him before pulling back gently and leading him to the pile of furs and pillows, "Then allow me to make your hunt complete my warrior, for I shall show you the gates of Valhalla and take you beyond."

Devin nervously gulped at her words as he allowed her to lay him down and begin kissing him with a passion that he was unaware she had felt for him. The night went on, and the two were undisturbed until the morning.

A Messenger of the Dead

It is a sad day… that day of woes,
the time of reckoning that always shows
I hear you calling, always out for more,
I see you bawling… always so sore…
Do you remember the times of heaven which each
of us shared? Can you recall the loving warmth
which came without care?
I recall the once upon a time, that far off land
where we laid down to die…
And as the darkness came to wrap out willing souls,
I heard you cry out, tormented… your sins
consuming you whole…
Now we are waiting, standing before our judge,
and I see you cast down… forever so low.
What did you do that I could not see?
How was it that you so betrayed me?
Was there confusion upon my heart which was
so dense that it tore me apart…
I would weep for you yet my heart will not bear,
so go now fallen… I hope you rest well down there…

December 31, 2008

Sarah nestled against Steven as they lay amidst the fur blankets and pillows listening to the old gypsy music outside of the tent. She trailed fingers across his bare chest while he dozed in the early morning hours, a smile trailing her lips as she thought back over the night's events which then caused her cheeks to blush. Steven leaned up and kissed her tenderly before lying back down and smiling up at her, "Today will be a great deal of cooking and singing and dancing, for it is the feast of the dead. So, do not be surprised if you see those who have passed on joining us here today and tonight."

Sarah nodded as she gave him a queer look, "Do the dead actually show up for this kind of thing?"

Steven nodded once, "They have before, I imagine it depends if they have something they need to say or do, but on occasion they will."

Sarah looked toward the exit of the tent and nodded some, "It would be nice to see my father once again, even if it's only to tell him that I love and miss him."

Steven drew her closer with an arm wrapped around her and smiled once more, "I am sure he knows, love."

Devin lightly ran his fingers through Valerie's hair as she slept against him. He smiled as he regarded how peaceful she looked in the moment. His mind began to wonder as something Steven had said on their way back had struck him as odd the night before. Steven seemed convinced that the spirit of Marcus was going to try and return and cause havoc this day or during the feast at night, but Devin was pretty certain that the gypsies put up wards to prevent such a thing from happening. Sighing he closed his eyes trying to put it all out of his mind, mumbling to himself as he did, "Bah, he worries too much anyway."

The majority of the day consisted of cooking racks of venison and other various dishes from stews to baked vegetables and breads. Sarah and Valerie spent their time with Anya as she taught them some about how to cook over or in an active fire while Steven and Devin gathered firewood and cleaned the deer for the feast. Everyone was working up until mid afternoon when the feast was about to begin. Steven and Devin took to the lake to wash up before the meal and were surprised when Anya and the girls shortly joined them. Devin grinned mischievously at Steven as the three approached and Steven merely shook his head, "You're going to be mischievous with a water elementalist in a lake, I think she'll whoop ya."

Devin shook his head some as he waited for the three to strip down and enter the lake before he began splashing Valerie playfully with water. Sarah moved over to Steven with Anya and watched with mild amusement. Anya smirked as she spoke to Steven, "He is aware that she is still learning how to control her powers right?"

Steven only snickered as he nodded and called out to Valerie, "Hey Val, just spread your arms a little and bring them together in a clapping motion aimed toward him in the water!"

Devin shot Steven a penetrating glance as he frowned, but it was too late as Valerie did as instructed and sent a wave of water crashing down on Devin. Her eyes widened as she quickly swam over to him as he splashed about sputtering and cussing in the water, "Steven! You're an ass!"

He snickered as Sarah laughed with Anya at the display, "Well, she has to learn sooner or later and I am pretty sure Devin can survive her."

The lot of them soon engaged in splashing each other and playing about in the water. The mood was light and merry, and for the time being even Steven seemed to have forgotten his worries for the evening.

As the skies darkened, music came from a circle of wagons and tents which surrounded a large bonfire. Upon one of the logs near the fire sat Sarah and Steven who were snuggled together closely beneath one of the fur blankets from their tent. Sarah nestled her head against Steven's shoulder as they listened to the old roman gypsy music, her eyes scanning the intricate decoration of the vardo wagons as she relaxed. The shadows of the bonfire danced and played along the wagons sides as Devin and Valerie danced hand in hand to the lively tunes. Steven smiled down at Sarah as he drew her closer to him with an arm around her. Grego tapped a tambourine in beat against his leg as the feast was being brought out to those within the circle around the bonfire.

Soon the tempo of the music changed and slowed, it became more somber and relaxed. Devin led Valerie to a log near Steven and Sarah and the two sat with smiles tracing both their lips. Devin then leaned over and spoke softly to Steven, "See man, I told you everything would be alright. You really should stop worrying so much otherwise that log might have you permanently affixed as its new bump."

Steven merely chuckled as he shook his head responding, "Shush you, the song is about to begin."

Soon the music was going at a slow and steady pace as Grego began to sing, "Once long ago mighty Thor was riding along when he came across some gypsies…"

The tambourine rattled as another man with a great beard and girth stood up and began singing as well, "Where be ye headed yon traveling band?"

Several of the men and women near the guitar players and drummers stood and sang, giving the song story an air of eloquence, "Where the wind blows us. And ye Odin's son who travels as he must?"

Grego sang once more, "Thor told of how he was bound to Valhalla to see his father…"

The group sang once more, "Please remember us to the Allfather. Tell him we wander the lands and ask him how we should live."

Grego picked up once more, "Thor agreed, ye but the gypsies believed he would forget them as soon as he would leave. Ye though we are crafty and one man eyed his horse and spoke out of need."

A young man from the group sung up alone this time, "I'll tell ye what noble Odhin's son. Make me a deal and we'll both be satisfied. Leave with me yer bridle made of gold, so when ye mount in your mind's eye us ye shall always hold."

Grego began to sing once more, "Thor did thus agree but in return a promise he had the man make that upon his return the golden bridle would once more be his. Then mighty Odhin's son went on his way until across some peasants he came in dismay. Felling lumber for a house were they, yet a mighty struggle were they having for the logs were too short for the walls they say."

The large man with the beard sung now once again, "What are ye doing there peasants this day?"

The group began to sing once more, "We try to stretch the logs, ye they will not give. Tell us what we shall do for a place to live?"

The large man looked at the group in an odd manner as he sung once more, "I shall ask Odhin, my father and bring word back to thee."

Grego began singing once more, "Thor continued on until a most unusual sight graced his eyes once more, two women taking water from one well just to another pour."

Now it was Tatiana and Anya who sung in unison, "Have pity on us mighty Odhin's son, tell us when we may stop doing this for we are worn and fear we shall wither away."

The bearded man motioned reassuringly to the two as he sung once more, "I shall ask my father, for he should know. Let ye not give in to despair and sorrow."

Grego began singing once more, his voice full and heavy, "When he reached Valhalla he asked for an audience. First, he asked to his father's health, and then he asked of the peasants and the women of the wells."

Grego looked over to Steven, which caused him to turn red as he stood and sang as well, "I gave those peasants that foolish task, because they had been so greedy and had took without need or thought to ask. Tell them that if they be more generous and joyous and kind that I will forgive them of their punishment and crimes. As for the women I have punished them for watering down the milk that they have sold, but I shall pardon them too should they be less greedy and to cheat so bold."

Sarah looked up at Steven rather surprised how smooth and honeylike his voice was in singing. Though she may have been more surprised that he knew the song and could sing more than anything else, for he had never done so before. Then the bearded man began to sing once more, "Aye Allfather, shall I tell them hence. Amends they will make and live a good life without regrets!"

Grego began to sing once again, "As Thor meant to leave, he paused as his horse and lack of bridle gave his mind a memory in which to cleave."

The bearded man began to sing again, "Allfather I had almost forgot, I promised to ask of the gypsies and how they are to live and lead their lot?"

Steven rubbed his chin thoughtfully, and then began to sing once more, "Ahh, they have never bothered me, those gypsies. And I like their songs and merriness, so go and tell them this. May they live by their own laws and their own ways. Where they pray, where they beg, and where they take without leave. It tis their affair and I shall not disagree."

Grego began to sing once more as Steven sat back down, still flush from embarrassment, "And Odhin's son set forth back from his journey. And ye he passed on the messages to the grateful women and overjoyed peasants. It was nay long before he reached the camp of the gypsy!"

The groups began to sing once more, "Thor is here! Pray tell, what did Odhin say?"

Grego sang briefly once more, "Off his horse did Thor clumsily slid, and upon hitting the ground did his anger go unhid."

The bearded man roared with song now, "The Allfather grants ye leave to live as you will. That where ye pray, where ye beg, and where ye take what ye may tis up to you and none other from this hence forth day. Now give me back my golden bridle, for words were given and I shall nay be idle!"

The young man sung up once more, a sly look across his face, "A golden bridle, you say? On my soul no such thing have we taken from you, may the moon cut me down if we have truly wronged you."

Grego and the group then sang together in unison, "After all the Allfather did say, Live as you may! Where you pray, where you beg, and where you take as you may! Tis now and forever up to you as of this day! And so a feast was given to appease mighty Thor, and he left with that and a song to remember forevermore. But the bridle of solid gold, with the gypsies forever remained never to be bartered, borrowed, or sold."

Now Grego sang alone, his tones somber and happy as the song came to an end, "Thus it was given to us to feast this eve, to remember Thor and the gods so bold. To remember the ancestors and those who have fallen. As the world was allotted to us to pray as we wish, beg as we wish, and to take as we need! So said the Allfather, so it shall be. May our ancestors and friends departed be welcomed this night to join us in feast!"

They all listened to the mood and melody of the song as it drifted across the area as if a soft blanket protecting them all from the cold of night and welcoming in any who would wish to join. It was the slow tapping of tambourines and drums combined with a somber fiddle and guitar that led to the mood as the shadows flittered about from the firelight. The conversation of those gathered were whispers if at all until the song was over. Steven even seemed to relax more as the music continued on until the flames of the bonfire flickered wildly and then turned a bright blue, casting an eerie light across the whole area. The music slowed to a halt as everyone stared at the flames in awe and surprise before Anya stood once more and spoke, "One from beyond the veil wishes to visit us this eve and partake in our feast. Shall we allow them admittance?"

Those gathered nodded and voiced their consent, though Steven noticeably tensed up at the notion. Anya nodded once to everyone's approval before she spoke again, "Welcome then spirit, seeker of the families feast. We bid you enter our happy circle this eve."

The flames rose briefly in before settling back to normal, though their color remained the odd blue. Anya was about to return to sitting when she paused and the color drained from her face. Instantly everyone turned to look in the direction in which she was staring to see a young girl no more than sixteen years of age with strawberry blond hair past her shoulders and jade green eyes. Her attire was the same as the other gypsies; however her features would have made some think that she was Sarah's younger sister. It was then Sarah's turn to gawk and stare as Steven rose from where he sat and walked over to where the young girl stood at the edge of the circle. As he reached her, he offered her his arm which she took before he led her into the circle to the spot in which he had been sitting with Sarah. As she sat down and let go of Steven's arm, he quickly retrieved a plate of food and sat down between her and Sarah, a somber smile upon his lips as he handed it to her gently, "Welcome, Ruby..."

Even Devin was staring at the situation with his mouth agape before Valerie reached over and gently closed it for him. She may have not known what exactly to make of the whole situation, but she was certain that being rude wasn't going to make it any better. Anya hesitantly returned to her seat as she managed a smile despite tears welling up in her eyes, "I have missed you, my daughter..."

Sarah looked between the young girl and the others for a moment in confusion before she noticed that Ruby was looking at her with a warm smile. Her voice was other worldly and a wisp of unnatural as she spoke to those within the circle, "Thank you all for welcoming me in this night my friends and family."

Ruby then addressed Sarah as she continued, though her voice seemed to send chills down the spine, "Sarah Roanoak, so you are the one my former beloved was destined to be with. I do hope you will take care of him well and him you for as long as you two shall live."

Sarah only blinked in astonishment at the young girl's voice, for it sounded so similar to her own in some strange way. Steven nodded and smiled as he took Sarah's hand in his own, "You know we shall, Ruby. It is a great honor that you have chosen to dine with us this eve, but I cannot help to wonder why you would leave your rest unless something else has troubled you?"

Ruby nodded as she delicately took a sip from one of the wooden cups filled with wine before speaking once more, "It is a warning I bring my former love, for the shadow that dispatched me in the past now seeks vengeance upon you. It has returned filled with venom and hate. It seeks to make your life as miserable as it feels its punishment is."

A frown creased Steven's lips as his expression deeply darkened, "I see…"

It was then Devin who spoke, having returned to his senses, "But naught was left of him, I had thought he was banished body and soul to the abyss to pay for his crimes?"

Ruby seemed to sigh softly, a sound which mimicked hundreds of fluttering butterfly wings, "One who knew him has called him back as a spiritual servant. You four must all beware and learn how to banish him and his companion once and for all lest they find a way to end all of you."

Devin fell silent as he looked to Steven whose expression was growing even darker with every word. It wasn't until both Sarah and Ruby embraced him at the same time that he seemed to stir and turned realizing that all eyes had turned to him. Ruby then gently whispered in his ear, "Don't allow your anger to rule you my love, or else they shall win."

Steven stared at the fire for a brief moment as he returned to himself and then nodded, "Thank you both."

Ruby reluctantly let go of him and smiled as she looked to Sarah, "You are his rock now, his guiding light. Let your love for each other protect you both and show you the way."

Sarah smiled warmly as she nodded, "Thank you, we shall definitely do our best."

Ruby continued to smile as she stood, trailing her grasp out of Stevens hand as he looked up at her fading form with a touch of sadness as she spoke to the group, "Thank you all once more for having me this eve, but my time is now up. Good bye, and know that my heart is always with you all."

She faded away then leaving only the scents of rose oil coupled with a spring breeze. Steven's eyes lingered on the empty air for a long moment before a tear trailed down his cheek as testimony to the heart wrenching pain that he still felt. Sarah drew him into a close embrace as conversation around the fire had fallen into silence for the rest of the night, as most of those gathered knew how close their relationship had been.

ABDUCTION

In the absence of humility, they are fallen…
Twisting in that spiral ever flowing down… down.
One cannot convey an absolute…
Tingly, quiet, and soft…
No more pain… no more suffering…
Quiet…
It always comes in threes… yes… the things which hurt…
Personal or not… it can become ever worse?
Still, on cool reflection… one may find…
All the misery one left behind…
'Tis truly just something to hold on to…
to cling and hope…
When knowing better, should one simply let go?

January 1, 2009

STEVEN ROSE EARLY as the sun began to crest outside his tent. He leaned over quietly and kissed Sarah gently on the forehead as she slept before standing and getting dressed. His steps took him outside the tent where he stretched gingerly and took in a deep breath of the fresh air. The events of the previous night were still settling in his mind and he found himself wondering where exactly he should start with all of it. Sighing heavily he wandered over to one of the barrels filled with water and gingerly splashed his face and washed his hands. He watched as the sun rose above the lake and the trees, his mind beginning to reason that the library at his home might be as good a place as any to start looking for the answers to the questions which were now forming within his mind. As he stewed on the whole lot, he felt soft hands trailing around his waist as a soft kiss trailed on the back of his neck followed by Sarah's voice in his ear, "Morning."

A smile crept his lips as he relaxed against her embrace. "Morning, love. Tear down today and then we can go home."

Sarah nodded as she rested her chin on his shoulder, "It will be nice to have an actual bed again and a shower."

Steven chuckled at her response as he turned around and smiled at her.

Olath observed the festivities from a distance with a deep scowl etched upon his lips. He didn't dare move closer for fear of being discovered and thus merely watched from afar. The whole grouping of events disgusted him and made his mind reel with images of how he would much rather see the whole lot catch on fire and burn to the ground with all of them in the middle of it. Grumbling he turned toward the dark apparition which seemed to float off to his side, "They are definitely the ones aren't they?"

It hissed dryly in affirmative response before Olath partially returned his attention to the festival across the lake, "It's time, then. Begin isolating them after this thime of celebration and false hope. I will see each of them fall. My plans will not fail again."

The spirit hissed once more with an eerie guttural laugh of approval.

January 3, 2009

Steven yawned loudly as he flipped another page in the book which referred to dark spirits and their creation in the world. Sighing heavily, he paused in his reading and looked at the piles of books he and Sarah had already looked through. He shook his head as he peered over one pile to see her sleeping soundly on the book she had currently started flipping through the previous hour.

"Ugh, I might have to make a phone call on this one. This is certainly not my area of study... we'll wait and see what Devin and Valerie come up with first at the local library," he mumbled to himself as he leaned back in the chair and rubbed his eyes gently.

Devin looked through the aisles of books with little to no luck on finding anything that he was truly looking for. Sighing in exasperation he made his way over to the table where Valerie was sitting and skimming through a book with frustration etched upon her features. She looked up with narrowed eyes but then relaxed when she realized he wasn't returning with more books for her to glance through. Devin sighed once more as he sat down and cracked open a book on Egyptian mythology, "I don't think we are going to find anything here."

Valerie only nodded as she flipped a page, "I agree, but we need to at least check to make sure."

Devin merely groaned in response before holding up the mythology book to reveal a scantily clad Cleopatra picture with a cheesy grin spread across his lips, "Think I can get you into something like that some time?"

Valerie looked up and instantly turned red before throwing a book at him, "Pay attention to what we're looking for here! And no!"

Devin only snickered as he ducked out of the way of the flying tome.

Steven sighed in frustration as he closed the old book. He casually stood and stretched before looking to the old grandfather clock to see the time and began grumbling, "Bah, the whole day is gone. Where is Devin anyway? He should have been back by now."

Sarah looked up from the book she had been flipping through and rubbed her eyes before checking her watch, "*Ugh*... it's already eight pm? I'll call Valerie and find out what's keeping them. Need a break from all of this anyway."

Steven merely nodded. "I'm gonna order some pizza for us then."

Sarah nodded once and stood stretching before walking out of the library. Her steps took her down the hall and up the stairs to the bedroom where she retrieved her cell phone from the night stand. Punching in Valerie's number she looked out the window and across the small lake which rested in front of the house as it rang.

"Hello?" Valerie's voice came through clear.

"Hey Val, it's me, you and Dev still at the library?" Sarah asked with a smile as she continued looking out the window.

"No, we're at the hospital. A bookcase fell on Devin at the library," Valerie answered in an annoyed tone.

"Oh gods! Is he alright? Steven is going to want to check up on him," Sarah continued.

"He's fine, just a minor concussion. No need to come here since the doctor is almost done. We should be back in about an hour or so," Valerie answered with a sigh still sounding annoyed.

"Alright, I'll let Steven know. See you both when you arrive," Sarah finished before hanging up as a concerned expression crossed her face.

Steven drummed his fingers on the kitchen counter anxiously as he awaited for both his friends and the food he had ordered. Sarah pulled a glass from out of one of the cabinets before moving toward the fridge, a half smile upon her face as she spoke, "You know Valerie said he was fine. I'm sure it was just an accident anyways."

Steven raised a brow as he glanced in her direction, "Mmmm… maybe, but I don't put too much stock in random accidents or bad luck."

Sarah shrugged as she opened the fridge and dropped the glass before screaming. Steven moved like lightning and was instantly by her side, his eyes narrowing at the grotesque sight before his eyes. Within the fridge sat Angela's decaying head. Worms and maggots crawled out from the empty orbs which once held her eyes. A deep scowl is on Steven's lips as he called for Alfred. The butler was there only a moment later and Steven gently handed Sarah to him, "Alfred, take Sarah to the study where it's safe. Oh, and when Devin and Valerie get here make sure they go in there as well. I'm going to clean up this mess and see if I can figure anything out about all this nonsense."

Alfred nodded as he led Sarah away. Sighing heavily Steven pulled out his cell and dialed the number of someone he wished by the gods he had never met. It rang for a moment before there was a click and a deep sounding cynical voice answering, "Ah, Steven… been a while. What do you want?"

Steven took a breath and cleared his throat before answering, "I need your help, Kriss. There's a demon or something damned similar lurking about and I'm not sure what to do about it."

A sarcastic chuckle crackled over the phone for a moment, "So what, you want me to come out and assist in the clean up? What's in it for me?"

Steven's lips dipped some into a scowl, "I'm sure we can come to an arrangement when you get her, Kriss."

Grumbling crackled over the phone for a long moment followed by an irritable sigh, "Fine. Expect me soon."

Steven sighed in slight relief, "Thanks I…"—click—"really appreciate it…"

Devin rubbed the back of his head tenderly as he sat on the couch beside Valerie in the study, his eyes glancing about some in slight irritability, "A bookcase, I mean seriously? Who does that?"

Steven glanced over from the other couch and merely shook his head, "It's obvious that someone or thing is starting to mess with us. We need to hurry and figure out what and how to deal with it."

Valerie and Sarah simply looked across the table at each other, both could tell that patience was running low and tempers were beginning to flare.

"I called Kriss. I figured he might be able to help somehow," Steven began.

"Are you serious? He's little better than a necromancer. Always talking to the dead and communing with spirits or whatever that creepy shit is he does. We'd do better off just continuing to look through books and figure it out ourselves… he asks for too much when it comes to his assistance," Devin retorted irritably.

Sarah and Valerie looked at the two of them curiously before both said at the same, "Kriss?"

Steven frowned noticeably as they seemed to inquire about the person they were unaware of, but it was Devin who answered with a disgusted scowl on his lips, "He's an expert on the damned… and any type of black magic. Hell, the line he walks with, what he knows, and does boarders on evil itself."

Steven sighed. "Devin just doesn't like the idea of asking someone who is schooled mainly in voodoo and other dark arts for help. He focuses in spirit summoning and exorcism and making the dead do favors for people. As far as I know, he's never hurt anyone though, even if his area of expertise is a bit dark."

Just as Sarah was about to say something the doors to the study opened and Alfred was showing in a gentleman who stood at an average height with short, nearly white hair. The eyes which echoed out from the face seemed almost like a soft golden color, though the features on the man's face were stoic and cold. High cheek bones echoed a Germanic or Russian descent, while his build gave him the appearance of a thin yet almost athletic frame. The clothes which draped his body were black and hinted of Armani. Everyone in the room seemed to be staring at the new comer as his gaze seemed to look them all over for a long moment before he made his way into the room and took a seat at the end of the coffee table on a large cushion. Valerie looked to Devin curiously as his scowl deepened, however Sarah was still staring directly at the new person to the room with curiosity. She noted that his features were very pale and almost seemed chiseled as if from stone. It wasn't until he spoke that she turned away looking red in the face from embarrassment, that and a bit off, as she realized that though the man's voice was deep and rich it held no hint of caring whatsoever for any of them.

"Stop staring girl, it's rude!"

Steven frowned and seemed to be about to say something when Kriss raised a solitary finger and looked at him, "You called me here, remember. Now, tell me what's been going on so we can get this over with..."

Steven took a long slow breath and began to recount the events of the past few months, his explanation going into as much detail as he could recall. Kriss merely nodded as he listened, his eyes drifting to Sarah or Valerie on occasion both which had taken to staring at him once more. Once Steven was finished reciting the past events along with Devin filling in some things he had experienced himself, Kriss leaned back on the cushion and gently stroked a clean shaven chin as he seemed to get lost in thought. Sarah suddenly spoke as she continued to stare, "Are you really a necromancer?"

Steven blinked as she asked Kriss the question, a slight draining of color from his face at her bluntness.

Kriss turned his gaze upon her for a long moment as if considering her question, "No, I do not raise the dead. I merely work with and speak to the spirits of the dead or those which have become something else. I can however, summon forth anything that I have a name for... perhaps you would like a demonstration?"

Steven coughed nervously, "I don't think that will be necessary Kriss."

Kriss grumbled some as he eyed Steven, "Mmmm, perhaps not..."

"Just tell me what it is you need to figure out what this thing is that is plaguing us and what you want for payment," Steven stated rather flatly as he eyed Kriss.

A twisted smile came across his lips as he eyed Steven once more, "Oh... well, the basics, amber gris, myrrh, sea salt... some hair from each of you... and... ah, a cauldron or large pot. We can discuss payment later... yes?"

Both Steven and Devin frowned noticeably, but it was Valerie who spoke up then, "And why can we not settle on a price for your, eh, services now?"

His golden eyes drifted to Valerie as he sneered menacingly at her, "Are you going to pay it little girl? Mmmm? I doubt you would even be worth the service I am about to perform for the lot of you. Perhaps you have something special you wish to give up as... a deposit? Hmmm?"

She blinked taken aback by his tone before looking to Steven and Devin who were both standing now, moving to get between Valerie and Kriss. It was Steven who spoke then, "I will make the payment, and you know this, leave the two girls out of it."

Kriss chuckled softly as he eyed the four of them, "Very well. Get the things I require and I will begin. Then we shall truly see what it is that plagues you."

Steven looked to Devin and nodded, "Dev, can you go out and grab the things he needs? I'll stay here and make sure nothing awry happens."

"Yeah, sure man," Devin responded as he looked at Kriss one last time before turning to go.

Valerie and Sarah stood and trailed after him, Sarah speaking as she followed, "We're coming too, need some fresh air anyway."

Steven only shrugged as Devin looked at him questioningly, "Right, well let's go then."

Valerie pulled into the parking lot for the new age occult store and sighed lightly as she parked her car. Devin was reading over the list which had been given to him from the passenger's seat and making a multitude of faces at half of the things named in the list, "I hope they have all of this stuff. Who in their right mind would even buy half of this stuff anyway? I mean, what the hell are you going to do with a jar of snake's tongues?"

Valerie snickered as she exited the car with Sarah in tow behind her, "It's a plant Devin dear, not actually the tongues of snakes."

"Oh!" Devin exclaimed as he followed the two into the store, "Witches, I mean real witches, are so odd when they come up with names for things."

Valerie only shook her head as she spied the crystal display case and quickly made her way over to it. Sarah merely looked about curiously as Devin went to the cashier with the list to try and figure out what everything on it was as quickly as possible. Sarah's steps took her down an aisle labeled fetishes and totems. Halfway through she paused and leaned over to examine what looked like a genuine shrunken head when she felt a cold chill wash over her whole body. A surprisingly deep voice with a dark undertone then caused her to jump, "You know, the art of shrinking heads has long been practiced by shamans living in South America. They live deep within the jungles… preying on any who would invade their territory."

She quickly stood and faced the speaker, her eyes graced with the visage of a young thin man with matted black hair and dark eyes, which harbored heavy circles under them. Her eyes narrowed partially at the stranger as she also noticed that his clothes were dirty and unkempt, colored in blacks and dark browns smeared with something that might possibly be dirt or something else. Finally she cleared her throat to speak, "No, I was unaware of that."

His lips twisted into an uncaring sneering smile as he spoke again, "Well, now you do... Sarah."

Sarah's eyes widened in fear and surprise as he spoke her name and she opened her mouth to scream when he raced forward faster than anything she had ever seen in her life and covered her mouth and nose with a cloth which smelled foul and greasy. She felt her mind slipping as her vision clouded and the strength left her legs.

"*Shhhhh* now... there is no need for all of that my little worm. You're going to help me catch a fish," Olath's sneering smiled widened as she succumbed to the drugs on the rag and her sight left her to a black of troubling unconsciousness.

Valerie made her way to the cashier's desk where Devin was scowling at six large bags full of herbs, minerals, and several other things of which he dared not guess as to their origin or usage. She leaned over his shoulder and giggled some at his discomfort, "Good thing you have two strong girls to help you carry all of this. Where is Sarah anyway? I haven't seen her in like twenty minutes."

Devin shrugged as he glanced back at her and responded sarcastically, "She went down the fetish aisle last I saw, maybe she's trying to find something to spruce up the bedroom."

Valerie only shook her head as she went to the aisle, "Only you would get magic and bedroom fetishes mixed up."

Devin snickered as he paid for all of the merchandise with the cash that Steven had given him. It was only a moment before Valerie was back at his side with tears in her eyes and a very worried expression etched upon her face as she held out a note toward Devin which had one of Sarah's earrings attached to it.

Devin's eyes narrowed as he opened the letter and let out a series of colorful swears, "Steven is going to kill me…"

Steven paced back and forth with the mostly crumpled letter in hand as Devin and Valerie sat on the couch staring at the coffee table in utter silence. Finally, braving Steven's temper Devin cleared his throat and spoke, "I'm really sorry man… we'll find her I pro—"

Steven only shot Devin a warning look which caused the two on the couch to shrink smaller before he spoke in icy tones, "Not another word; take this note to the police, get them to do their damn job for once. I'm going to help Kriss prepare because now we need his help more than ever."

Devin merely nodded as he stood and took Valerie's hand easing her to rise as well and follow him out of the room. As the two made their way down the hall, a loud crash followed by an anguishing scream echoed from the study. The sound itself hinted to an unknowable suffering teetering on the edge of despair and it tore at both of their hearts.

Revisiting the Past and Reunion

In the absence of emptiness do we crawl along our paths,
in the turmoil of strife do we face our own wrath...
What is this noise which surrounds me here, is it life, or
just death drawing near...
Have I lived a thousand lives to understand this thing, or
am I just hoping for a simple summer's rain...
Why do we draw nearer when we push each other away,
why do try to care when all we do is cause so much
pain...
How can there be love if it is so cruel,
yet when I feel it I feel so unreal...
Am I just a tool... a simple spoke and wheel...
Are we to continue falling when there is
no end and no fuel...
Try me... Try me again...
Let me show you that some things don't end...
Trust me and take me away...
Away from life, away from the misery we face each day...
Help, and let me give you a hand...
Let us not crumble into nothingness again...
Feel me and know that I am warm...
I am here and alive...
Not dead or unborn...
Would you leave me if I had my way... am I too con-
stricting or cruel in each day...
Would you stay with me if I professed my love...
Would you turn your back and give a simple shrug...
Why can't you hear me when I am screaming inside...

Why can't you see me when I bleed and cry...
What is it that I have to do to get through to you... am I
fighting against myself...
Or am I losing too...

NO LIGHT REACHED Sarah's eyes as she hazily came back to consciousness. Confusion and fear began to register in her mind as she felt her body swinging by her wrists through cool damp air. She could feel her arms stretched above her head, her wrists tightly bound by both rope and metal which held her up a few inches off the floor. Her body tensed up instantly as she began to recall what has occurred as the store and she began to cry out into the darkness, "Help! Somebody help me!"

A soft sarcastic chuckle was the only response that came from the unending void of darkness around her accompanied with the echoing drips of water upon a stone floor. Then a raspy voice whispered close to her ear causing her to shiver and shake uncontrollably as she felt a cold finger trail down across her spine, "No one is going to hear you here. So scream out to your heart's content. After all, it's not as much fun if you remain silent the whole time..."

Sarah shivered more as she began twist and turn to try and get away from the cold touch on her skin, "Don't you touch me, you disgusting pervert!"

Her mind spun with fear and panic, she had to get out of here, get away, such were the only thoughts coursing through her head other than a growing foreboding feeling which was penetrating into her very core. Once more the voice reached her ears as she felt the cold fingers once more trailing along her naked skin from her sides and across her stomach, "My aren't you a feisty one... trying to struggle even when you are all tied up and all hope is lost to you. I've been watching and waiting for this moment for a long time... Sarah... oh yes, and I am going to make sure you feel every moment of it before your lover arrives so that I can cut out your heart in front of him!"

She screamed, the sound echoing off of stone walls and vanishing into the darkness only accompanied with maniacal laughter.

Devin paced in the lobby of the police station impatiently while Valerie kept shooting him looks which stated, "Sit down and relax already." He had already been waiting half an hour and Devin wasn't exactly the most patient person in the world, it wasn't until the sound of a door opening and the echoing of footsteps coming from down the hall that he took pause and watched the hall entrance behind the desk expectantly. Soon Frank entered the waiting room via the hall and gestured for Devin and Valerie to follow him back. Valerie timidly stood and began to follow at a casual pace where as Devin nearly sprinted across the room to catch up to Frank. They all walked down the hall in silence until Frank reached his door and opened it and gestured for the two to sit in the chairs in front of his desk. He followed the two into the room and then moved around the desk to take his own seat before looking them over for a long moment and finally speaking, "Alright you two, what cha' got for me?"

Devin leaned over the desk and handed Frank the note which they had found at the shop before speaking in a bit of a shaky voice that indicated both anger and worry, "Sarah was abducted from the new age occult store while we were there shopping. That note was left with one of her earrings attached to it."

Frank carefully took the note and unfolded it reading it to himself.

> *You may have stopped my companion last year, but you will not be so fortunate with me. I have taken your friend, the wolf's lover. Do not expect to stop me; you cannot even begin to fathom what will happen if you do, for by the time you arrive I will have her beating heart in my hand to show you the futili-*

ties of your efforts. If you wish to find me then just check where your voice echo's in the darkness and screams never reach the outside air, a place abandoned to the past and forgotten in the decay of societies miseries.

—Silk

PS I enjoyed your friend Angela, she begged up until I cut her heart from her flesh.

Frank looked up from the letter and between the two youths in front of him, for a moment as a grim expression traced over his features darkly, "Who else has touched this and how long has it been since you found it?"

It was Valerie who spoke up then as Devin seemed to be turning red with anger and frustration, "Not but an hour ago. So far only I, Devin, and Steven have touched it since we found it."

Frank nodded grimly as he picked up the phone receiver on his desk and pushed a button on the console for it, "Hey Jimmy, come up here from the lab. I got some evidence to log and I want it examined and checked for prints."

A heavy sigh escaped Frank as he hung up the phone and looked back at the two once more, "I want you two to head back to Steven's place and stay there. I'll have some people come out and watch the grounds around the house to make sure the rest of you are safe while we find this sicko and rescue your friend. And don't do anything rash, and I mean *anything*, understand?"

Devin nodded knowingly as he stood, though it did little to relieve his concern or worry, "Yeah, no problem Frank."

Kriss had set about the study laying down lines of salt and mumbling incomprehensible words from some long dead and forgotten language. His tone was deep and almost guttural as it seemed to vibrate and echo throughout the room. Steven watched silently and shivered, for though he felt torn apart inside with the recent events, there was still something about his friend's incantations and magic that made his very skin crawl and chill through.

"My type of magic seems to disagree with you, but then it could just be your distress over the current situation—strong emotions, especially negative ones—give way to negative reactions with any type of magic," Kriss mumbled as he continued working on some elaborate diagram.

Steven sighed heavily as he rubbed his temples tenderly before responding in a despondent tone which gave him away more than he would have liked, "Maybe both… I just feel clouded, overwhelmed, and most of all helpless to do anything at the moment."

Kriss seemed to chuckle softly to himself as he continued working diligently, "I've been in your situation before… more than once even… I imagine that's why I have become so cold and uncaring over the past few years."

Steven quirked a brow as he leaned forward in his chair and stared across the room at Kriss, "So how do you deal with it?"

Kriss paused sighing in exasperation as he turned to look at Steven a moment, "At first I only sought revenge… I ended the lives of those who are responsible for my loss and my misery… but after the third time, I resolved myself to being alone. I realized that despite all my power, my gifts I could not protect the ones I loved all the time. It was… no, is because I am too weak and I have yet to find someone who can protect themselves… so I've simply given up."

Steven merely blinked, genuinely surprised at the answer he was given. The words had caused him to fall silent for a long moment in thought as he contemplated them and the reasoning given to him. The very idea of Kriss giving up on anything positively astounded him beyond words or rational thought, but not so much as learning that Kriss had lost so many people he cared for to evil individuals and circumstances. Besides, Steven couldn't bring himself to think of Kriss as weak in the slightest, after all he had witnessed him do spells in the past that caused what Steven himself would consider miraculous results in themselves. He just shook his head quietly as he thought on it, dwelling on if it were the right course of action or just a consequence of loss and despair.

Frank left the station with a full squad of officers; he knew the trail would be a little cold but he at least hoped to gain a lead on where this mad man might be. Though he had very little to go on, he did at least have a place to start. The squad cars sped across the city toward the new age shop which Devin and Valerie had spoken of, sirens blazed and lights flashed ensuring that none would get in the way of official police business. The drive was too short it seemed to Frank, given that the building in question was on the other side of town from the station. Still, that was not what really shocked him upon arrival; it was the fact that as they all pulled into the store's parking lot the store was merely a charred burnt out husk of a building which was still just barely smoldering at its foundation. Frank pulled up right to the entrance of the former building and exited the squad car surveying the scene before his eyes as he cussed profusely at the blackened and smoking foundation stones. The only sign of life from the place were several barely smoking piles of rubble from the interior of the structure. He shook his head still swearing for a long moment before turning and yelling at one of the officers nearby, "Get forensics and an arson unit here yesterday!"

The officer ran to his squad car and radioed dispatch making urgent requests as Frank began pacing absently back and forth in front of the building, his irritation still smoldering within.

Valerie drove down the long wooded drive to Steven's estate, occasionally glancing at Devin as he sat brooding in the passenger's seat.

"What do you think is going on? I mean, a shop like that just doesn't burn down to nothing in a matter of less than an hour without the fire department being notified and no one hearing about it," She said as she parked the car in front of the mansion.

Devin only grumbled as he exited the car, "I dunno, I don't even know what to think of all this… or how we're supposed to fight it."

Valerie only sighed shaking her head as she followed him into the house. The hall to the study was filled with moved furniture and walking down it was a tight fit at best. Whatever was being prepared was going to take up the entire study, Valerie reasoned to herself as she squeezed in between things making her way toward the room. Steven sat on one of the misplaced chairs in the hall with his head in his hands, his hair was disheveled and his clothes were unchecked and out of sorts. Devin made his way over to his friend and placed a hand gently on his shoulder offering up what little support he could at the time. He knew that though Steven was perfectly still on the outside, inside he was falling apart at the seams.

Valerie paused a moment to look between the two of them and then entered the study quietly, though it was there that she instantly froze, her voice caught in her throat and her eyes stared transfixed in wonderment at the sight before her. Symbols and line decorated the room's every surface, their hue was a soft glowing blue and they all intricately intertwined in some complex pattern which made the mind spin and imagine things of tales of old and legend. For an instant, fairies danced in the air followed by the melody of an elven choir which caused them to take flight amongst the soft blue lights. The illumination provided from several candles only seemed to add to the ambiance of the environment, causing shadows to play across the walls in secret forms of revelry and enjoyment. The air seemed to feel heavy and electric as Valerie's eyes drifted across the length of the room to settle on Kriss who stood in the center and momentarily looked up at her from his work; it was only a flash but she swore that his eyes shimmered as if they were made of gold.

She blinked once, seeing him normally and attributed it all to a trick of the lights and glowing symbols in the room, though his voice as he spoke seemed uncommonly chilled and annoyed at the disruption of whatever it was he was doing, "Have you come to assist me, little herbalist, or are you just going to stand there gawking like a child who has never witnessed true magic in her whole life?"

Valerie faltered for a moment in speaking as she continued to regard Kriss with mute curiosity, "I… uh, yes. What do I need to do?"

Kriss considered her for a long moment, his eyes tracing over her as if she were more of a tool than a person to be considered and it made her shiver as if a draft had entered the room. It was a only a moment before he reached down to a bag and dug out some sort of thin blue outfit which she couldn't quite make out. His voice still had a bit of a cold edge to it as he spoke to her once more, "Can you dance?"

Valerie shrugged as she continued to stare at the outfit, uncertain of what it entailed, "I suppose I can, what exactly do you want me to do?"

Kriss seemed to nod as he tossed the outfit at her and began pointing at certain points around the elaborate diagram on the floor, "You will change, instruct the other two that we are not to be disturbed until this ritual is over, and then you will return and dance in the pattern I am specifying now. You must step exactly as I instruct, the music in the air will give you the rhythm to follow, and the fae will give you the proper movements if you watch closely enough."

She blinked once more before beginning to speak again when something washed over her and caused her to pause and look about the room once more. It seemed filled with fairies and the music of something long forgotten, something ancient and lost to the world of today, yet it rang clear in her ears now. It made her heart skip a beat and race, her legs wobble weakly, and her skin to sweat. It was a feeling of passion and power, a combination that made her mind spin in anticipation. Kriss frowned as he clapped his hands once, "Keep your mind about you as well, for if you mess this up, then both of us will be dealing with some dire consequences that neither of us want."

Valerie shook her head to clear it and nodded, for though everything still seemed present it was also distant now. There was something terribly old and unsettling about all of this and she couldn't quite put her finger on it, but planned on asking him once it was all over where he had learned such things. Her steps took her to the door of the study where she poked her head out and looked to Steven and Devin who were conversing quietly in the hall.

"I am about to help Kriss with this odd ritual, he has instructed that you two stay in the hall and wait for it to come to a finish and then we will invite you in," Her voice shook with undertones of uneasiness, for she didn't understand why she felt nervous, perhaps fearful of making a mistake.

Devin frowned and began to move toward the study door when Steven caught his arm gently and shook his head to him as he turned back to look. Devin's scowl deepened as he turned back toward Valerie, "Alright, fine, but if he tries anything funny just scream and I'll be in there faster than jack flash."

Valerie only nodded mutely as she returned to the study and closed the doors quietly before turning to see that Kriss was staring at her a bit more intent than she liked. She shivered just a little as she began to slip off her clothes and change into the outfit which had been tossed at her. It seemed to be an open sided skirt of soft blue silk with gold lining that represented several odd symbols and a cut off top which served more as a bra than any sort of clothing that Valerie knew. The set was matching and very well crafted by hand from what she could tell as she handled it and put it on. Carefully she stowed her regular clothing off to the side out of the ritual area and looked at Kriss once more who nodded approvingly at her before speaking, "Good, it is very fetching on you… I can see why you have stolen away Mr. Noirlion's heart now. It's too bad he will never be allowed to marry you or anything."

Valerie blinked several times at his words, "What do you mean he could never marry me? Why not?"

Kriss paused in his final drawings just briefly looking up at her once more, "You are from two separate families, all of which are sworn to a certain duty and forbidden from intermingling since there is the chance that only one child will be born. And one child from two families would place the sole inheritance of power and the role of both families on one person, thus giving that person entirely too much power. It would be a crime against the pacts which have ensured the survival of the families you serve and anger the gods themselves. Haven't you ever wondered why Steven and his little girlfriend seem to have so much trouble?"

Valerie took a slow breath as she thought about it for a moment, "I did wonder, but they aren't married… at least not yet. Besides, I and Devin haven't any such issues and we're in the same boat, aren't we?"

Kriss chuckled softly for a moment, "No, not quite. You see, Steven suffers from a curse, as does Sarah. It was placed on them long ago when they decided to marry and take power from their families even though they were the second born which is also forbidden. Thus the gods struck them down and sent them forward to be reincarnated into this life to make amends for their sins as it were. They are meant to live through this life and suffer because of their choices to go against the vows made by their families so long ago… Now, if you would start here…"

Valerie moved to where he pointed, but her curiosity was sparked now as she eyed him a bit more carefully, "And how do you know all this?"

Kriss grinned as he gestured about the room for a moment, "These are the symbols you will be dancing to and around, do not fail here. As to answer your question... well, I know many things. You will begin when the music starts anew."

It was only a moment before the music seemed to start anew, the wood flutes and chimes of a forest long forgotten filled her ears and her eyes drifted hazily to a fairy which seemed to dance in front of her. She moved following the fae's example, and proceeded around the room in an elegant and remarkable manner. Her mind danced with her, the music filled her soul and made her heart beat with the tunes that echoed to her. After a moment, she caught herself singing, softly and in a language that made no sense to her own ears. Valerie's voice sung, of its own accord, and the song made her weep uncontrollably as she continued to dance as it rang out across the room, "Tha mi sgìth's mi leam fhìn, Buain na rainich, buain na rainich, Tha mi sgìth 's mi leam fhìn, Buain na rainich daonnan...

Kriss listened until she finished the verse and he chimed in from the center as Valerie continued to spin and dance about the room singing her verse over and over again, but his voice reached her ears as well, deep and rich, oddly soothing as he sang, "'S tric a bha mi fhìn's mo leannan, Anns a' ghleannan cheòthar, 'G èisteachd còisir bhinn an doire, Seinn sa choille dhòmhail."

Soon the two were singing the whole song in unison as Valerie seemed to dance with fever across and around the room to the odd sigils in what seemed to be a preset pattern. Their voices melded with a soft choir and tempo which matched the wood wind instruments, drums, and strings which rang through the air only to be heard by their ears, "Tha mi sgìth's mi leam fhìn, Buain na rainich, buain na rainich, Tha mi sgìth's mi leam fhìn, Buain na rainich daonnan. 'S tric a bha mi fhìn's mo leannan, Anns a' ghleannan cheòthar, 'G èisteachd còisir bhinn an doire, Seinn sa choille dhòmhail. Tha mi sgìth 's mi leam fhìn, Buain na rainich, buain na rainich, Tha mi sgìth 's mi leam fhìn, Buain na rainich daonnan. 'S tric a bha mi fhìn's mo leannan, Anns a' ghleannan cheòthar, 'G èisteachd còisir bhinn an doire, Seinn sa choille dhòmhail."

As the last chorus ended, Valerie was standing nearly face to face with Kriss, her breath labored and her eyes staring into his, though she was weeping uncontrollably now and had no idea why. Her entire form shook and sweat soaked through the barely covering clothing. Her heart was racing and for an instant she began to lean toward him, her mind lost in some hot haze as she attempted to kiss him. He merely smiled as he touched her forehead and she slumped to the ground as a feather falling from a ledge high above a valley, his words echoing to her as she drifted into blackness, "There will be none of that now, little herbalist, your boyfriend would be quite cross with me if I allowed you to just follow your instincts due to a ritual created by the fae…"

With that Valerie collapsed, her mind drifting off into realms of vision and the unknown. Her thoughts swam for a brief moment in heat and passion before clearing and showing her that which was to be seen.

Damp darkness, that's all that reached Valerie as she tried to look about. Her mind spun, her heart was still racing, but where was she? She shook her head defiantly trying to clear it to no avail. Everything seemed unfocused and misty, but she could still walk. Her steps were soft, quiet; they made no sound even though the echoing of water dripping and chains shaking reached her ears. Still, even that sounded off to her, as if she were under water. Ahead she saw light, yes, she was certain it was light. Blinking rapidly she gasped, the form of Sarah hung in the center of a dimly lit room, the smell of earth, water, and smoke assailed her nostrils and she coughed. Something else was in the air here, it was foul, and it smelled metallic and wet. Turning her attention back to Sarah, she felt her breath catch in her throat. She was covered in blood and Valerie couldn't believe the sight before her, cuts lined her friend's naked form hung up by chains and rope. She could only watch as Sarah swung to and fro sluggishly, hearing her whimper softly in the darkness. Valerie gritted her teeth as she looked around more, the light was coming from a window, way up in the ceiling it seemed, but it was more like some sort of an elaborate bay window. Valerie scowled some, no, it wasn't a bay window, maybe something one would see in a large warehouse. She was uncertain; everything seemed so foggy and vague. It all seemed so real but not all at the same time. She tried to take a slow breath to steady herself when something across the room caught her eye, something darker than the shadows in the area. It moved, it was fast, and it was rushing across the room toward her. It was blacker than night, its eyes shimmered like a glowing crimson as it flowed across the room. Nothing but hate came from this thing of shadow and darkness, and it wanted her as its plaything. As it drew closer. she found herself unable to move, her body wouldn't respond to her commands. It reached out with a singular boney finger toward her as its mouth opened releasing a foggy cloud that stunk of rot and decay. Her eyes widened as her soul filled with dread and she opened her mouth to scream just as it came close to her skin when a bright light erupted causing it to howl in a horrid wail which caused her ears to ring and her mind to reel as everything went dark once more.

Valerie sat up screaming, her eyes wide. She felt a hand on her shoulder and on her head lightly along with the soft hushing of Kriss in her ear, "Shhh now, you're awake now."

Devin and Steven stood over her with Kriss as they sat on the floor, both affixed disapproving looks upon their face as they looked to Kriss in what could be nothing but utter agitation nearing on anger. Valerie looked around, gradually calming down though there was clearly a look of utter fear on her face until she regained her bearings Devin quickly knelt down in front of her and took her hands in his own carefully, "Are you alright?"

Valerie took a slow breath and nodded before she turned to Kriss, "It's a warehouse or something similar, there was a large window in the room, partially broken out. The whole area smelled like smoke and earth, and there was water dripping all around.

It echoed, so I think the walls are made of stone, maybe a really old warehouse?"

Kriss nodded as he looked to Steven, "Perhaps you should inform your officer friend while Devin here helps bring her all the way back to reality. These things are trying on the seer."

Steven nodded as he held a hand out to help Kriss up and the both walked out of the study, though his eyes remained on Kriss for a long moment before he spoke, "I don't know how you do the things you do, but thank you."

Kriss merely nodded once, "It's fine, now give the cops a head start before you rush off to the old industrial section of town. I have a feeling that you'll find your answers there, but be wary, whatever tried to hold her spirit there is nothing to be trifled with… it took almost all my strength to pull her back here."

Steven pulled out his cell and began to dial the local police station's number as he watched Kriss slump into a chair and closed his eyes. The phone only rang for a moment before the operator picked up and he spoke, "I need you to connect me to detective Frank, and hurry, this is important."

Steven spoke on the phone for several minutes before he returned to the study. Devin and Valerie were in a close embrace which caused Steven to clear his throat to get their attention. Devin turned quickly and managed a smile, "Well?"

"Frank is on it, he says to wait here but of course all of us know that we aren't going to so he called his officers away from the house for a few minutes. We have about an hour to try and catch up to him and the squad he has with him and hope that this can all be resolved without any further issue…" Steven answered as a dark expression clouded his face.

Devin frowned as he examined Steven's expression, "You sound like you are unsure of something?"

Steven shook his head, "I just… I'm not sure if I can go through it again, the same thing as last year. Let's go save her and put this S.O.B. in jail or the ground."

Devin nodded as he looked to Valerie who also nodded, both with a determined expression on their features.

As the three left the house, Kriss opened one eye partially and smirked to himself before mumbling, "And so it has begun."

Tentatively he stood and pulled out a black robe from his bag and put it on pulling up a hood which hid his face just before he vanished entirely.

Death or Demise

How can I embrace such sensation, to speak so simply
and confer what I feel within the depths of my soul?
How is it possible to show… what truly lies deep inside
another… would it really impact you then?
I am at an end… a simple impasse… forever falling…
Perhaps if you look back on a lonely rainy day…
you will see me… hearing the soft patter of drops upon
your window and the slight chill within the air…
Here we can begin… forever searching…
trying to see within…
It is a soft whisper then… caressing…
as you rock slowly in a chair…
Staring forward, and realizing nothings there…
The soft sound of creaking wood…
followed by the wind in the trees…
It is speaking… forever taunting me…
Then you get the urge… crawling up and wrapping
your arms around your knees…
Feel your heart begin to race… the pounding in
your ears… skip… beat…
and panic comes nipping at your heels…
Slow… slow… can you calm down…
listen to the swirling wind…
Calm… calm… yet again… tis naught…
Just breath… caught instead…
Then…
Twisting…
Turning…
Down…
In your guts again…

As the breaths quicken, you struggle to
catch up to the sound…
But there is no air to satisfy you or take leave…
no… no…
Force the pace…
Breathe deeply and hope for release…
Stare forward once more and see… that this…
is not your hopeful peace…
only to realize that in front…
what you see truly comes from within…
Is it now that you are sinking, lost from control…
Drowning, churning, a never ending…
swirl… down… twirl…
Stop!
Stop… there you see the shadows taunting…
Laughing…
Rejoicing in ones misery…
And it never ends… just keep hoping and
bracing for the fall…
I know I'm not perfect, but I keep trying despite it all…
You may never know… how deeply… all of it goes…

STEVEN'S PORSCHE PULLED into the run-down parking lot beside an abandoned warehouse of overly large proportions. His car was followed immediately by Valerie's as the two vehicles parked beside an empty patrol car. Steven shivered as he exited the car and began to look about taking in the gruesome scene before his very eyes. Five empty patrol cars sat parked in various positions around the entrance of the warehouse, lights still flashing without the sounds of the sirens. The silence itself was eerie enough but the sight of blood strewn about the area made it even harder to bear. Several policemen laid strewn about as well, the looks of them hinted to being tossed about like rag dolls and then squeezed to death as if in a winepress. The scene's horror etched itself in his mind as he began to scowl noticeably. His eyes traveled to the building up from the carnage on the ground. It was old, the stone work itself hinted to it being at least built around the mid to early 1800s. The roof was still composed of old stone slate and the windows rod were iron and hand-blown glass, though they seemed shuttered from the inside of the ancient building. Vile black and red moss crept along the exterior masonry as if some horrid disease were trying to envelope the building itself. Water dripped from the stone slate roof all around the building, but it was the sound of Valerie vomiting behind Steven that pulled him out of his revelry of disgust and caused him to turn and to look to his two friends somberly.

Devin patted Valerie on her back gently as she lost her lunch to the pavement due to the spectacle of horror before them all. He looked to Steven for a long moment as he felt the fire within his soul rising up in anger.

"We're going to end this, Devin, I promise you that," Steven said in cool even tones as he looked back toward the building.

"You've got that right. I'll burn this whole place to nothing but ash if it comes to it," Devin replied as his eyes drifted angrily to the dead cops littered on the ground.

Steven merely nodded as he mumbled to himself, "If it comes to that…"

Valerie eventually composed herself and looked between the two for a long moment before taking a deep breath and speaking in shaky tones, "Let's go get Sarah and fry this bastard for everything he's done to us and our friends."

Steven and Devin nodded once at the same instant to Valerie before the three of them began to head toward the entrance of the old warehouse. The door itself seemed ominous and imposing to the three, but a gurgling cough pulled their attention off to the right of it.

"Frank!" Devin exclaimed as he rushed over to the bloody officer's side who was still clinging to life.

Valerie was only a step behind Devin and was soon kneeling beside the officer as well. She carefully took Frank's hands into her own and closed her eyes concentrating. It was only a brief moment before both Valerie and Frank were encased in a soft blue light; its warmth seemed to radiate a welcome relief to the cold and damp area where they were at. Devin watched nervously as Steven remained at the entrance.

Steven looked between the three and the door before he kicked it open with barely containing his anger for a brief moment before turning to Devin and speaking, "You two follow me once Frank is stable and good to go. I'm not going to leave Sarah alone in there a second longer than I have to."

Devin nodded as he watched Steven enter the building with a look of both determination and desperation.

A soft old gentle voice reached Sarah's ears as she hung, drifting in the darkness, "Love of my brother, I will heal you and release you. Take this chance amidst the upcoming chaos to join the others and put an end to this evil which holds all of you in rapture."

A click resounded throughout the room as Sarah fell to the floor, her vision and mind quickly cleared as she looked about to examine her surroundings. She found herself blinking several times as she tried to make sense of all that was around her. Ancient trees loomed high overhead, soft sun light cascaded through their branches to warm her skin. The floor was that of a forest, covered with moss and delicate flowers and ferns. She blinked once more before turning quickly and looking in all directions to try and find whoever had set her free. It was all forest, and it seemed to stretch forward in every direction with no sign of clearing. The only thing which finally stood out to her was an ancient mossy cobblestone path which led away from where she currently sat and into the depths of the forest. Taking a slow deep breath, she shivered and pulled a cloak tighter about herself. It was then only a fraction of a moment before she looked herself over and noted the long sixteenth century style dress she wore colored in an earthy green tone along with a thick brown fur cloak; she realized that she was no longer nude or held captive by some madman. It all seemed so familiar to her, yet foreign and alien at the same time.

Taking another slow breath she stood and began to make her way along the old cobble path toward wherever it would lead her.

Footsteps echoed within the musty darkness, as cold eyes fixed themselves on empty ropes and chains which hung from the ceiling. What followed was a scream of nothing but pure hatred and rage at the situation which could turn the hottest soul frigid with fear as it echoed out through the darkness.

"Find her! Find her now or I'll shove you right back into that hell I dragged you out of!" Olath screamed at the shadowy apparition which seemed to cringe at the threat before slipping off into the surrounding darkness.

Olath's eyes narrowed as he looked about in fuming anger before he took a deep slow breath to refocus himself.

"So, you all have some mysterious helper. 'Tis no matter, all of you are here now and it's time to start my little games with you all. None of you will survive... I promise that much," he mumbled to himself as he seemed to vanish into the darkness itself.

Devin and Valerie jumped noticeably as an infernal scream echoed out from the warehouse causing a chill to run down both of their spines for a moment. It was only a moment before Devin seemed to smirk and spoke in sardonic tones, "Seems that Steven's making someone angry. I think it's about time we join him, is Frank going to be alright now if we leave him here?"

Valerie nodded with a small smile, "Yeah. I think so. He's sleeping now, but I am fairly certain his injuries are only minimal now."

Devin only nodded once in return before he headed into the building with Valerie close in tow behind him.

Steven blinked after entering the building and a dark frown crested his lips as he looked down what appeared to be a long corridor of mirrors. He eyed the reflections suspiciously for a long moment. The only thought which occurred to him was how insane a person would have to be to turn an old warehouse into a mirror maze and torture cabin just to mess with anyone attempting a rescue. Still, he progressed with caution, for something about all of it stirred in his gut telling him that something was terribly wrong with this hallway. Each step he took seemed to take him farther and farther down the hallway, but by his judgment he didn't think that he was moving at all. His scowl deepened further as he picked up his pace and then paused, his reflexes causing him to duck an instant before one of the reflections of himself reached out from the mirror swinging a sword where his head had been a moment before.

He cursed to himself under his breath as he peered at the reflections which now seemed to be mimicking his movements once more, but he knew that they were no ordinary mirror images of himself now. He sat for a moment kneeling on the ground as he considered his options, running or walking blindly down this corridor was a poor choice when he didn't know where the next attack might come from, but he wondered if breaking them would truly bring him bad luck. Sighing softly in resignation, he stood and turned to the mirror on his right and swung as hard as he could. His fist connected with the mirror and it shattered into several pieces as did the rest around him, leaving a dark and damp corridor with little to no light within it. Steven's eyes narrowed as he continued on, his steps echoing softly as he walked.

Devin paused for an instant after he entered the door and looked around at what appeared to be a crumbling stone path leading through a large abyss of a hole in the floor. His brow knotted as he turned to speak to Valerie when he paused in mid sentence, "Well, this looks to… Valerie?"

His eyes scanned behind him as he merely saw a ledge leading off and down into darkness with no Valerie behind him whatsoever. Devin cussed profusely under his breath as he began to realize what was happening, "So, the bastard is trying to separate us with some illusion or something."

He leaned down and tested the edge of the path and found that his hand did in fact go down past the ledge, and he began to wonder how much of it was real after all. Sighing irritably, he began to walk along the craggily path noticing ever so often that the further he went the warmer and brighter it got as if the depths below him were starting to light a fire. His eyes turned down for a moment as he caught glimpses of flames below and his skin felt the heat of them as they seemed to be rising up slowly around him and the path. Devin's eyes narrowed as he picked up his pace and continued along the path, though he kept his concentration on the fire which was now climbing ever higher up toward him.

Valerie blinked repeatedly as she looked about in awe and confusion after entering through the door finding herself on a small island surrounded by nothing but blue ocean and a harsh salty breeze. Her mind turned and spun as she tried to get a grasp on what was happening, but none of it made any sense to her. How could she be on an island in the middle of the sea after walking through a warehouse door? She shook her head for a moment and began looking about more, noting that the island seemed to be circled by several large fish with fins, then it struck her that they were sharks. She backed up slightly from the edge of the tiny isle and began to notice that the water was creeping up steadily along the shore, and the thought occurred to her that if the island became submerged that she would become dinner for those nasty fish.

Her eyes looked about once more frantically as she tried to figure out a way to get past the situation, though nothing was occurring to her and she could feel panic rising up in her gut. Her steps took her back until she was standing at the center of the small isle of sand and she watched in fear as the water rose ever so slowly over the sandy shore. Her mind began to give in to despair when she heard a cold uncaring voice whispering to her from somewhere nearby but unseen, "Get a hold of yourself little herbalist, it's only an illusion and only as real as you let it be. This is a place of water, use that water and dispel the things around you… open your eyes and truly see!"

She turned about several times and then paused considering the words from a familiar voice before closing her eyes for a long moment and taking a deep breath. Her own voice mumbling to herself as she began to concentrate, "Only an illusion… open my eyes…"

She focused and concentrated all of her will into disbelieving what was around herself, repeating that it was all an illusion, a falsehood of her imagination, and then opened her eyes to see a damp dark corridor that smelled of mold and stale water. She blinked several times then took a few steps forward before realizing that this was truly what was past the door before turning back to see the entrance to the warehouse behind her. A slight smile traced her lips and then she wondered what happened to Devin and Steven and if they were also caught in some terrible illusion themselves.

Devin scowled as he wiped sweat from his brow while continuing down the now fiery path, it all seemed so real, but he knew that it was just a trick in his mind. Taking a slow breath he paused and closed his eyes as he felt the flames beginning to lick at his feet and legs.

"This is not real, just an illusion placed in my mind… there is nothing…" his breathing quickened as he tried desperately to concentrate despite the pain which was rising up from his feet and legs now.

He was nearly about to give up as he felt the fire rising higher and burning him when it all stopped and he felt soft reassuring arms wrapping around his waist and all the pain seemed to fade away with the heat around him. Hesitantly Devin opened his eyes and looked down to see Valerie hugging him tenderly and that the two of them were standing in a dark and damp hallway which stank of mold and decay.

"Thank you. I thought I was about to go there for a moment with all that fire rising up around me," he said returning the hug with her gently.

"You looked like you were about to collapse, just standing there shaking and sweating. We need to find Steven and Sarah, are you feeling alright now?" Valerie answered as she looked up at him for a moment in concern.

Devin nodded just slightly as he looked about trying to gain his bearings, "Yeah, let's go."

Steven continued down the long corridor when he paused and frowned to himself, it was too long to be possible. His eyes looked about once more and he frowned noticeably, magic was at work here, he just wasn't sure what kind. His scowl deepened as his frustration began to get to him and he could feel his temper rising before he yelled out, "Where are you coward, hiding behind spells and illusions and sick jokes! Come out and fight me!"

His words seemed to echo down the corridor as laughter returned echoing back with cold words, "Oh, I am not hiding from you young, Nightwolf, in fact I am quite close to you. Not that you could tell…"

Suddenly Steven felt a stabbing pain along his right side as a long gash formed through his clothes and across his skin. He jumped back nearly stumbling as the pain shot through his entire body for a moment, his eyes searching the darkness about with no success at identifying the malefactor which had attacked him. His eyes narrowed as he strained to listen to everything around him, then something whispered through the air to him, a soft scraping sound of metal upon stone. His movements were just a second before the slash that he narrowly avoided to his other side. He strained his eyes and then began to see a shadowy figure close by in front of him, cloaked in darkness wielding a blade, its expression one of twisted joy and malice.

"Damn you! Where is Sarah?" he shouted at the barely visible figure which lunged for him with the blade once more unsuccessfully.

Soft hissing laughter came from the shadowy figure as it took up an offensive stance once more before answering in a voice which continued to echo all around Steven in the dark musty hall, "Oh, you mean the little red headed girl? Oh she's dead… wonderful fun though while she was alive… I made sure to take her in every way I could think of before killing her."

Steven's expression changed to that of pure rage as he lunged at the shadowy figure, lightning crackling around his fists as he leapt screaming the whole time, "I'll kill you!"

The figure laughed maniacally as he moved aside and out of the way into what appeared to be one of the walls, "You haven't got the strength to kill me boy… just like your other friends who are probably dead as well. You are all weak willed…"

A loud resounding thud echoed from where the voice originated and the walls seemed to fade away causing Steven to blink as he saw Sarah standing over a now unconscious Olath with what looked like a cast iron frying pan in hand. He stood staring for a long moment as all of his rage drained away from his features before taking a step toward Sarah who was now rushing into his arms. They embraced, tears coming to both of their eyes without restraint as he leaned in and kissed her tenderly.

"Are you alright my love?" He finally asked as they began to regain their composure.

Sarah merely nodded mutely for a moment resting her head on his chest for a long moment before looking up at him and smiling, "I am now, I knew you would come for m—"

Her expression changed instantly as a sickening squishing crunch resounded from behind her and the two of them looked down to see the tip of a blade protruding from her stomach. Steven's looked up instantly and behind her to where Olath was standing now holding the blade which he had shove through Sarah's back with a sickening grin decorating his dirty features. His movements were swift as he drew the blade back out and made to strike again when Steven moved like the wind halfway across the dark room holding Sarah still in his arms.

"You dirty bastard! I'll burry you!" Steven shouted angrily across the room as he gently lowered Sarah to the ground and stood, his eyes glowing a slight fluorescent blue as lightning seemed to crackle around his fists.

It was then that Devin and Valerie ran into the large room and eyed Steven standing over Sarah while facing off with Olath in a display of what seemed to be raw anger. Devin grabbed Valerie's hand and dragged her into a run as they made their way across the room to Steven in what seemed like a desperate sprint. It only took them a moment as they watched Steven speed across the room launching bolts of what seemed to be lightning from his fists that Olath was parrying with a black darkly glowing blade.

Devin looked from Sarah to Valerie and nodded. "Take care of her please; I am going to help out Steven."

Valerie only nodded as Devin ran to Steven's side and began launching fire from his own hands at the insane laughing boy with the sword, "You alright man? Val is helping your girl, so don't worry about that, just focus on this bastard and we'll get him alright!"

Steven nodded once as he launched another attack which Olath parried with the blade while dancing about in some sick fashion and then parrying one of Devin's attacks as well. The blows went back and forth for some time before Olath grinned sickly and snapped his fingers on his free hand causing a dark shadowy apparition to appear beside him, his voice grating and deep as he commanded it forward to attack the two. Steven scowled as the spirit lunged at him with gripping talons for fingers and dodged repeatedly being put on the defensive now.

Devin continued focusing on Olath, though his breathing was becoming labored and he was finding it more difficult to concentrate the longer the battle went on, the only thoughts registering in his mind were never to give up, never to admit defeat. With his mind centered on winning, Devin lunged carelessly and missed just as Olath brought the sword's blade down across his back causing him to scream out in pain. Steven gritted his teeth as he launched a blast of lightning at the fiend in front of him and tried to move past it while it seemed to howl in pain itself, but it was only a ruse as the fiend lashed out slashing across Steven's other side and tossing him across the room like a rag doll. Sarah opened her eyes to the fight before her and cried out trying to get up, but Valerie kept her in place still trying to heal her, "There's nothing we can do to help them right now with your injury! Let them fight, they're a lot tougher than they look, I bet."

Sarah whimpered as Valerie looked over with growing worry and concern on her face. Both of them were on the ground now, with their opponents approaching them with nothing but death in their eyes. She said a silent prayer to herself for any help that the gods could provide as she returned her attention to Sarah's injury as if trying to will her powers to work faster given the situation.

Devin rolled over on the floor, his face twisting with pain as he rolled again to avoid a thrust of Olath's blade. Cursing left his lips as he realized the horrible position he was now in, his eyes only briefly drifting toward Steven who laid crumpled against one of the walls with the black fiend closing in on him and he began to wonder if this was really going to be the end of them both.

Kriss appeared outside of the large warehouse and inspected its moldering appearance with a hint of distain. This place radiated the magic he kept sensing and judging by the cop cars and the dead police it was certainly the right place. He found himself pausing as he noted the one police officer leaned up against the building sleeping soundly with what looked like minimal injury and surmised that the three must be inside now trying to find their fourth. A slight smirk trailed his lips for a moment as he entered the building and paused, eying Valerie as she stood with a blank yet terrified look etched upon her face. Chuckling softly he placed a hand on her shoulder and leaned in whispering softly into her ear for a moment before he released her and continued on down the hall, his black robes seeming to move to some unknown breeze that didn't exist in the cold musty hall.

His steps took him about the large warehouse as paused for a moment and eyed his surroundings, something seemed off. Then he noticed it, a shimmering along one of the walls. He moved over with a silent quickness and reached through the shimmering space and pulled Sarah out of whatever world she had been temporarily placed within and stared at her with his penetrating golden eyes as she stared up at him in horror.

"Don't be afraid of me, girl, I am not your captor… now, you need to go find your lover before he is caught up in the illusions here as well," Kriss said as he turned her in a direction and gave her a simple shove, "And use this."

Kriss tossed her a cast iron frying pan which she caught and looked at in slight confusion before looking up to see that he had vanished from sight.

He continued to move through the shadows unseen as he surveyed the entire building, his eyes watching both the spirit and the man as they moved about until the fighting began. He watched with mild amusement until the two were slashed and tossed about the room before he emerged from the darkness himself and stepped forward into the little bit of light which illuminated the room.

A large grin stretched across the barely visible features of his face as he spoke in a clear loud echoing voice that seemed to resound throughout the room, his hand raised toward the dark fiend which looked over Steven's unconscious form, "*Barra gigim xul! Edin na zu asar sarrat irkalli ensi! Ana harrani sa alktasa la tarat, eseru annu utuk xul!*"

The fiendish spirit wailed and screamed in agony as if some invisible searing blade had penetrated its essence before several glowing red chains seemed to leap out from the ground and wrap around it with fierce intensity and heat. The spirit continued to lash out at the air and the chains to no avail as the ground opened up with a shaking and rumbling noise followed by the screams of those who were tortured in the underworld for the horrid crimes committed in life. It let out one more despairing scream as it was dragged down into the earth before the ground closed in around it.

Olath's attention turned from Devin to the howling spirit and he screamed out in anger, "Who dares to attack my spirit! I'll destroy you!"

Kriss's haunting laughter seemed to echo throughout the room as he faded back into the shadows before his voice echoed through the darkness, "You will now, will you? I don't think you even have the power to lay a single blow on me, little boy..."

Olath spun about with a sickly insane grin on his face as he slashed bout with his blade, "You don't frighten me, I don't care what shadows you hide in… I'll hit you eventually."

Kriss's laughter echoed once more as a slicing sound echoed through the air and Olath dropped his blade with a howl of pain. Blood began dripping to the floor from Olath's right arm as it fell limply at his side, his eyes darted about madly as he scrambled to grab the blade back up with his left hand, panic beginning to register on his features. Another swift slicing and singing sound echoed throughout the room followed by another howl of pain echoing out from Olath's mouth as he leapt back from the blade, his left hand falling limp and bleeding profusely now.

"You… you can't beat me! The legions of the underworld are at my command! I will summon them to destroy all of you!" Olath screamed out in crazed desperation.

Kriss's voice echoed once more throughout the room following a long silence from Olath after his mad outburst, "You want the legions of hell… then I will give them to you! *Uggae, maskim xul, ningishzidda, ati me peta babka! Usella mituti ikkalu baltuti*!"

His words echoed throughout the room as a dark foreboding seemed to fill the entire area with dread and the stench of death. Olath looked about the area in fear and panic as he recognized the chant used and then howled in terror as a large skeletal gate seemed to materialize from the damp musty air and began to open before him, "NO! No! I will not be imprisoned and sent to the abyss! I am too powerful! No!"

Fiendish apparitions and skeletal undead demons poured forth from the gate and set upon Olath, the only sound was that of his screams of terror and pain as they dragged him through the fiery gate to whatever hell they were from.

Sarah, Valerie, and Devin stared in disbelief as their attacker was dragged away until the gate closed with a resounding thud that echoed of a finality that was never to be tempted. Their attention turned to the black robed figure who was now carrying

Steven over to them and unceremoniously dropped him to the ground at the girls' feet before turning away.

Sarah called after him as he walked from the room, "Thank you... whoever you are."

Kriss chuckled some and simply raised a hand in a wave of farewell as he left the room without so much as another sound.

The three looked down at Steven who seemed to be bleeding out at a fast rate, all of them with worry and concern on their faces. Valerie quickly set to work on healing him and looked to Sarah and Devin, "We're going to need an ambulance. I don't think I can do more than stop his bleeding with these injuries."

Devin nodded once as he pulled out his cell and dialed 911, his conversation with the operator was quick short and frantic before he hung up and looked down at Steven. Valerie was doing her best to try and heal him and Sarah was holding his hand as she wept fearfully for his life. Devin frowned as he looked in the direction of where that robed man went and began to wonder who he was. It was only a few minutes before the sound of sirens and quick footfalls echoed throughout the building. Paramedics were soon at their location and lifting Steven onto a gurney while the other three were covered in blankets and escorted out of the building. As they exited, their eyes were met with a surprising sight as several ambulances were there loading up the policemen onto gurneys as well as Frank covered in a blanket sitting on the back of the ambulance they were being led to.

"Devin! My god, are you kids alright?" Frank exclaimed with a wince and a cough as they stopped at the back of the car.

"Yeah, well, all of us except Steven. He got cut up pretty badly by that bastard in there. But your policemen, we thought all of you were dead," Devin answered in confused and astonished tones.

Frank coughed once more as he leaned in, "So did I, but they started moaning and moving after I came to, so I started calling the ambulances. I'm told their injuries are pretty severe but that they'll all live. Did you kids get that bastard that did all this?"

Devin only nodded as he looked at Frank, "Yeah, he won't be a problem anymore. I'm not sure if you'll find a body though, Frank, he got pretty tore up too."

Frank merely nodded as he motioned them all into the back of the ambulance with him, "We can talk on the way to the hospital; I want to know everything."

The three nodded as they climbed in the back of the ambulance and headed to the hospital.

EPILOGUE

Steven sat on the hospital bed looking out the window with an irritated scowl dipped from his lips. He hated being this helpless, just sitting around and feeling useless aggravated him to no end. A deep sigh echoed out from him as he looked to all of the get well soon flowers and cards which were laid out on the desk beside his bed and he shook his head. He had no idea what happened after he was thrown, and no idea how they all survived the ordeal. The questions were tearing him apart as they twisted within his mind, but his silent revelry was interrupted as Kriss walked in and sat beside his bed. Steven blinked in surprise as he looked Kriss up and down for a moment, "Didn't expect you to visit me in here."

Kriss chuckled softly as he looked out to the window for a moment, "I'm not here on any pity party or to wish you to get well. I already know you are going to live... I simply wanted to stop by and make sure you understand what my payment is going to be for my assistance."

Steven scowled noticeably before he responded, "What do you want?"

"Oh nothing very difficult. I just need you to go retrieve something from South America when you are all better," Kriss answered handing Steven a set of old papers and a map before he stood and began to leave.

"That's it? Why do I get the feeling you're not telling me something, Kriss?" Steven called to him as he reached the door.

Kriss turned and grinned at him slyly as he chuckled once more, "And keep it when you find it... I'm sure it will come in handy one day. Chow."

Steven eyed the papers for a long moment as he looked through them, his mind thinking over what could possibly be so important in South America.